"Isn't this the kind of woman I'm supposed to be, the kind of woman you like, the kind of woman who would boldly kiss you just because she could?"

Philip tensed, feeling aroused and confused. Then Anne took his tunic in both hands and turned him about. He let her handle him, let her push him against the wall. He wanted to understand her strange mood—but he also recognized the darkness within himself, the lusting part that wanted not to understand, only to feel.

"This is what the Lady Rosamonds of the world know all about," she whispered, her face below his. "I'm just beginning to learn."

"If that's what you want," he said in a low growl, "then let me teach you more."

He turned her about and pressed her into the ivy-covered stone wall, feeling every soft inch of her body along his. He took her mouth in a kiss, arching her ̶̶̶̶̶̶̶̶̶̶̶̶ that she had no choice but to succu̶̶̶̶̶̶̶̶̶̶̶̶ ed to seduce her co̶̶̶̶̶̶̶̶̶̶̶̶d at his back, she ̶̶̶̶̶̶̶̶̶̶̶̶nd met him with ea̶̶̶̶

Other AVON ROMANCES

Julia Latham

One Knight Only

AVON
An Imprint of HarperCollinsPublishers

This is a work of fiction. Names, characters, places, and incidents are drawn from the author's imagination or are used fictitiously and are not to be construed as real. Any resemblance to actual events, locales, organizations, or persons, living or dead, is entirely coincidental.

AVON BOOKS
An Imprint of HarperCollins*Publishers*
10 East 53rd Street
New York, New York 10022-5299

First Avon Books paperback printing: December 2007

Avon Trademark Reg. U.S. Pat. Off. and in Other Countries, Marca Registrada, Hecho en U.S.A.
HarperCollins® is registered trademark of HarperCollins Publishers.

Printed in the U.S.A.

10 9 8 7 6 5 4 3 2 1

To Ginny Aubertine, fellow Packeteer and forever friend, thank you so much for showing me your wisdom, and guiding me with a shining example of a woman changing her life for the better. I so admire you!

ONE KNIGHT ONLY

Chapter 1

Yorkshire, 1486

The last time maidservant Anne Kendall pretended to be a noblewoman, she'd been locked in a tower bedchamber, and only had to keep up the masquerade for one person. Now she was able to ride her horse through the colorful pavilions of the tournament on the grassy park on the plains near York, her head held high, wearing the finest garments, projecting the confidence of a wealthy, powerful woman. She was impersonating Lady Rosamond Wolsingham, daughter of a duke, widow of an earl, and a woman who knew too many secrets, the kind that desperate men might kill for.

Anne could never forget the risk of danger involved.

But she had her small retinue of soldiers near her at all times, as well as Lady Rosamond's maidservant to help with her masquerade. They surrounded her as she moved through the crowd of knights and squires, their ladies and their servants, heading toward the walls of the town and the inn that awaited them.

Anne had already honed her impersonation by spending a week under the tutelage of Lady Rosamond, then visiting the first castle on the lady's husband-hunting list. Thank goodness Lady Rosamond had something in mind for Anne's journey to London. How else to keep all eyes focused on Anne, instead of the secret journey that Lady Rosamond was taking?

But this tournament had not been anticipated. There might be people here who knew the countess, who would realize that Anne was not she. So Anne bowed to the wishes of her soldiers and wore a veil attached to her headdress to obscure her face. She had not meant to take any chances by watching the tournament, but as they rode past a field surrounded by a cheering crowd, she could see two armored combatants swinging swords at each other. The fight looked intense enough for a battlefield, and one knight even lost his helm during a blow. But the reeling man only shook back his brown hair that glinted red in the setting sun, laughed, and continued to attack his opponent bareheaded. He was a reckless, brilliant fighter with little care for his own safety.

Anne felt a chill of recognition. Sir Philip Clifford. Here was one man who could identify her, might even unthinkingly call out her name. She turned her head away and tapped her mount's flanks to hurry into town. But inside her, something hot and smoldering reawakened, and she cursed her weakness where Philip was concerned. She could not afford to be distracted—especially not by memories of him and the anger it evoked inside her.

The tavern on the ground floor of the inn was over-flowing with cheering, laughing, drinking men and women, and Philip Clifford was determined to enjoy every minute of it. Today he had bested every knight in sword fighting, and he was using part of his winning purse to keep the celebration going. He knew a deep satisfaction in keeping his name in the public eye. If he continued his winning streak, he would most certainly come to the attention of King Henry. He intended to be the king's man, perhaps his champion, to live at court and make a good marriage. The king had only come to power the previous year when he defeated King Richard in battle. Would not such a man need to discover men he could trust? Philip could be such a man.

Pleasing a monarch had not always been his goal, Philip thought, sipping his tankard of ale and tugging on the skirt of a blond serving maid as she pranced by. She laughed over her shoulder at him and winked. He used to hold himself to a strict morality, focused on being as worthy as the knights in the League of the Blade, the shadowy group of men who took action when they saw a wrong being committed. He'd grown up listening to his mother's stories of the great League and its worthy deeds.

But he'd given up that quest. After everything he'd accomplished in the service of his friend John Russell, newly married and now the earl of Alderley, Philip still hadn't earned an invitation to join the league, although John had. It had been time for Philip to move on. He'd taken to the roads of England, looking for any chance to show his talent, to earn prize money and the notice of the king.

Sometimes that road was lonely. He'd been a man always part of a company, first a soldier, then a knight. But now he owed his allegiance to no man. More than once a pretty maid had eased his nights. But even that had begun to seem lonely. He wanted his life to have meaning. So when the maidservant brushed by him again, her hand lingering on his shoulder, he smiled, but did not offer an invitation.

Several women brushed past him, even a merchant's wife, and he made a game of reaching for them, only to send them away laughing. When it happened again, he swept his arm around the woman's waist and hauled her across his lap. There was a roar of approval from the crowd, and Philip leaned over to smile at his captive, but to his surprise, she was wearing a veil that obscured the lower half of her face. Upswept black hair was tucked back beneath a small headdress, and below that, he could see wide, fathomless black eyes.

Inside him, everything stilled in recognition and desire. Anne Kendall. He had not seen her in many weeks, but his body remembered. When he'd first met her, he'd believed her to be Lady Elizabeth Hutton, and she'd been dressed as finely as she was now, with long silk skirts. Her garments slid like water across his legs, his thighs pillowing her, his arm holding her as if she were a lover. She was delicate and strong all at once, as a woman should be who'd fooled a viscount for days and kept him from marrying her lady. 'Twas a shame she was only a maidservant.

Before he could even frame a question, she put a finger to his lips, and then gave him a bold smile. "Well, Sir Knight, are you making a play for my bed?"

He arched a brow in surprise, but couldn't respond because a man pulled her off his lap and held a dagger to Philip's throat.

Still wearing a smile, Philip raised his empty hands high. "I have no quarrel with you, friend."

"Keep your hands to yourself," the man growled. He was of middling years, but with the stocky frame of a man well used to battle. "My lady is not for one such as you."

"Perhaps she wants such a choice," Philip answered, hearing the approval in the laughter of the rest of the room.

He looked at Anne, but she only smiled boldly and shook her head as two well-armed men led her out of the public room. The first man stood above Philip, glared menacingly about the room as if threatening them all, then sheathed his dagger and left.

Philip's fellow revelers gaped at him.

Then he cocked an eyebrow. "Doesn't know what's she's missing, eh?"

He forced himself to participate in the laughter.

Sir Peter, one of his opponents in the tournament, called out, "She's knows something of it. That one's a widow, Lady Rosamond, I hear tell."

Philip kept the smile on his face, although his stare focused on the knight. "Who was her husband?"

"The earl of Wolsingham. Tragic accident, it was, and her husband so young. But no one can contain a woman like her. She's rich on her own merit. I hear on this journey she's looking for a new husband."

Philip glanced at the door Anne had disappeared through. What had she gotten herself into?

Anne was hustled into her small bedchamber and found Margaret, Lady Rosamond's servant, laying out Anne's nightclothes across the bed. The maid, tiny and freckled, with sandy brown hair, looked up wide-eyed. Seeing all three soldiers escorting Anne inside, Margaret gasped and gathered the garments behind her back.

Anne began to grin, but it faded when she saw the frown on the face of Sir Walter, the captain of her small guard. There was little open space in the chamber, filled as it was with a bed, a coffer with extra bedding, and a small hearth, but he took up the rest with the dominating force of his character. He was a grizzled man out of his youth, but before his elder years. His hair was short and gray, and he always seemed to have graying stubble on his face, regardless of whether he'd recently shaved or not. But he had the broad shoulders of a warrior, and she wondered at the life he led.

When he wasn't serving his duty to the League of the Blade. Surely he was used to being in command.

She didn't know the last names of her knight escorts. The League believed in anonymity.

"You must be more careful in so public a place," Sir Walter said sternly.

The other two knights, Sir David and Sir Joseph, sat down on stools on either side of the door, crossed their arms over their chests, and tried to look equally as stern.

"Sir Walter," Anne said calmly, "what would you have had me do? I played my part. I know we were supposed to avoid York, but the heavy rains forced us to halt."

"But the tournament—"

"Aye, the tournament could not be planned for. I am suitably veiled, and we're leaving in the morning."

She thought briefly of mentioning Philip, and then decided against it. Perhaps he hadn't recognized her after all. Or was he embarrassed by how he'd treated her not two months ago? She could only hope for that.

Young pages brought up the bathing tub and hot water she'd ordered, filing past the frowning knights uncertainly. Anne gave them each a smile and a coin, and asked them not to return until morning.

As the knights left to retire to their chambers on either side of hers, Sir David, blond and so tall he had to duck beneath doorways, said, "Lady Rosamond, you do remember how best to protect yourself?"

Anne looked about and spotted just what she needed. "I promise to push that coffer against the door."

"Very good."

Sir David rarely smiled: all the knights took their duties very seriously. It was difficult to get to know her traveling companions when social niceties had to be pried out of them. The League must train them all to focus on their tasks, to never be personable—no last names, no jokes, and no companionship. Without familiarity, no one could get hurt. That made sense to her.

That brought thoughts of Philip, somewhere here in the same inn. The last time they were together, she had been feeling far too lonely to make wise decisions.

Margaret helped Anne unlace her gown. "Do ye need anythin' else, milady, before I retire to me chamber?"

Margaret was a cool, remote young woman, ever dutiful because she knew that this masquerade would help her mistress, Lady Rosamond. Though at first she'd hesitated calling Anne "my lady," she had gradually become used to the need of it. But Anne understood that Margaret thought she was a poor substitute for her mistress.

In exchange for her services, Margaret had requested her own chamber. After all, Anne and she were both of the serving class, and equals. The Bladesmen had reluctantly acquiesced in their need of her.

"Margaret, you may find your bed," Anne said. "Thank you for your help this day."

When the girl had gone, Anne pushed the heavy coffer against the door, angry with herself for feeling torn. She would not think of Philip. He was a connection to her past, to a time when she'd first realized she'd liked being needed, when she'd helped save Elizabeth from an unwanted marriage. She was needed now, urgently so. She had a mission and a focus, and it was a good feeling.

She had once thought Philip needed her, and with him she had shared her feelings of newly blossoming passion, ignoring her better sense. She'd been in a weakened state, she silently reminded herself; her parents' rejection had left her feeling angry and adrift. She had to stop dwelling on it.

The bathing tub was a rarity, deep enough for a woman to sink into, and the pages had been generous with the amount of water. She soaped herself leisurely, then settled back to enjoy the comfort and warmth while it lasted. She closed her eyes and let her thoughts drift away.

The shutters covering the window suddenly rattled. Frowning, she opened her eyes in time to see one of the shutters slowly open. A foot appeared on the windowsill.

With a gasp she sat up, clutching the linen cloth to her bosom. This had happened to her once before, she thought, feeling a flood of anger. Another foot appeared, then a hand gripping the sill, then a face peering in from above. Although the light of the candle did not easily reach the far wall, she already knew who it was. Her traitorous heart began to beat madly.

Philip Clifford.

He dropped into a sitting position and ducked his

head inside. Grinning, he said, "Might I come in? I just missed having the contents of a chamber pot dumped on my head."

"You could have just knocked on the door!" she hissed, sinking down as far as she could in the water. The cloth and the water obscured her, but she felt dangerously exposed.

"I didn't knock the last time," he countered.

"The last time I was a prisoner, and desperate for company—and I was not bathing!"

He dropped to the floor, but came no farther, for which she was grateful.

"Well, that's why I came—not because of the bathing part, although that is an interesting bonus."

He glanced lower than her face, and she wondered what he could see.

"Aren't you a prisoner again—*Lady Rosamond*?"

His voice deepened with suspicion—with worry? She didn't know him well enough to know the difference.

But she knew what his kiss tasted like, how his hands could work magic on her body.

She took a deep breath to steady herself against the memories. "I am here quite willingly."

"You were willing the last time, too, but you were still a prisoner."

"The soldiers are my guards, not my captors. Thank you for your concern, Sir Philip, but you should leave now."

Instead of leaving, he walked forward into the candlelight. His features sharpened. He was not a man of softness. He was composed of angles: prominent, lean cheekbones, square jaw, and heavy forehead above his brows. His body, though muscular, was thinner than some of his bulkier opponents, and therefore deceptive. She imagined many men thought the advantage of their substantial weight alone could defeat him. But he was powerful and strong, and she felt an embarrassing warmth remembering how he'd swept her onto his lap in front of the entire tavern—

—And how he'd stalked her for days at Castle Alderley when she was at last free of captivity, playing a powerful game she'd felt reckless enough to enjoy.

Now he was studying her, from her face to her wet knees, which were the only things that showed above the soapy water. His eyes were a vivid green, like a grassy field under a sunny sky. Why was she feeling so intimidated by him? She knew where she stood with him—she'd been a pleasant diversion, although she'd thought he'd wanted something more permanent from her.

And now she was naked. He wouldn't take advantage—would he? She remembered his restlessness, his disquiet. Elizabeth Hutton, the lady she'd grown up serving and who had married Philip's good friend, had told Anne that Philip had not been invited to join the League of the Blade, as Lord Alderley had. Though on the outside, Philip had seemed the same amusing man, she'd sensed that something had shifted on the inside, as if the refusal had changed him in some subtle way.

What would he do if he found out that she herself had been asked to work for the League?

Oh, she wasn't a member yet, but by the end of this, she planned to be. She would convince them that she was talented enough to be the first Bladeswoman.

Yet she couldn't tell Philip anything about the League or her mission—she'd vowed to keep Lady Rosamond's secrets.

He suddenly leaned over the tub, bracing both hands on the rim as he looked down at her. To her frustration, a hot feeling of awareness shot through her. He'd seen more of her body, given intimate kisses that even now made her want to shudder with remembered pleasure. She forced herself to ignore the sensations.

She couldn't sink any lower, so she returned his stare coolly and kept her voice level. "Why are you not leaving?"

"You know I cannot leave you here like this, masquerading as someone else."

"I'm not—"

"Do not doubt my intelligence, *Countess*. That *is* what you're pretending to be." He pointed to her gown now hung on a peg in the wall. "Those rich garments aren't yours."

She pursed her lips and narrowed her eyes. What would he do if he did not hear the truth? Could he accidentally ruin things for her—for Lady Rosamond? If the wrong people discovered the masquerade, then the countess could be in real danger.

Perhaps he would accept *some* of the truth. She met his gaze, striving for sincerity. The water was growing cold, and it was difficult to maintain one's composure while stifling shivers—and being stared at by a man who knew how to wield his gaze like a sensuous weapon.

"Aye, the garments," she said. "They belong to another woman, Lady Rosamond Wolsingham."

"So I was told."

"They know who I am in the public room?" she asked in astonishment and growing worry. "No one here was supposed to know that identity."

He narrowed his eyes. "You chose York deliberately?"

"Not me, I—" Then she stopped.

"Does John—Lord Alderley—know about this?"

She hesitated, then realized she was betraying too much. She shivered.

He obviously noticed. Leaning even closer, he whispered, "I'll allow you to leave the tub if you tell me everything."

"Are you *daring* me to stand up?" she asked, putting her hands on the rim as if to push herself to her feet. It was a bold gamble, but after all, she had nothing to lose, no dowry, no future, only what she made of this masquerade.

Philip straightened, and she insisted to herself that she felt relieved.

"You'll catch your death lingering in there," he said.

"Well, whose fault—"

"Do I have your word you'll tell me the truth?"

"Aye."

Some of it, she amended silently.

Chapter 2

Philip stood above the bathing tub, staring down at Anne in the soapy water. The moment was frozen in time, her hands gripping the tub, droplets sliding from her shoulders and down to the upper slopes of her breasts, hazy in the water. He guessed she didn't realize how much he could see, and wasn't about to let her know. It was difficult to keep his gaze mostly on her face, when he could see the vague shadow of dusky rose nipples, and a darker shadow where her thighs met. He'd tasted her skin, had even parted those thighs, but his honesty had stopped them from having the ultimate pleasure. Since then, his desire for her had never gone away, only smoldered in the deepest recesses of his mind, waiting for this chance to come flooding back.

"You need to turn away," she said.

Her gaze was demurely low as she spoke, but then she raised it to meet his unflinchingly.

It took every ounce of strength to go to the window and look out over the dark stable yard, lit by the occasional torch. He could hear her moving about, the brush of linen as she dried herself, and the rustle of garments being donned.

"I am now clothed," she finally said.

When he turned back, she was sitting before the hearth, wearing a silk dressing gown that flowed smoothly over her curves but hid her skin from him. She was brushing her hair out before the fire, spreading the heavy curls to dry them. He had never seen her hair let down, though he had dreamed of it. As a maidservant, she had to keep it out of her way to work.

Once again he found himself fascinated by the color of her hair, so midnight black that the highlights seemed tinged with blue. Her hair was matched by her eyes, dark as well, hinting at secrets. Her hair framed her face, pale and delectable as cream, with spots of color on her cheeks and lips. Her very moist lips.

"Will you do nothing but stare at me?" she asked quietly.

"I am deciding what I can believe of your words."

"I have never lied—"

She broke off when he quirked a brow at her. Blushing, she glanced back at the fire and continued the hypnotic brushing of her hair. He was uncomfortably aroused by her slow movements, by everything about her.

"Very well, I've lied," she continued. "But 'twas for a good purpose. I saved my lady's life by pretending to be her, locked in the tower, so that she could move about the castle and find a way to save herself. I helped Lord Alderley—her betrothed, your friend—did I not? And you have lied as well."

"Aye, we both did what we had to for our friends. I, too, pretended to be someone else."

"You made a good clerk."

She smiled in that calm, smooth way that made her seem always in control, never bothered by anything. He wondered what kind of training a lady's maid had to become like her, so talented at pretending to be above her station. He knew she'd been raised and educated at Lady Elizabeth's side, that the two were friends more than mistress and servant. But still . . . there was something about Anne that just exuded confidence. And it still drew him, though he should know better.

He walked closer, unable to help himself. With every brush of her hair, he could smell the soap she'd used. It would be so easy to forget his questions.

Had that been her plan?

He braced his hand on the mantel and frowned down at her. "So why are you pretending to be Lady Rosamond?"

"Because she asked me to."

"You know her?"

"She was a lady-in-waiting to Elizabeth's mother when I was serving at the Castle Alderley."

"Why would a noblewoman need such a pretense?"

Anne was watching the fire, not him, which made him even more suspicious.

"Her reasons are her own," she finally said. "But I am to travel to London, interviewing potential husbands along the way."

"Interviewing potential husbands?" he scoffed. "Surely you could not know what would please Lady Rosamond."

"She gave me a list."

"But I suspect something deeper, and I think John knows what it is."

She looked at him swiftly, so sincere that he was impressed.

"Why would you think Lord Alderley is involved?"

"Because when I asked you if he knew about this, you hesitated. Now either this has something to do with his wife, which is why he might know, or something to do with the League of the Blade, of which he is now a member."

Mention of the League filled the room with a tension that hadn't been so obvious before. Philip knew he was on to something, even as Anne shook her head.

"The League of the Blade?" she echoed.

Her amusement was almost flawless. He was impressed despite his suspicion.

"Aye, the League," he answered. "They knew about your masquerade as Lady Elizabeth. Who else would have thought to ask you?"

"Elizabeth told Lady Rosamond—"

"Nay, Lady Elizabeth would never put you in this kind of danger willingly. This had to be something you were asked to do, and you agreed to it."

"'Tis a joke, a lark! Not something dangerous."

"Then why do you have armed guards following your every move? Where are they now?"

She lifted her chin in a show of stubbornness. "Their chambers are on either side of mine."

"So the famed Bladesmen did not hear me invade your bedchamber?"

"Why would they think someone could come down from the roof four stories above the ground?"

Philip simply smiled at her in triumph, and then she seemed to realize that she had not corrected his assumptions.

"I mean the guards," she quickly corrected herself.

"The Bladesmen."

Once he would have felt a strange hollow in the center of his chest knowing that the Bladesmen had asked another person he knew to join them. Anne was certainly capable, and he did not begrudge her the opportunity. Only recently he'd finally met some of their members, had trained with them, had fought at their sides. He had thought he'd proven himself in their eyes. But although they had asked his good friend John Russell, now the earl of Alderley, to join their ranks, they had not asked Philip. Though it had been difficult, he had let his dream of membership go. He would not live his life trying to reach some mysterious standard.

But what had the League gotten Anne involved in? Surely it could not be something innocuous.

"So the Bladesmen are guarding you on your husband-hunting journey," he summarized.

She sighed, continuing the slow brushing of her hair.

"You are impersonating Lady Rosamond at her behest, because she will not—or cannot—do it herself."

She only nodded.

"I cannot believe you would accept this situation if you did not know the truth of the matter."

He dropped to kneel before her, so she'd be forced to look at him. Her eyes widened at his nearness, and he put his hands on her knees. There was a warmth to her that was so distracting, and he felt her trembling. He focused his thoughts.

"What is happening, Anne? You cannot believe I would leave you in such a situation. I owe Elizabeth and John that much. I respect your skills, but I cannot understand the risks you're taking. There are men who will take offense when they discover they've been misled."

She lifted her chin. "They won't discover. I trained with Lady Rosamond for many days, learning her mannerisms, and how she'd behave."

"Such training is necessary for a joke? A lark?"

She looked at her lap, remaining silent. He took her clenched hands in his.

"And what about the men who expect an experienced widow? How will you handle them?"

She pulled her hands away. "As I handle any man too forward in his behavior," she said sternly.

"As you handled me?"

Glaring, she said between clenched teeth, "How dare

you—" And then she broke off, taking a deep breath. "Lady Rosamond picked men she didn't know."

"How could she predict how strangers will respond to you?"

"Philip, you must stop this," she whispered. "You will not sway me. This is too important, and they cannot do it without me."

"Do what?" He leaned against her knees, cupping her face in his hands. He was taking advantage of the attraction that always sparked between them, but he needed to discover the truth and keep her safe. He kept telling himself he owed that to John and Elizabeth, but something inside him knew it was more personal that. It was about Anne, and his worries that she was being taken advantage of. And what he owed her for the liberties he'd taken.

They stared into each other's eyes. The firelight brightened half of her face, left the other half in shadow. He could feel the pulse of her rapid heartbeat against his skin. She trembled faintly, and he stroked her skin with light touches as he held her. And then she pulled away.

"You must not speak of this to anyone," she whispered hoarsely.

He nodded, finally close to understanding everything.

"The king's life is at stake."

He sat back on his heels, feeling stunned and turned upside down.

It was her turn to reach forward, to touch his shoulder. "I need your oath, Philip, that what I speak of goes no further than this chamber."

"I swear you have my silence," he said solemnly.

"Several weeks ago, at a tournament in Durham, Lady Rosamond overheard three noblemen discussing a plot against King Henry."

"Were they King Richard's men? Though Henry killed him in battle, there are still many who believe he was the rightful heir."

"She doesn't know their motivations because she doesn't know *them*. She saw their faces, but did not recognize them and therefore doesn't know their names." Anne rose to her feet and paced away from him.

Philip slowly stood up, frowning as he considered the dilemma. To his surprise, it was difficult to concentrate while watching her walk with smooth, athletic grace, the skirts of her dressing gown undulating around her legs. She was tall for a woman, but with feminine curves in provocative proportion.

He turned away so he could think. "So Lady Rosamond needs to relay her information to the king."

"And since she only *saw* these men, she'll have to identify them in person."

"Is she in danger because they saw her?" He faced her again, eyes narrowed as he thought of what Anne had become involved with. "Are they using you to lure out these traitors?"

"Nay!" She came to a stop, eyes wide with sincerity. "They would never put me in such danger. Lady Rosamond is certain that the traitors did not see her. They don't know what she knows. The League doesn't want to take any chances, so they're escorting her to London in secret. But they don't want her to seem to disappear, just after she announced her search for a husband."

"So they came to you for help."

She nodded, and a pleased smile softly touched her face.

"Anne," he murmured, coming toward her. "'Tis obvious you were glad to be asked. Your talent must have impressed them."

Instead of being soothed by his comment, she looked wary.

"But do you not see how dangerous this is?" he continued. "You are out in the open, while Lady Rosamond is allowed to hide. You don't know what these traitors know. I could have been one of them, coming right in the window, and you couldn't have stopped me."

"You're wrong, Philip. I am just here to distract people from the lady's disappearance."

"They didn't even give you a whole troop to protect you!"

"How could they? Wouldn't that look incredibly suspicious, and draw attention that Lady Rosamond doesn't need?"

"But three soldiers?"

"Three knights, trained as Bladesmen. And it was four, but one of their number broke his leg in a fall and had to be sent home."

When Anne finished speaking, she could not help but remember Sir Walter's frustration at being down a man. He had said that contacting another Bladesman would take too long. Though he had betrayed no emotion, she knew he was worried about being able to keep her protected.

And here was Philip, a skilled knight, who'd already worked with the League.

She almost groaned aloud at the thought of spending each day with him, risking a fall back into her behavior at Alderley, where he was all she could think about when her world was falling apart. She would not tell Sir Walter about him. She had to stay focused on her mission, on becoming a member of the League. Her foolish desire for Philip would only get in the way.

And yet, if someone were injured or killed because they did not have enough men . . .

She sighed. She would have to tell Sir Walter of Philip's visit and leave the decision up to him. It was the correct move for a woman who wanted to prove that she could be impartial. But oh, how she hoped that Sir Walter would refuse. For if Philip was in her party, he might discover her plan to join the League. Would he try to stop her?

"Philip, I am confident in what I'm doing," Anne said.

"And I'm just supposed to ignore what I've learned."

She put a hand on his chest.

"You gave me your vow," she said harshly. "Do you plan to break your word and tell someone?"

Had she misjudged him?

"Nay, of course not. But I cannot just go on worrying about you, not knowing."

He certainly hadn't worried about her when he'd been seducing her.

"Are you staying in this inn?" she asked.

Frowning, he nodded. "For a few more days."

"Then I promise I will contact you if I need to." She took his arm and guided him to the window.

When she would have released him, he hugged his arm close, trapping her hand against his side.

"Anne, you know I am not simply concerned about you because of what happened between us."

Anger blushed her cheeks. "I know."

For a moment of silence, he said nothing, and she tried to remove her hand.

He pressed it tighter to him, leaned over her. "Anne—"

"Nay, you mustn't," she said angrily. "I should never have assumed that I could be more than just a willing maid to you."

"Anne, you weren't—"

"Believe me I am grateful that you had enough honor to tell me you would not marry me before we'd consummated our relationship."

"I didn't feel honorable."

"You were honest."

When she'd been naked in his arms, so close to the satisfaction of joining with him, his revelation had left her feeling humiliated and furious. But when she'd fled from him and calmed down, she'd been glad to know the truth before she'd found herself in love with him—or worse.

"I am sure you will succeed in your quest for a nobly born wife at court," she continued impassively. She pulled her hand away from him and stepped back.

"Would you accept my apology?" he asked.

"I already told you I did."

"Then why don't I feel as if you meant it?"

What could she say?

Philip nodded as if he understood, and then reached out the window and tugged on the knotted rope that hung from the roof.

He bowed his head. "Send for me if you need me, Lady Rosamond."

With his back to the wall, he boosted himself up onto the sill, and then leaned out, catching onto the rope. Her stomach churned at the mere thought of him hanging out over hard earth, four stories up, but all she did was clasp her hands together.

He put his legs over the side, braced his feet on the lowest knot and swung out over the ground. He began to climb nimbly up to the roof, out of sight.

She waited as long as she could, and finally she leaned out and peered up. He was gone, and she saw the last of the rope slithering as it was pulled up over the roof and disappeared.

She barred the shutters and stared about her deserted chamber. At first, she'd thought it an incredible luxury to be alone. The only time she ever had been was when she was held captive in the tower, and that wasn't the same. Each night she told herself that she was a rich, titled widow, who could do as she pleased—sleep as she pleased. It was part of her preparation for *becoming* Lady Rosamond.

But suddenly Philip's absence made the room seem cold, barren. She hated feeling like this, as if she were a desperately lonely woman. She wasn't desperate. She had a plan for her life now, and it didn't involve Philip. She would prove to the League that she would be a valuable, *permanent* member.

And if she had to deal with Philip, then so be it.

Chapter 3

Anne barely slept. Well before dawn, she was awake and dressed, and even managed the lacing at her back with some awkward tugging.

"Milady?" Margaret, who usually awoke her, knocked softly on the door.

After pushing the coffer back into place, Anne opened the door and smiled at the girl's surprised expression.

"You are up early, milady."

"I need to speak to Sir Walter. I've begun packing away my things. If you could finish for me, I'll return as quickly as I can."

"Of course, milady."

It was on the tip of Anne's tongue to ask Margaret to withhold her formality, but she could not. Using the correct titles kept everything in line, made everyone remember how important it was to keep up the appearance of who she was supposed to be.

And perhaps Margaret, so diligent in her duties, would rather not become any closer to Anne. Just because Anne had been a friend to her mistress Elizabeth, didn't mean that Margaret wanted the same thing with Anne.

Anne walked next door and rapped softly on the wood. It was opened immediately by a scowling Sir Walter, and she almost took a step back.

His eyebrows rose. "My lady?"

"Aye, I know, I am up early. Might I speak with you in private?"

"It would not be seemly for a noblewoman to—"

She pushed past him. "But I am a widow, used to getting my way. I care little what others think of my behavior."

He slowly closed the door. "Of course."

The chamber was even smaller than hers, but Sir Walter had it to himself since Sir James's injury had necessitated his departure.

Anne stood beside the bed, already neatly made up, and took a deep breath. "Sir Walter, if you could have one, would you want a replacement for Sir James?"

He blinked at her, rubbing a hand across his newly shaved chin. "Of course, but by the time the League could be contacted, and another man sent, we might already be to London. We will have to manage with three guards. Did we not already discuss—?"

"Aye, we did," she said heavily. "But I felt that it was only fair to tell you that there is another knight staying at this inn who has worked with the League before."

He cocked his head. "And how did you recognize another of my order?"

"He is not a Bladesman. Do you remember the man who pulled me onto his lap last eve?"

"I do." His voice deepened with seriousness.

She thought he would begin to protest, but he just waited, his demeanor more and more disapproving.

"I know him. More to the point, he recognized me."

His expression did not change, but she sensed a hardness about it.

"How do you know—"

"Because he came to my chamber last night."

She finally had her reaction, and it was a cold anger.

"And how did he enter if you had a coffer before the door?"

"He came in through the window."

His gray eyebrows plummeted in a frown. "You did not scream for me?"

"But I know him, Sir Walter, and so does the League. He was second in command to Lord Alderley. His name is Sir Philip Clifford, and he has already worked with the League."

"But he is not a member."

"Nay, he is not."

"I have heard of Sir Philip, because I was given information on your past."

"You have?" she said suspiciously.

"You are his concubine?"

She took a step back in shock. She hoped her hot blush was attributed to his words, rather than her own guilt and anger. "Nay, do not think such a thing. He only came to find me because he was worried about why I was"—she lowered her voice—"masquerading as Lady Rosamond."

"And what did you tell him?"

She lifted her chin. "I tried to dissuade him, but he knew something was wrong. Finally I realized that if I did not tell him the reason, he might try to find out on his own, which could endanger our mission."

He briefly closed his eyes as he spoke through gritted teeth. "So this stranger knows everything."

"He knows what I know—which isn't all that much," she added quickly. "I felt it only fair to tell you what happened. He *did* help rescue me from captivity, and reunite Lady Elizabeth and Lord Alderley, Sir Philip's friend and now a member of your League." She took a necessary breath.

"Sir Philip is not a Bladesman for a reason."

She waited silently, hoping that Sir Walter would not want to ask Philip for help. And then she felt a little guilty, knowing that the League had meant a great deal to Philip. But she had the opportunity for her own success, and she did not want to lose it.

"At first he had not proven himself worthy," Sir Walter said, "but now he has a growing reputation as a man who takes unacceptable risks, who acts before he thinks—not the mark of a Bladesman. His approach to you last night only proves it."

"And how do you know this of him?"

"Because I have been privy to any information that concerns you."

"And they send you regular missives on everyone I've met?"

He did not answer, and she put her hands on her hips in frustration, trying not to imagine what tales he might have heard of her—and Philip.

He sighed. "Lady Rosamond, you have presented me with an unwelcome dilemma. On one hand, Sir Philip is a gifted swordsman and an intelligent man. He would prove useful on our journey. Yet always I will worry if he will somehow betray us, whether deliberately or not."

"He would never do such a thing." Anne could have groaned. Now she was defending him! "He doesn't even know I have come to you."

"You are very clever, Lady Rosamond."

She winced. "I did not mean to be clever, only honest."

His eyes sharpened. "And you don't seem to wish his presence."

She said nothing.

"But neither of us can do what would satisfy us personally. I will send Sir Philip a missive, asking him to meet us at Micklegate Bar, outside the city walls. If he agrees to journey with us, we could use his help. And I will at least be able to keep an eye on a man with too much knowledge."

If Anne had hoped to make a good impression on the League, she was failing. Gritting her teeth, she could only nod.

"You will bar the shutters from now on."

"I promise."

Anne left Sir Walter's room, feeling hot with anger and humiliation. It was done, and she could only go forward. If Philip agreed to join them, she would keep her distance, and never let things get out of control again.

The portcullis slowly lifted, its sharp points retreating up into the gatehouse. Philip slipped beneath, leading his horse. Fog shrouded the early gray morn in darkness, hovering above the Ouse River, making it hard to see. He stationed himself near the gatehouse and waited.

He must truly be over his desire to join the League, because even though his boyhood heroes were again coming to life, he felt no eagerness, no excitement. Only curiosity—and worry for Anne's sake. Why had she told them about his visit? They could not be happy that he knew of their mission. Yet still they wanted to meet with him. He wondered how far they would go to protect themselves.

He'd spent his life striving to be someone—first a soldier, and then when he was lucky enough to be named a squire, he'd seen his chance to serve his master well. Knighthood had been unexpected, and had made him realize that *all* his dreams might come true, if he worked hard enough.

But not his dreams of the League; he was a practical man, and knew that it was time to go on with his life. Reassuring himself about Anne's protection would be a start—and would ease some of his guilt. He only hoped that they did not try to detain him.

A small party came through the town walls, three men and two women riding, with three packhorses being led behind. As the men looked about alertly, the taller woman pushed back the hood of her cloak, and he saw that it was Anne. A feeling of intense awareness moved through him, a heating of his blood and an uncomfortable erection. He always knew when she was near him—no wonder he had pulled her across his lap in the tavern. The sooner he could continue his own journey, the better.

Philip led his horse nearer, and as one, all three men put a hand on their swords, as if they had not asked for this meeting.

"Peace, gentlemen," Philip said. He bowed to Anne. "Lady Rosamond."

One of the Bladesmen, broad and powerful, rode toward him and dismounted. It was the same man who'd held a knife to his throat when Philip had accosted Anne.

"I am Sir Walter. Lady Rosamond told me of your unwelcome visit to her chamber."

Unwelcome. She was still very angry.

Philip nodded. "I was concerned for her. It was too easy for me to make my way into her chamber."

Walter frowned, but did not glance at Anne. "I have requested that Lady Rosamond bar the shutters from now on. My assumption that she would know to protect herself in this way was wrong. It will not happen again."

There was a subtle hint of menace in his voice— was he warning Philip to stay away from his charge? Or warning Anne? Philip didn't like leaving her like this. He would follow at a distance and see for himself that she would be fine. He owed her that much. But he wouldn't tell that to this proud Bladesman.

Walter cleared his throat, a crack in his calm facade. "I lost a man to injury recently. I know of you, Sir Philip. Would you join our party in protection of Lady Rosamond?"

Philip didn't bother to hide his surprise. "Why not another Bladesman?"

"We are unable to alert one at this time."

He cocked his head. "Alert?"

Walter scowled. "You know of us and our mission. Do you wish the position or not?"

It was obvious that hiring Philip was barely better than using a stranger, at least to Walter. Or perhaps it was a way for the knight to keep an eye on Philip, who now knew too much. His own plans would have to be put aside. Philip glanced at Anne, but she betrayed no emotion and did not protest. Surely she had to be against his inclusion. It would be awkward; they would be together much of the time. At Alderley, he'd barely been able to keep his hands off her, though she'd been under his own friend's protection. Now, on the open road . . .

Yet Anne needed him, and he owed her for the mistakes he'd made.

He must have studied her too closely, for Walter's frown grew even more ominous.

"What is your answer?" the knight demanded.

"What does the position entail?"

"Guarding Lady Rosamond at all times until the journey is over."

"And where will we be traveling?"

"And how is that your concern?"

Philip opened his mouth, but then thought better of it. He would be under this knight's command. It would be best not to antagonize him.

"You are, of course, correct," Philip said. "Might I know how long this employment will last?"

"Several weeks; perhaps as long as two months."

"Ah, I see."

"Will it bother you to be away from the excitement of the tournaments?" Walter asked, a touch of sarcasm in his voice. "To do your job well here, it is best not to be noticed at all, except as a force of strength for our lady."

So he had heard of Philip's recent adventures. And he didn't seem to approve. Well, Philip was no longer living for the approval of the League of the Blade.

"I was long trained as a soldier before I was a knight," Philip said. "I understand the duties you have laid out, and I can follow your orders. I accept the offer."

Walter only harrumphed, as if the answer was never

in doubt. Maybe it wasn't, Philip thought, glancing at Anne. She sat prettily on her horse, no sidesaddle for her. The real Lady Rosamond was obviously not a typical female. Neither was Anne. She was an enigma, a maidservant who could pass as nobility with ease. He couldn't read her expression, and he found himself far too interested in learning how to do so.

"Since you are obviously leaving today," Philip said, "I need an hour or so to store my armor and pay my accounts. Shall I meet you down the road?"

Walter nodded.

Philip smiled. "And you would be heading . . . ?"

"To Ferrybridge, where we cross the River Aire."

"And into Pontefract itself?"

"Nay," Walter said. "My lady does not wish to journey there."

It was a decent size town with a royal castle, Philip thought. Not someplace a fake widowed countess could blend in easily. "I understand," he said. "I shall meet with you in but a few hours."

To Anne, the hours seemed to trudge by slowly. The three Bladesmen concentrated on their surroundings and spoke little, which made her dwell on the fact that she'd disappointed them. Margaret was not easily coaxed into speaking. So Anne was forced to admire the greenery of the fertile plain of the Yorkshire countryside and the view of distant mountains in the west. She wouldn't allow herself to think about Philip.

But at last he joined them. Sir Walter stopped for a mid-morning break to let the horses graze and introduce his fellow knights. Anne wanted to ignore Philip, but knew that would be too suspicious. He was not as handsome as Sir Joseph, nor as tall as Sir David, or as broad as Sir Walter. His brigandine, the traveling armor protecting his chest and back, outlined the width of his chest, with a cloak thrown back from his shoulders. Once she had been held against that chest, felt the overwhelming stirrings of desire she'd never felt for another man. With a groan, she closed her eyes. She could not think about that. Determined to be professional, she met his gaze—and he looked away from her smoothly. She was relieved. He, too, could play at these parts they'd been assigned.

Philip was introduced to the other two knights and to Margaret, who all gathered around awkwardly. Anne could see their suspicion and their worry.

Sir Walter said, "You knew Lady Rosamond before?"

Philip glanced at her, an eyebrow raised. He would have to get used to never calling her by her real name.

"Aye, for a few weeks only," Philip said, "when she performed a great deed of service for Lord Alderley. But you have already heard about that."

Sir Walter nodded and passed to Philip a wedge of cheese. As usual, no one spoke as they stretched their legs in the little clearing beside a stream. Anne stooped to drink from her cupped hands, but faltered when she saw Philip leaning against a tree on the other side of the clearing, watching her. For a moment she stared at him, caught in some indefinable spell, so aware of him, yet truly knowing so little *about* him.

What was this? she asked herself angrily. Wasn't her remorse enough to shield her from such awareness of him?

When they mounted, he was the first one at her side, saying nothing, but offering his linked hands for her to step into. She steadied herself on his shoulder, as she efficiently swung her leg low over the horse's back and tucked part of her skirt beneath her. Riding astride like a man had not been hard to master, and she enjoyed the higher degree of control over the animal. But there was always the problem of rearranging her skirts, and she quickly tugged them over her lower legs before Philip could see too much. But he had already turned away.

She wondered if he would ride at her side, and tensed as they fell into pairs, but as usual, silent Margaret rode next to her, and Philip guided his mount to the rear beside Sir Walter. Anne released a slow breath. So far, so good.

Philip rode behind Anne, glancing up and down the road as they headed south. In the distance behind them, he saw a farmer's cart, and far ahead of them a shepherd guided his sheep in their crossing.

"You look for danger?" Walter asked him.

Philip glanced at the knight, who was at least ten to fifteen years his senior. There was experience and care in the lines that bracketed his eyes and mouth, but Philip had also glimpsed the fine hem of the man's shirt beneath his jerkin. This was a man of wealth; his bearing of great dignity. Was he more than a knight? With the Bladesmen, one never knew.

"Am I not supposed to keep watch for our lady?" Philip replied.

"Aye, do it well," Walter said, his sharp gaze scanning the flat countryside.

Philip let the silence lengthen for several minutes, studying the group. Occasionally Anne pointed out something in the distance to her maid, but other than that, no one spoke. He didn't think he could keep silent for so long, so he might as well make that clear.

He slowed his horse, and when Walter noticed, he did the same.

"You saw something?" the older knight asked sharply.

"Nay, I thought to put to you my questions, if you don't mind."

Frowning, Walter said, "I'll only answer what I can."

"Lady Rosamond told me some of the details of this journey."

"Told you freely, or did you force her to tell you?"

Philip smiled. "My curiosity could not be contained, I will admit. 'Coerced' would be a better word. I was concerned for her safety."

"No one suspects our true purpose," Walter said blandly. "Lady Rosamond is a woman well known for her eccentricity, wealth, and intelligence. This journey was well anticipated. We have traveled in peace, if not always comfort."

"And you are used to comfort?"

The knight only glanced at him, and then looked forward again.

"Ah, too personal a question for a Bladesman such as yourself. Very well, I will focus on the mission, and not the players. Assuming you are acting on orders from above, does it not seem to you a dangerous task to ask an innocent maiden to involve herself in?"

Walter did not look at him, but Philip saw his jaw tighten.

"Sir Philip, these are dangerous times in the early reign of a new king. The League cares little about the nobility of the people it helps, but in this case, all will benefit by the stability of the monarchy. The danger to our Lady Rosamond is only the usual dangers of travel on public roads. No one knows the truth of our mission, and we are taking great care that her identity remains a secret."

"The veil she wore didn't hide her very well from me."

"Because you rudely pulled her close. A more restrained man does not do such things."

Philip withheld the urge to laugh. So he was not "restrained" enough for these knights. "Every man in the kingdom cannot be a gentleman. Especially these traitors."

"That is why we took great care with the planning of this journey."

"Ah yes, the list of approved noblemen to visit.

How will you know if your noblemen have unexpected visitors?"

"One of my men will journey in advance to each residence, announcing the lady's impending arrival, and determining the safety of the household."

"And what are our duties while Lady Rosamond is interviewing prospective grooms?"

"We guard her at all times. We only remain one or two nights at each place, to reduce the risks. And then we move on to the next."

Philip lowered his voice. "And how do we know when this journey is no longer necessary?"

"I will receive word when the other mission is complete."

"And how is the other mission to work?"

But Walter only gave him a cool glance. "Such is not our business."

"So even you know not?"

"Sir Philip, I suggest you give more attention to the dangers of the road."

A dismissal if he had ever heard one. "I can do more than one thing at a time," Philip said, using the same bland tones favored by Walter. "For instance, the farmer's cart behind us has been passed by a lone rider cantering toward us."

Walter quickly swiveled in his saddle, and then turned back to Philip.

Philip only smiled.

Though Walter called to the forward knights to be on guard, the rider passed them with only a salute.

"Probably a messenger," Philip said.

Walter wasn't in the mood to talk after that.

But this was no pleasure journey, Philip thought, scanning the countryside once more. If the traitors discovered the plot, the only warning Walter and his men would receive would be an attack. And though a large army would be too suspicious, traitors would surely hire desperate—and deadly—men.

When they stopped for the midday meal, Philip watched one of the knights—David or Joseph?—help Anne from her horse. He thought it best not to help her himself this time, although he was dismayed to discover it had still been his first inclination.

But he was her soldier now, one of her protectors. It wouldn't do to lust after the lady, although that was another of his inclinations, even after everything that had happened. There was a wall of duty between them now, and Philip would try to respect it. He was vain enough to admit to himself that he wanted the League not to regret hiring him.

Margaret spread a cloth and bade Anne to sit. The maid spread out their fare of biscuits and dried apples and more cheese. Although as countess, Anne should have been served, Philip watched in amusement as she and Margaret both handed out portions to each of the knights. The knights stood about together, as if they silently communicated with each other while they ate. After so many hours of silence, Philip needed to use his voice. He sat down on the edge of the blanket beside the two women. Margaret eyed him in surprise and suspicion, while Anne looked wary. She even shifted away from him. Could she still be interested in him, after how he'd hurt her?

"Would you like more, Sir Philip?" Margaret asked.

"I haven't finished my portion yet." Philip took a bite of his apple and chewed, and his gaze slid back to Anne.

He enjoyed watching her too much. When he'd first met her and thought her Lady Elizabeth, John's betrothed, he had envied his friend. Anne had seemed warm and intelligent and beautiful, a rare trio of talent. When Philip had discovered the masquerade, and realized that Anne was Elizabeth's maid, she had become even more intriguing to him, for she had fooled not only him, but also a power-hungry viscount. Over the next few weeks, he had discovered that the warmth and intelligence were all hers. But there had also been a sadness about her that he hadn't understood and couldn't ask about. There had been desperation there, too, something he could now admit to himself that he'd shared.

And it had all sparked into heated encounters that still haunted his dreams. She had been a woman of rare passion, and he'd thought they were simply enjoying each other. But before he'd taken her, he'd had a feeling of foreboding, that in her innocence she had not understood their relationship. He had not considered it meaningless, but he would never forget the look of surprise, and then humiliation she'd showed him, before her pride had smoothed her expression. He did not want to hurt her like that again.

If she was still sad about anything, she didn't show it. Her dark eyes glimmered in the sunlight as she bit into her biscuit.

He considered a safe topic. "How were things when you left Castle Alderley, Countess?"

She didn't even look surprised when he used the title. She had been well into her character for two weeks now.

She gave him a considering look but did not smile. "Did you know that Lady Elizabeth is expecting a child?"

Surprised, he leaned back on one hand. "Nay, that is good news. John must be quite full of himself."

"I think not. He has become overly cautious of Elizabeth since the news was announced. She was quite put out that I was leaving her to fend off his caution all alone."

"What did they think of this journey?"

As Margaret sliced more cheese, she made no secret that she watched and listened.

Anne hesitated. "They understood my need to be of help."

"John did? Well, of course he would, being of the League."

"You know that he was only recently invited to serve," she pointed out. "He has not yet even gone away for his first training. But he seemed to understand—"

She broke off, lowering her gaze so that he could no longer see her troubled eyes.

"Understood more than your need to be of help?" Philip pressed.

Chapter 4

Anne told herself that it was ridiculous to be bothered by Philip's questions. Of course he would be curious about why she'd accepted this assignment, how his good friend, Lord Alderley, her new master, had reacted.

But she didn't want to explain about her family; the subject was still too painful. He did not deserve to know that, lately, being someone else was better than being herself.

She gave him Lady Rosamond's bright, bold smile. "Lord Alderley understood that I was bored."

He frowned. "Bored? I don't think that was what you first meant to say."

Margaret was leaning toward them in open fascination.

Anne glanced at her. "Would you mind packing away the food?"

Margaret nodded in disappointment. "Aye, milady."

Anne was still unused to other people obeying her as if she were nobility. When she'd pretended to be Elizabeth, only Elizabeth and Viscount Bannaster had ever seen her performance—and Philip, of course. But none of them had had to behave subserviently to her. Sometimes it was a powerful feeling, knowing that these four knights and another maid had to do her bidding.

But she had to distract Philip. "Speaking of Viscount Bannaster," she began.

"Who did?" he asked, a grin tugging at his lips.

She felt an angry blush heat her cheeks. She forgot that she'd said nothing aloud. "Your discussion of Alderley made me think of him."

"Then by all means, do so."

She wasn't going to allow his humor to lure her. Philip was a genial man, well able to make people relax. Even she, who should be on her guard. His warm green eyes reminded her too much of carefree summer days, when all he'd had to do was look at her to heat her blood and make her want his every intimate attention. She gave him a quick frown, but all he did was tilt his head with studied innocence.

"Viscount Bannaster?" he prodded.

"He was on the original husband-hunting list."

"I'm sure he would be happy to know that," Philip scoffed. "After all, he failed trying to win Elizabeth."

"Well, he's off the list now, since I alerted . . . the people who need to know."

"You already rejected him once in your guise as Elizabeth. Wouldn't it be amusing if you could—"

"Sir Philip, such conjecture is pointless," she said sternly. "We won't be seeing Lord Bannaster."

"What a shame."

Even when they talked of other things, his low voice rumbled through her in startling—and unwelcome—ways. Days, perhaps weeks, of his personal attention stretched before her. She would somehow have to learn to guard her emotions. Such a skill could only help her work with the League, she reminded herself.

She looked up to see Sir Walter and his men cinching the horses' saddle girths in preparation for the resumption of the journey. Margaret closed the saddlebag, then stood looking off in the distance, her expression sad.

"Does she miss her lady?" Philip asked.

The intimacy of his voice startled Anne. Obviously he wanted no one else to hear him.

Anne knew she should stand up, move away, but strangely, she couldn't. They weren't alone, but somehow it felt as if they were. She didn't allow herself to look at him. But he was such a solid, warm presence beside her. How was she going to ignore him?

"Aye, she misses her old life," she murmured. "Margaret well understands the equality of our stations. She is not meant to serve one such as me."

Didn't Philip know that how he'd treated Anne at Castle Alderley had also served as a reminder of her inferior position?

"Are you not both serving the purposes of the League?" Philip asked. "Surely she has accepted her part in this play."

Anne gave him a quick glance. "Aye, I know you're right."

"I'm always right."

He didn't quite smile, only looked at her too intently, as if he was trying to read and understand everything she kept hidden.

Sir Walter called to them, "Come, Lady Rosamond. I will soon send Sir Joseph ahead to announce our presence."

"We are near Birkin Castle?" she asked, ignoring Philip's outstretched hand as she got to her feet.

"Several hours' journey yet. Perhaps we will reach it before nightfall."

"And this is Lord Milforth?" she continued.

While Sir Walter nodded, Philip looked puzzled. "Is he not a baron? And beneath a countess's notice?"

"He's very wealthy," Anne said.

Philip seemed unconvinced. "But he's also old."

Anne shrugged. "And I am a widow. I cannot afford to be choosy."

Late that afternoon, the men were debating making camp rather than trying to reach their destination. Twilight was approaching, and the road was narrowing into a turn. Just as Anne was insisting that she didn't mind sleeping outside, especially now that the rain had stopped, Sir Walter raised a hand. Instantly, the four men were silent, hands on their weapons.

Margaret gave a little gasp, her eyes shadowed with fear. Philip and Sir David drew behind them, and with just a look, Sir Walter sent Sir Joseph riding ahead.

Anne said nothing as she huddled within her sodden cloak. She glanced back at Philip, but he was not watching her. He had already drawn his sword, and was looking behind them into the distance.

Suddenly Sir Joseph shot around the turn in the rocky road, and Anne gasped as someone jumped down on top of him from a low cliff. But Sir Joseph didn't go down, and with a thrust of his elbow, was able to drop the villain to the ground, where he rolled several times and lay motionless. Sir Joseph galloped quickly to rejoin them.

Three thieves were riding toward them from the front, and three moving onto the road behind. Anne fought her horse's restlessness as the four knights surrounded Margaret and her. She told herself to be calm, because her horse would sense her turbulent emotions. But how to be calm when they were under attack?

"If we fall, my lady," Sir Walter said, "leave us and ride for safety. We are not an hour from Birkin Castle." As Margaret began to cry, Sir Walter tossed his dagger to Anne. "Take this to use if your need becomes desperate."

Anne stared at the weapon in shock. She pulled herself together, knowing that a Bladeswoman had to be prepared to defend herself. And then the attackers were upon them, engaging the knights. Philip and Sir Walter each had two men to contend with. Margaret's horse reared up, and Anne reached out and caught the reins, pulling down on the animal's head. She clutched her dagger in the other hand, grateful to be riding astride so that she could restrain her horse easier. All around them was the crash of metal, the grunt of men, cries of triumph or pain.

For a moment, Anne lost sight of Philip as he was forced out of the protective circle by his two attackers. But Sir David defeated his own foe and came to Philip's aid, luring away one of the thieves. Anne could finally breathe again, though raggedly. Horses neighed in a dance orchestrated by the pressure of each knight's legs, often going up on two hooves to attack their opponent's mounts. Whoever they were, the thieves did not possess the same training. One by one they fell, until the last two broke and fled, galloping away on their mounts, hunched low over their saddles.

When Philip rode after them, Sir Walter shouted his name, but Philip could not have heard him. Anne watched in fear as he took the turn in the road and disappeared from sight.

"My lady, are you well?" Sir Walter asked.

Anne nodded and dismounted. She tried to hug the sobbing Margaret, but the girl only pushed her away and shook her head, hugging herself. 'Twas a forlorn sight. Anne turned to the three knights, all of whom breathed heavily as they examined their mounts and then each other. Sir Joseph had a gash across his upper arm, but there was not much blood. Sir Walter's eye was already swelling and turning purple.

Sir David touched the blood at the corner of his mouth with his tongue. "'Tis a good thing they didn't touch your pretty face," he said to Sir Joseph. "Then what would you have done?"

Sir Joseph only grimaced.

Anne was watching Sir Walter, who stood apart from the group, staring down the road where Philip had disappeared.

"Do you think he's all right?" she asked quietly.

Sir Walter frowned, but didn't look at her. "He was a fool to leave us."

"Perhaps he thought by catching the last thieves, he was guaranteeing our safety."

"If they *are* thieves."

Anne stared at him in growing worry. Could someone know that she was not Lady Rosamond? Or did they think she was the countess, and that she knew of traitors to the king?

Philip returned not long after, and Anne knew a shiver of relief. She wanted to demand what he thought he was doing, but it was not her place. His horse was winded, and Philip himself had blood seeping through the hair above his ear.

As Sir Walter stepped forward to meet him, Philip swung down from the saddle, shaking his head. "I could not catch them. They know the area too well, and seemed to disappear."

"'Twas foolish of you to follow them," Sir Walter said harshly.

Philip stared at him in surprise. "I thought we would want to know who attacked us. If someone has guessed the truth—"

"Regardless, these women are our main responsibility. What if a larger force was waiting nearby, hoping to separate us?"

Philip nodded, his expression impassive. "I did not think of that. It will not happen again."

"You obey me, and not your own instincts."

Philip nodded again.

Margaret, who'd been helping Anne tend the men's injuries, now took a damp cloth to Philip, who bent down so that she could part his hair and examine his wound. Anne gladly turned back to Sir Joseph, whose arm she was bandaging.

"Have we been discovered?" Sir Joseph asked of no one in particular.

"They were decently armed and trained, more so than common thieves," Sir David said.

The knowledge that they might be more than thieves made Anne's neck tingle, as if someone hidden were watching her.

Sir Walter frowned, looking off into the distance. Dark shadows had begun to lengthen over the ground as twilight stole upon them. "I would hope they were thieves, but I cannot assume so." He glanced at his two fellow Bladesmen. "See to the bodies. Perhaps we will have a clue there. Sir Philip, you and I will continue to guard against another attack."

Now that the men were no longer being treated, Anne knew she should console Margaret, who was still trembling. But Anne wanted to see what Sir David and Sir Joseph were doing, what they would learn from corpses.

She walked toward them, glancing cautiously at Philip and Sir Walter. But the two men were focused on the distant hills, and not her. She was close enough to the other two knights to watch them line up the four bodies and begin to search their garments. It seemed a gruesome task, but she made herself watch. Finally they looked at each other and shook their heads.

"What about the man who jumped from the cliff to attack Sir Joseph?" Anne called.

They shot her admiring looks, then ran slowly down the road, looking into ditches and behind clumps of ferns. When they gave a shout, Philip and Sir Walter joined Anne to watch as the other men carried the last attacker between them. They set him down on the side of the road, near the horses.

"He is alive, but barely," Sir David said, shaking the thief's shoulder.

Though Margaret stayed near her horse, leaning against its neck, Anne forced herself to look down at the injured man. Blood oozed from his mouth and nose, and even his ears, she realized as she shuddered. But at last, the prodding roused him, and he blinked in confusion. When he seemed to focus on her, Anne held her breath.

"Who are you?" Sir Walter demanded.

But the man just blinked at Anne and murmured hoarsely, "But . . . you're not . . . Lady Rosamond. He said . . . we were to watch Lady—" With a strange gasp, he died.

Anne felt a shiver of fear, and hugged herself. She felt suddenly vulnerable on the open road, with darkness creeping on them. "They were looking for me," she whispered.

Sir Walter gave a grim nod. "It seems our mission is not so secret after all. We have to reach shelter. The castle is only an hour ahead—"

"Wait," Philip said. "They thought she was Lady Rosamond, and *he's* the only one who got close enough to see that she wasn't."

Sir Joseph nodded. "That is true, but it also means that someone was looking for her."

"He said they were *watching*," Philip pointed out. "Joseph, you must have surprised them, and they were forced to attack rather than flee, so we would think them thieves. If they were just watching for Lady Rosamond, then perhaps they don't really know what's going on."

"Neither do we," Sir Walter said. "We must assume that the traitors know someone overheard their discussion."

For a moment they all looked at each other in silence. Margaret spoke in a shaky voice. "Does this mean that my lady is in greater danger?"

Anne tried to smile reassuringly. "Nay, I think it means that they still believe that *I'm* your lady."

"And *you're* in greater danger," Philip said to Anne.

She straightened her shoulders, trying to keep her

voice from trembling. "But as you said, if they were only watching, then they must not know who overheard them."

Philip crossed his arms over his chest. "But they consider you a suspect. We'll never know when they might try this again."

"We will remain vigilant," Sir Walter said.

"Vigilant?" Philip repeated in disbelief.

"And vigilant with our noble hosts," Sir Walter added. "Now that we know that Lady Rosamond is suspected, we won't know if one of these noblemen we're visiting might be a traitor himself."

"They would not be foolish enough to do something within their own walls," Philip said between clenched teeth, "not when everyone knows that Lady Rosamond is visiting."

Sir Walter nodded to him. "Exactly. But at least these men have been handpicked because they didn't know our lady."

"Yet this soldier knew her," Philip said. "This is too dangerous for A— Lady Rosamond."

"We can't stop our journey," Anne said. "After all, this is just conjecture. There is too much at stake. But I appreciate your concern for me."

Sir Walter said, "Sir Joseph, ride ahead again, to prepare the castle for our approach. Be very cautious."

Sir Joseph grunted his assent, mounted his horse, and rode away. Anne watched him go, fearing for him, but understanding that Sir Walter would want three men guarding her.

Turning back to the other knights, Sir Walter said, "Let us move the body with the others. We'll hide them as quickly as we can, because we won't have time to bury them."

Philip's frown was thunderous as he looked at the backs of the retreating knights. Then he came to Anne, standing right before her. She didn't want to look in his eyes, see the concern that might make her emotions overcome her. She tried to look around him, keep her gaze focused on the knights. But then he put his warm hand on her shoulder and squeezed gently. She almost leaned her cheek against his hand, just to touch him. How could a little fright make her feel so confused?

"Look at me," he said in a low voice.

She finally did, and he studied her with narrowed eyes, where compassion flickered. "Are you really capable of going on? Or are you putting on a brave front?"

She gave him a cool smile. "I will be fine. I was just . . . startled."

"This is more dangerous than you thought it would be." He leaned closer, his face just above hers, and whispered, "Just say the word and I will take you away from here."

The brief thought of being alone with him, safe, distressed her. One attack, and she was already questioning her commitment? Disappointed with herself, angry at his ready compassion, she ducked away from his hand. "I will finish what I started. But you have only just begun. If this is too much for you—"

Philip rolled his eyes and stalked away from her, going to help cover the bodies. Not for the first time, Anne found herself wishing that she hadn't told Sir Walter about him. Surely she would handle herself better when faced with Sir Walter's brusque assurance, rather than Philip's compassion. But her fears were still there, burrowed beneath, ready to alter everything she did. Philip was right; this mission had suddenly become far more dangerous. But if she were to prove herself to the League, she had to accept and learn from it.

Philip was shocked and uneasy at the welcome Anne—Lady Rosamond—received when they approached the castle. A line of knights and soldiers stood along the battlements, and in the gloom of twilight, he could not make out their intent. In that instant, his battle readiness took over, in case they were archers about to turn away this false countess. He moved to draw his sword, saw the other three knights do the same—and then the castle soldiers began to cheer and wave. He realized that the gatehouse stood opened to them, festooned in ribbons and flowers, with hundreds of torches lit, making dusk as bright as day.

Anne and Walter exchanged a look, and then she rode into the lead of their small party, with Walter just behind her. Philip thought that was foolish. What if someone who knew the real countess had escaped Joseph's notice? What if Lord Milforth had hoped she was already dead?

But no, the dying attacker had only said that she was being watched.

When the party rode beneath the portcullis, Philip's tension increased, but all he saw were several dozen people, some dressed as simple farmers, others obviously servants of the castle. All shouted and waved as if Lady Rosamond could be their savior.

Philip glanced at Margaret, who rode at his side. She looked as if she might shake herself right out of the saddle. He tried for levity to ease her fears. "Is Lord Milforth that desperate to marry that he has to resort to this?"

She gave him a faint smile and muttered, "Men."

As if that explained everything. Philip continued his scrutiny of the crowd. Was there someone here not happy to see Lady Rosamond?

All held back to a respectful distance, then quieted when their lord appeared at the top of the stairs near the entrance to the great hall. He raised an arm in greeting, instead of coming down to meet Anne himself. Was he lame, and did not wish to display it?

As Philip and his fellow knights dismounted, young grooms rushed to lead their horses away. He absently helped Margaret down, not taking his eyes from Anne. She'd been assisted by a man from the castle, who was dressed in a short gown and hose, and carried himself as if he were one of the lord's closest councillors.

"The steward?" Philip murmured to Margaret.

She shrugged. "At the last castle, the viscount himself lifted her from the saddle and carried her across the muddy courtyard so that she wouldn't ruin her slippers."

Philip arched a brow in disbelief.

"I told ye—men." She made the pronouncement as if it were her final word on the subject.

Her hand on the arm of the steward—or whoever he was—Anne ascended the stairs to meet the baron. Philip fell into line near Walter, and together they followed close behind. Anne allowed the baron to take her hand and kiss it, then rest it on his own arm as he led her inside. He was not lame, and moved at a good pace. Philip saw that although the baron might have had thirty years more than Philip, the gray in the baron's hair was sparse, and the smile he granted Anne showed his interest, which looked perfectly innocent.

But many men were capable of behaving as others expected them to do.

Inside the great hall, Walter drew aside the steward, motioning Philip and David to follow Anne. Philip knew he would be explaining about the attack on the road. The steward listened, his expression shocked, then gestured for several soldiers. Philip didn't think they'd find anything, but one never knew.

The air was cooler inside, smelling of fresh rushes scattered on the floor. As Philip's eyes adjusted to the dimmer light, he still found himself as tense as if before a battle. Joseph was waiting for them, and he, too, drew close to Anne.

Philip turned to watch two musicians serenading Anne as she walked through the crowded hall. From behind, he glared at anyone who came too close to her. Trestle tables were already set for the coming dinner, but Lord Milforth did not bring her to the head table.

"Would you care to bathe and rest before we eat, my lady?" he asked.

Anne smiled broadly at him. "You'll find I'm not a woman who requires much rest, Lord Milforth."

There were several titters of laughter scattered through those nearby. Lord Milforth smiled in obvious surprise.

"But I would like to wash away the dust of the road," she continued. "Have chambers been set aside for myself, my men, and my maid?"

"Aye, my lady. Please allow Gwen to guide you. We will all await your return, when you and I can know each other better."

When Anne accompanied a young girl toward the stairs at the end of the great hall, Philip started to follow.

Walter, who had joined them again, stopped him. "Sir Philip, you and Sir Joseph remain here and see to the safety of the hall. Sir David and I will escort Lady Rosamond."

Philip did not like limiting her guards, but of course someone had to keep watch for mischief. He nodded and glanced toward Joseph. Although the young man was already drawing his fair share of admiring gazes from the women present, he ignored it all to watch over the crowd. Obviously well trained, he had helped save Anne's life, and Philip was grateful.

"Joseph, when you arrived earlier, was everything as it should be?" Philip asked in a casual voice.

The knight glanced at him. Though his face was almost too pretty for a man, his pale blue eyes were narrowed in a keen study of Philip that betrayed uncommon intelligence. In a low voice, he said, "Aye, there are no unexplained recent arrivals. And no missing soldiers, although of course I could not question everyone in such a brief time. I will continue to, while we're here."

Philip nodded. "I would help, but that might seem too suspicious for both of us to make such inquiries."

"Of course." Joseph clasped his hands behind his back and went back to examining everyone in the great hall.

When Anne returned, Philip felt some of his tension ease. Walter and David stood close behind her. She floated down the stairs in a green gown sewn with embroidered gold braid from the hemline all the way up. The neckline pointed so enticingly to her breasts, well covered, but without revealing evidence of a smock. Rather scandalous, Philip thought, but he along with every other man present approved. On her head perched a tiny frame from which hung the sheerest veil over her dark hair, pulled back with a ribbon, yet tumbling down her back almost as freely as any maiden. Even more scandalous, considering her widowed state.

Anne held her head high, walking slowly down the stairs as if enjoying her own display. In no way did she indicate she was not what she seemed, or that she might be nervous. She held the admiring glances of every man present, and Philip knew he was one of those. How could he not, when he knew what she truly was, how very different she was from the woman she portrayed?

Anne walked to the raised dais and the head table, where Lord Milforth met her.

Philip followed Walter toward the nearest trestle table, and considered how he could do his part. There were certainly enough maidservants to charm; if he flirted enough this eve, he might be able to learn something about Lord Milforth—and the men he associated with.

When Philip was seated, and bowls of warm water were being brought about to wash, he found that he could hear Anne's conversation.

The baron handed her a towel to dry her hands. "Lady Rosamond, I feel quite privileged to be chosen to receive a visit from you out of all the many eligible men in England."

Anne smiled. "My lord, you were one of the first I considered. My late husband spoke so highly of you."

Philip saw the baron smile in pleased astonishment; were her words fact, or was Anne free to embellish? What a bind it must be to work within the confines of a real woman, known to many.

"I told my son this would be a good idea," Lord Milforth continued.

Philip felt some of his tension return. The son had to

be convinced about the necessity of Lady Rosamond's visit?

"Your son is here?" she asked in astonishment. "But he is not at the head table with us, is he?" She looked down at the other three men seated with them, all with the appearance of upper staff.

"Nay, Charles is with his men," Lord Milforth said, and pointed. "I had to convince him that your visit was important."

Philip followed the gesture and saw Charles, not much younger than Philip himself, seated with the other knights. He glowered at his father, avoided even looking at Anne, and took a long swig from his tankard of ale. Could he be a traitor? Was he angry that his men had been discovered on the journey—or just angry that his father was looking for a new wife? Charles would bear watching.

Anne touched the baron familiarly on the arm. "Be sure to tell your son for me that we are just meeting each other." With a laugh, she sat back in her chair. "Although I can see we'll have much in common. 'Tis obvious you are a skilled warrior, like my first husband."

Anne's flattery seemed to achieve the effect she wanted, for Lord Milforth smiled with pleasure, then appeared sincere as he said, "You are recovering well from the shock of his death."

She smiled at a valet who offered her a selection from a platter of broiled fish. Then she turned back to the baron. "Aye, my lord, a wife expects death from battle or illness or old age—but an accidental death, a fall down tower stairs? The spouse left behind takes a long time to recover—as you well know."

"Ah, it has been many years since my dear wife's death."

And just like that, Anne had engineered the conversation back to Lord Milforth, and away from the personal life that was Lady Rosamond's. Someone had taught Anne well.

"I am glad you have a son, Lord Milforth," Anne said. "Were you in need of an heir, you would have been within your rights to refuse my visit."

"My lady, your lack of proof that you can bear children concerns me not in the least. My own dear wife took many years before she conceived our son. You are very young yet."

"Believe me, my lord, should we marry, I will do my best to prove to you my eagerness."

Laughter erupted all around them, and Philip couldn't help but participate. He enjoyed listening to ribald humor from the innocent maid that Anne really was. Her confidence in herself astounded him—how had she come about it? What kind of family did she have that gave a lady's maid such a belief in herself?

But Walter was frowning at him. Did he think Philip paid too much attention to Anne, instead of the rest of the supper guests? Although Walter might not understand what Philip was about to do, he knew he could prove his worth. The next serving maid who passed him got a smile full of the charm he knew how to ladle.

Anne was thankful when Lord Milforth concentrated on his meal. It was exhausting thinking of ways to be bold. And she didn't like the disgusted looks given her by the heir himself, who had obviously chosen to slight her by sitting elsewhere. At first she suspected him in the plot against Lady Rosamond, but the more she considered it, the more foolish it seemed. Why would he be so obviously against her, if he meant her harm? That would make him too suspect. Nay, he just seemed like an immature young man who wasn't ready to have his mother replaced.

Though she was playing a part, it was growing far too easy to imagine herself as Lady Rosamond, in command of her place in life. She was beginning to feel that she had more in common with the nobility than with her own fellow maidservants.

One of those maidservants was a beautiful young woman with red hair and a saucy expression; it was obvious she had an eye for Philip, who surely saw the glances cast his way as she poured ale from a pitcher. He was not of the same sober bent as the Bladesmen, because he had no problem returning her grin and lifting his tankard to be filled. The maid leaned on his shoulder as she did so, and he was granted the press of her body along his.

Anger bubbled inside Anne, and she resented it. She was disappointed with herself that she felt distracted by Philip's behavior. It was too easy to remember being the focus of his intense gaze.

She didn't like watching him flirt. The maidservant

was gesturing broadly to include the whole table, and more than one knight looked on Philip with envy that he had her attention. Her simple gown was too tight and too low across her bosom, and he was at the perfect viewing height. She sat down in his lap, and they whispered together. If Anne was this jealous over a serving maid, she prayed she would not be around when he courted a gentlewoman.

"Lady Rosamond, do not frown so," said the baron.

Anne felt unnerved that her expression had been so obvious. Had Sir Walter noticed? She didn't want him to think she wasn't intent on her part.

"Your knight is not abusing my hospitality. Maud is used to the attention of men. She is harmless."

"As is Sir Philip," she returned quickly, smiling.

But she wasn't so sure. Philip now had his arm around Maud, his hand on the girl's hip. What was he doing?

After dinner, when the minstrels were tuning their instruments, and several of the knights had opened a game board of Tables to play, Lord Milforth turned to her expectantly. To her surprise, his smile widened, and he put his hand on her knee. She couldn't very well turn him away, but out of the corner of her eye, she saw his son Charles gaping at them. She could not allow this situation to get out of hand.

She saw Philip glance between the head table and Charles. He met her gaze. Did he understand that someone would have to mollify Charles?

She turned to the baron. "My lord, allow me to entertain you after your gift of such a fine meal."

He started to rise to his feet—what did he think she meant?—but she gently pushed him back, smiled wickedly, and walked away.

Chapter 5

Philip and the rest of the guests in the great hall watched with anticipation as Anne sauntered slowly between the trestle tables. He knew that the Bladesmen were just as ready as he was to come to her defense, but no one tried to touch her. Maud, the maid Philip had been flirting with, gave a pout as the attention of the men shifted from her.

Anne approached the minstrels, and then after a few quiet words, took one of their lutes and began to strum it, her head bent forward in concentration. The veil fluttered in a soft draft, her eyes were closed, and Philip felt the image at a very deep level, as if she were a painting come to life. Hundreds of candles glowed on her ivory skin, highlighting each wave of her hair. She was so very beautiful. And when her strumming took on the notes of a merry tune, he thought of the unexpected talents she possessed.

Smiling, she walked among the people of the hall, playing a song. When she began to sing, her voice was deep and husky, reverberating through him at a depth he didn't want to think about. If he weren't careful, he'd be looking at her with the same worshipfulness as some of the others in the hall.

But not the Bladesmen. Their gazes were cool, roaming deliberately over the assembled guests. Philip did the same, and immediately saw Charles Milforth, the man's expression caught between a scowl and relief. Was he glad Anne had left his father's side?

Suddenly, Maud was in front of Philip, smiling wickedly, catching his hand and pulling him to his feet. There were cheers and whistles as she danced her way around him, and he had no choice but to swing her about with feigned eagerness.

He knew Anne watched them as she sang, though she did not miss a note.

After a few turns about the rush-strewn floor, Philip noticed that Charles was on his feet, his back to the performance. Philip handed off the twirling maid to David, who must have been trying to get out of the way of the dancers. David looked startled, but Maud only gaped up at the sheer height of him, grinned, and took his hands.

Charles kept glancing back at the merriment in the hall, then at his father, who clapped in time to the music.

Philip moved swiftly between the guests until he reached the young man. Picking up a tankard of ale from the tray of a passing valet, he lifted it to Charles. "A toast to the future of your good family. 'Tis a shame I probably won't see it."

Charles frowned at him. "What do you mean? If they marry . . ." His voice trailed off.

"Your family's future will not necessarily include my mistress."

The young man glowered at his father. "Not if he has any say about it."

"But he doesn't, does he?" Philip answered with certainty. "It is my mistress's choice, and believe me, she entertains and flirts and smiles at every household we visit."

Charles looked as if he wanted to believe him. "You truly believe she will be allowed to make her own decision?"

"Who is to gainsay her? Though the earldom has passed to a cousin of her late husband, Lady Rosamond is rich in land and monies of her own, and need not marry again. There is no desperation on her part, and we have many more noblemen to visit."

Charles considered him thoughtfully. "My thanks for your honesty."

Philip lifted another tankard and clinked it with his. "And my thanks for the ale."

Remaining beside the young man, Philip turned to watch the dancing. Anne looked away quickly, as if she'd been aware of his conversation with Charles. She began another song, bolder, with a second meaning that had many in the hall laughing uproariously.

Disgruntled, Philip wondered where she'd learned it—or from whom.

He suddenly realized that Walter was watching him,

eyes narrowed. Philip cocked his head, but all the older knight did was glance at Charles, smile faintly, then turn back to watch over Anne.

Ah, approval. What every knight lived for, Philip thought with grim amusement.

When it was finally time to escort Anne to her bed-chamber, the merriment in the hall had begun to wind down. The lord's son had found his bed long before, and the baron himself had to be awoken from where he sat slumped in his chair.

Philip fell into line with the Bladesmen, allow-ing Walter to lead them all through the torchlit cor-ridors of the castle. As usual, Margaret met them in Anne's chamber, ready to assist her mistress out of her garments.

As Anne's door closed with her inside, Walter said, "Sir Philip, you may take the first duty."

Philip nodded. "Of course."

"I will have the next man come to replace you when the candle burns down two hours." Walter looked about, as if seeing that the corridor was deserted. "Do not be surprised to find two of us gone for several hours this night."

Philip whispered, "What do you mean?"

"We cannot take the chance that soldiers will again be waiting to follow us as we begin our journey. We will search the countryside for clues."

"But the castle gates were closed hours ago."

Walter's smile was faint. "We do not have to worry about gates."

Philip longed to ask him how they planned to leave, but Anne's safety was more important. "Did Milforth's soldiers return from hunting for our thieves?"

"Aye. They were not found, of course."

"Of course. I do not believe Milforth is involved."

Walter studied him. "Why do you say that?"

"Because Joseph discovered that no soldiers had gone missing, and I spoke with a maid, who indicated that everything was as it should be."

"That is good to know," Walter said, inclining his head.

Anne, restless and too anxious to sleep, leaned against the door, but she could not hear what was going on in the corridor. She didn't want to be alone with her thoughts, to remember what might have happened today if her soldiers weren't experts in their craft. She opened the door, and both men turned. Philip watched her too closely, and she almost changed her mind.

"I will not be able to fall asleep," she admitted. "I was going to ask to be accompanied on a walk—"

Philip spoke first. "I will do it, my lady. We have found nothing to fear within these walls."

Anne almost winced when Sir Walter glanced speculatively at Philip, but he said nothing. How could she beg for Sir Walter's company in Philip's place?

Reluctantly, she said to Philip, "You will do."

He inclined his head and took a position behind her, as a bodyguard should. She could feel him there, reliable and stalwart, keeping her safe from harm—but she could not protect her emotions from him.

Whatever communication Sir Walter was able to impart with his eyes, he did so to Philip. She glanced over her shoulder, but Philip only arched a brow at her.

"My lady, when you are ready."

She started to walk, not really knowing where she wanted to go, only knowing that she needed air to clear her head—and she didn't want to face more people asking if she favored Lord Milforth. So at the first circular staircase, she went up several flights. Philip was silent behind her, offering no criticism, as if she were truly his lady. Why were her feelings of anger toward him fading away under the onslaught of seeing him every moment of the day? She wanted to hold that anger between them as a separation, but she was losing the struggle. Lately, she was far more upset with herself than with him. How could she blame him if he acted upon his desire for her, when she could think of nothing else?

At the top, the final doorway led out onto the walkway lining the battlements. She took a deep breath, and the air was warmer than inside the castle, but in a comforting way. She started to walk, looking out over the dark countryside. Torches were interspersed here and there, ringing the battlements, lighting the darkness in shallow round pools that flickered in silhouette with the flames.

"Is something bothering you, Lady Rosamond?"

Philip's deep voice at her back did not startle her; she could never forget his presence.

"Nay, it is just that a bedchamber can be too silent. At first, I thought it a rare treat to sleep alone, but now I find that I miss the reassurance of someone at night."

He made a choked sound, not quite a smothered laugh, and then she realized how that could be interpreted.

"I meant my mistress," she said with annoyance.

"Or your ladies?" he added.

"Aye." She blushed. Of course Lady Rosamond had no mistress.

"If you'll permit me to speak freely . . ."

Suddenly his voice was even closer, and when she turned around, he was right behind her, his head above hers. She stood her ground, angry that he was not keeping to the boundaries of his duties as bodyguard. By torchlight, she could see the arch of one raised eyebrow.

"I cannot very well stop you," she answered tartly.

"Of course you could, but I know that you are a woman who enjoys conversation. Surely you have not forgotten those many days alone trapped in Alderley's tower."

She turned away again, not wanting to be seen so close to him by the soldiers who walked the length of the battlements. She put her hand on the cold stone and looked out into darkness. "An easy deduction on your part."

He was standing at her side now, but far enough away for propriety. "Of course. But I wanted to offer you a compliment. Your performance here is quite astounding."

She told herself to accept the praise, but she couldn't shake her suspicion, and her words came out more sternly than she'd intended. "As in you never thought I, a mere lady's maid, would be capable of it?"

"I wasn't implying so because of your position in life. Most people could not easily portray others, even if they're of the same class. You have a talent at mimicry that impresses me."

"Thank you." The whole purpose of this was to deceive everyone. The fact that Philip thought she was good at it should reassure her. Did the Bladesmen agree with him?

"This husband hunt is a brilliant way for you to draw just enough attention."

"Now you're no longer complimenting *me*, but my lady."

"So I shouldn't waste my time?"

She shrugged. "Whatever you say."

"You are not so easy to talk to anymore."

She gave him a cool glance. "Do you blame me?"

"Nay, you have reason to be wary, and not just of me. Every moment of your day is full of the tension of keeping your secret, worrying about being discovered—or attacked—and protecting something that has implications for the entire kingdom."

"And now you know why I needed this walk."

"Do you like pretending to be someone else?" he asked.

She bit her lip, uncertain how to answer. He hardly deserved her confidence. And she wasn't about to tell him of her plans to join the League permanently. He would believe it was his manly duty to protect her from such a dangerous decision. " 'Like' is the wrong word," she said slowly. "I am confident in my skills, and proud to be able to help."

"And glad to be away from Alderley?"

She glared at him. "I never said that. Alderley is my home, where my dearest friend resides."

"But you are a lady's maid there, and here you're the focus of everything."

She didn't answer—what could she say? He was right, but she didn't want him to know it.

"What about your own family?" he continued. "Do they know what you're doing?"

Inside her, a crack of pain opened whenever she thought of her family. "I didn't tell them. They . . . did not react well when they heard that I'd exchanged places with Lady Elizabeth."

"But she asked you to," he said in disbelief. "You were obeying your mistress."

"But apparently I was hurting my chances at marriage, because according to my parents, a man nearer my own station might believe I thought myself better than he."

"That makes no sense."

She only shrugged. "They are simple people, with one view of the world. If they knew I was getting paid for another masquerade . . ." She trailed off, knowing they would think her a harlot. She knew Philip was watching her, trying to see beneath her words, but she didn't look at him.

"I am glad you're being compensated for the risk you're taking."

She tried to laugh, and it sounded stilted. "Are you being compensated enough for these risks? Today's attack might not be the last."

"Lady Rosamond, you need not concern yourself with me. I am here to help protect you."

Perhaps he was as good at mimicry as she was, for she found she didn't believe him.

"You can't just be here for me," she said in disbelief. "You were winning tournaments and making a name for yourself."

"Perhaps this, too, can someday have the king's attention, even more than a tournament win. I'll have my chance at court to make a better life for myself."

"You mean by making a good marriage." How else did a knight rise in influence and property if not with dower land? He had told her so, and she had been forced to accept it. She had her own goals now, but inside she still could not conquer the slow bleed of resentment.

"Aye, I want a good marriage," he said, looking away from her and out into the dark countryside.

She wondered if there was a deeper reason it was so important to him. She knew nothing of his family, and was not about to ask, though he'd proved curious enough about hers. The wind picked up, and she hugged herself against the chill.

"Don't you?" he added.

The glance he gave her was far too penetrating.

Marriage was not on her mind, but she had to pretend it was so. "You assume someone would want to marry me."

Oh, that sounded too personal, too bitter.

He inhaled swiftly, but only said, "John told me that your father is a yeoman farmer. Since he owns his own property, surely you have a dowry."

She gave him a bright smile. "Nay, I'll only have what the League gives me. It will have to be enough. Shall we go inside?"

When she turned to walk away, she realized that he didn't follow her, only stood with his hip against the battlements and studied her.

Philip watched the stiff, proud way that Anne held herself as she turned to face him. The wind caught her hair, fluttering her veil, teasing out individual curls to fly free. He wanted to put his arms around her, to comfort her. Without a dowry, any marriage she made would be poor indeed.

"What happened?" he asked quietly.

She came back toward him, keeping her voice soft, although the nearest guard had to be fifty yards away.

"And why do you think a simple lady's maid would have a dowry?"

She said it lightly, but he wasn't fooled.

"Ah, let me guess," he said. "Your parents weren't happy with your masquerade, so they took it away from you?"

"Nay, they took it away when I would not marry the man they chose for me. They thought to punish my disobedience, but it did not work."

Why did he feel that there was more to the story than what she was saying? Yet learning of her family was too intimate. And he was trying to stay away from that with her. "So this is why you accepted the assignment."

"It was not the money." She turned her head away. "I cannot believe I am discussing this with you of all people."

He laughed softly, not offended.

"It was the chance to help that seemed so important," she said.

"And I wouldn't understand this?" he asked. "Aren't I helping you?"

"You're helping yourself, too."

"Aren't we all? Except perhaps the Bladesmen, whose anonymity earns them no credit."

"How am *I* helping myself?" she demanded.

"By meeting as many people as you can with hopes of advancement, the same as me."

"So I want notoriety?"

"That is too strong a word."

"Not for your motive," she shot back.

He caught her arm when she would have turned away. She felt warm and soft and slender. "I didn't mean to make you angry," he said. "Perhaps we were helping each other back at Alderley."

They stared at one another, and in the darkness, it

was easy to remember their furtive efforts to be alone, to take solace in their intimacy because everything else was too painful. It was hard to believe he'd been so upset by the League's rejection. But back then he'd had no idea what direction to take his life, and he'd felt lost. He wondered if she felt that way now.

She licked her lips, and he didn't like how easily his body responded. There was always an unwanted thread of desire between them, hovering, waiting for the right moment.

"Helping each other do what?" she demanded. "Commit a sin because we were not married? Using each other to forget that life wasn't the way we wanted it to be?"

"I am so sorry for hurting you."

Without responding, she swept past him, as regal and remote as a queen, and he had no choice but to dutifully follow. How many times must he apologize to her? And why did it matter so much to him?

He followed her down to her bedchamber. When she tried to enter alone, he pulled her behind him and went in first. Though Lord Milforth might be innocent, that didn't mean that someone might not come in through the window, as had been done before. He examined each shadowy corner, searching behind the changing screen and the coffers set against the wall. The shutters were barred securely from the inside.

When he turned around, he found her with her back to him, standing before the fire. She hugged herself, as if she were frightened—or sad. Was today the first time she'd ever been in a life or death situation? Suddenly, it was more important to touch her than to keep his distance, and he came up behind her, so close that their garments brushed. Her skirts swayed about his feet. When he whispered her name, she stiffened, but did not try to escape. He slid one arm about her waist and whispered, "You became too cold up there. You'll catch your death."

He gave her the warmth of his body, turning just enough so that she did not feel his erection as damning evidence of his base interest. His front to her back, he willed the warmth that jumped between them. He could smell the faint scent of some type of flower in her hair, and he nuzzled against it. She was still shivering, but he no longer believed it was from the cold. Gently, he pressed a kiss to her neck, and her trembling grew more intense as he licked a tiny path up the delicate shell of her ear.

She whispered his name and leaned back fully against him, turning her face up to his. Her eyes were heavy, almost closed, her lips parted, inviting him to lean over her shoulder and take the kiss she offered. Her lips, so long forbidden to him, tasted even sweeter than he remembered. He ached to let his hand sweep up her rib cage, to feel the soft fullness of her breast. When he was with Anne, pressing delicate kisses to her lips, he remembered nothing of himself or what he wanted in life. There was only her, and the desire for her that never went away.

When he opened his mouth over hers, intent on taking more, she broke away, whirling to face him.

Instead of tears, this time her eyes flashed fire.

He reached for her, but she stepped back. "Anne—"

"Nay, this was such a mistake."

"And it was mine," he insisted.

"I should have pushed you away," she said bitterly.

"You have far more control than I have. Pushing away is what you should do to any man who tries to touch you so familiarly."

"You think I have no experience at that?" she demanded angrily. She lowered her voice. "I am a maid, used to men believing that they can make free with my body."

He swallowed, feeling uneasy. "You believe that of me?"

"What would you call how you behaved not two months ago?" Before he could apologize again, she held up a hand. "Aye, fine, I accept that you feel guilty and sorry about it—and that it meant nothing to you. But you would never treat the Lady Rosamonds of the world the way you allow yourself to treat me."

"You believe I think less of you just because I've kissed you?"

"That is how you made me feel." She waved a hand and turned away. "Believe what you will. Just stop using me whenever you don't want to face something in your own life."

He frowned at her, feeling anger begin to overtake his guilt. "And what do you mean by that?"

Over her shoulder, she said, "Exactly what I said."

Aye, he'd used her when his life had seemed bleak at

Castle Alderley. He'd thought they'd used each other, but she didn't seem to see it that way. But what did kissing her now have to do with facing something in his life?

"You may leave now," she said. "*Then* there will be nothing in this chamber for me to fear."

Chapter 6

When Anne awoke the next morning, she lay still amidst the softness of the goose-feather mattress, absorbed the feeling of the clean sheets, and smelled the sweet fragrance that was a part of the cushions. Lord Milforth was treating her well. It would be so easy to become used to such luxury.

As she dozed, her mind went to Philip as it often did, betraying her. Oh God, she'd kissed him again, let him seduce her better sense away. She remembered being in his bed, amidst sheets that smelled like him, sharing the heat of his body. Sadly, her anger had faded, and it was only the intimacy that snared her, the memory of heated flesh touching in ways she hadn't imagined. Sometimes she wondered if her fevered imagination would leave her alone if she'd actually gone through with the act, made love with Philip as her body had demanded.

Her knights were waiting for her below, and it was difficult to be at mass with him, when her mind would not leave its sinful meandering. She avoided Philip's gaze, telling herself that she didn't want Sir Walter to suspect anything. But really, she felt like a coward.

After breaking her fast with Lord Milforth, Anne gladly left him to business with his tenants, politely dissuaded the maidservants who wanted to show her the weaving room, and went out to walk the inner ward. Her four knights were with her, the ever-present guard, and she thought they looked a little fatigued this morn. But of course she had slept while they'd guarded her door. She led them to the tiltyard and found a bench where she could sit and watch the soldiers and knights train.

"Ah, the famed discipline of which I've heard so much about."

There was an edge of sarcasm to Philip's voice that Anne found curious.

"How have you heard so much about us?" Sir David asked. "Before I was approached, I thought this . . . association was a legend."

"As did I," Sir Joseph offered.

Anne glanced over her should and said quietly, "And I'd never even heard of it."

Sir Walter studiously ignored the conversation and watched Charles Milforth sword fight.

"My grandmother was saved by a Bladesman," Philip said.

This was the first Anne had heard him mention his family. She was afraid to move, for fear he would be distracted.

"She was a lady of the court?" Sir David asked.

"Nay."

"Then where was she from?"

Philip suddenly stepped from behind her and walked toward the tiltyard, saying over his shoulder, "I had best show Charles Milforth the error of his ways."

Sir Walter's hand was clenched on the bench beside her shoulder. In a low voice, he said, "He had better know what he is doing."

"He befriended Charles last night," Anne offered, hoping to reassure the captain.

Charles smiled grimly when Philip approached, and then found him a blunted sword. In the ensuing match, Anne could not take her eyes from Philip. She could see the muscles in his arms bunch with each slash with the sword, as perspiration made his shirt cling to him. There was an intensity in his gaze that seemed far too familiar to her—he'd looked at her the same way when he'd been pursuing her. What he wanted, he tended to get, she thought, but not where she was concerned. She had turned him away, taught him a lesson. She should have learned her own lesson, but here she was, staring at him hungrily. She told herself to be objective, to examine his knightly skills. Strangely, the two men seemed almost evenly matched. Perhaps Philip was having the same trouble concentrating as she was.

"Sir Philip is not challenging him," Sir David said softly. "It is obvious he is holding back."

Anne narrowed her eyes as she stared at the combatants. Charles thrust forward and Philip jumped aside, and then swung his own sword, which Charles neatly parried. She could see nothing unusual in their maneuvers, but apparently the Bladesmen did. They recognized Philip's skill, perhaps the first step in realizing he could be a valuable member. Maybe Philip's dream of the League wasn't as dead as he'd thought. She hoped she wasn't competing with him for it.

"My lady," Sir Walter suddenly said in a quiet voice. "I want you to know that it seems whoever has been watching you, is no longer in the vicinity."

She clasped her hands together, pretending to watch the combatants, when all of her attention was focused on the knights behind her. "And how do you know that? Two of our attackers escaped, did they not?"

"Because last night, although we left you well guarded, we went out into the countryside and searched."

Her eyes went wide. "How did you leave the castle in the middle of the night?"

"We have our ways."

Teach me, she thought. *I want to know every skill you possess. I can do it all!* Aloud, she said, "I tried to persuade Lord Milforth to reveal anything he might know, but I believe him to be innocent."

"As do we, but I appreciate your dedication."

Besides portraying Lady Rosamond, she could be of even more help, she realized. She had access to every nobleman on her husband-hunting list, in a way that the knights never could. She would look for clues in their speech and mannerisms that might betray nervousness, talk that might hint at allegiance to others than the king. She would prove her worth to the League.

And then she glanced at Philip, perspiration dampening his dark hair, his body taut as he crossed swords with Charles above his head and held him there. Oh God, he was too much of a distraction.

That evening, Lord Milforth grew bolder. There was much drinking and dancing, and Anne found herself in his arms for far too long. He held her close and whirled her around with a young man's energy, and she finally had to tease him by pulling away and flirting with her eyes. Then she moved on to the next man, joining hands and allowing him to swing her about the floor.

She was passed from man to man, and when one lifted her into the air to turn her about, she caught her breath, feeling a bit frightened. If he was too drunk, he could drop her. When he staggered, she gave a cry—

And there was Philip, catching her against his chest, taking her from the arms of the knight who'd imbibed too much. For a moment, she was held against his warm body, feeling the hardness of muscle and bone, the very solidity and strength that was Philip. She looked up into his face, and he wasn't smiling. His green eyes glittered and she found her breath was far too shallow. When he swung her to her feet, she was almost disappointed. He caught her arm, whirled her about, and then passed her to the next man.

"No lifting her," Philip growled at her newest partner.

The man gulped and nodded.

An hour later, as the merriment continued, Anne slipped away from her table, hoping to escape Lord Milforth's notice. Guests and servants suddenly came between her and her knights, and she felt fear begin as a twinge between her shoulder blades.

Someone slung an arm about her waist and she stiffened.

"You cannot be leaving," Lord Milforth said into her ear.

His voice sounded slurred and slow, and she knew he'd had too much to drink. Her unease prickled to life.

"It has been such a long, tiring day, my lord," she said, striving to sound happy. "You have shown me how much I could enjoy living here."

"You could enjoy other things as well."

His arm tightened, and she had no choice but to follow where he led, praying that his son was not watching. She wasn't yet ready to scream for help—but would anyone even hear her over the sounds of the minstrels, and the laughter of the people? And Lady Rosamond wouldn't scream; she would be enjoying herself.

He pulled her into an alcove just off the hall. A window inside showed the cloudy night sky obscuring the moon. He tugged a cord, and a fall of curtains separated them from the hall, muffling the sound of merriment.

"A lovely view," he murmured.

She kept her gaze on the countryside and tried to smile politely. She guessed he was not referring to the scenery when his lips touched her throat.

"My lord, you cannot take what has not yet been offered," she said, teasing him to lighten the moment.

His mouth was warm behind her ear, and she tried to duck away. He allowed her room in the span of his embrace, but did not release her. Yet she was able to face him and put a hand on his chest.

He smiled. "I have heard that you are a woman who needs to know the truth of a man."

She cocked her head. "And I am discovering that by being with you." *Especially right this moment*, she thought grimly. Where were her knights? Philip had barely taken his eyes off her all day, and now she could have used his aid.

"Nay, truth in other ways," he murmured, pulling her closer.

Anne resisted, both hands flat against his chest, but the distance between them slowly closed. She felt his body against hers first, and then he cupped her head and held her still for his kiss. She kept her lips firmly shut, hoping he would realize that she would not give in to such poor tactics. His open mouth was wet, and when he licked across her lips, it took all she had not to shudder.

A sly voice deep inside whispered that Philip's kiss had been masterful, pleasurable.

When Lord Milforth finally lifted his head, he looked down on her with curiosity, then satisfaction. "It is obvious that your first husband did not kiss you well—I shall look forward to teaching you better skills."

She was Lady Rosamond, who would only laugh throatily as she said, "I like to be in charge of a first kiss—and you missed that experience."

She swept the curtains aside and found Sir Walter not a foot away, obviously waiting for her. She felt relieved, yet disturbed that he had not come to her rescue. But would Lady Rosamond have wanted to be rescued from an amorous embrace?

"Lady Rosamond?" He said the name as a question.

She smiled and looked back at a befuddled Lord Milforth. "I am fine, Sir Walter. But I think 'tis time for bed."

Lord Milforth hastened after her. "Lady Rosamond, I realize that I was in the wrong. Please do return."

She simply waved her fingers good-bye, and allowed Sir Walter to lead her through the dancers toward the main staircase. Her other knights fell in line, and she led them all to her bedchamber like a mother duck.

At the door, she turned and gave them a tired smile. "Your work was diligent tonight, gentlemen. My thanks."

Sir Walter stepped toward her. "Lady Rosamond—"

She put up a hand. "Nay, I am too tired to discuss anything tonight. Tomorrow. We are leaving after mass?"

He nodded.

Philip was looking between them with suspicion, but she didn't want to tell him anything. With her luck, he would forget his vow to obey the Bladesmen and go after Lord Milforth.

Philip found himself with the first watch again, and he began to pace after the other knights retreated to their chamber. He still could not forget the hollow feeling of fear when he couldn't find Anne in the great hall. He and the three Bladesmen had separated to look for her, and although it was only minutes until Sir Walter escorted her back, it had seemed like a lifetime. Where had she been?

Young pages brought up buckets of water for Anne, and Philip remembered the last time he'd seen her in her bath. He felt dismayed that he could not banish the sultry image from his mind, even when he knew how dangerous their situation was. Every time the door opened, he stood right across the corridor, as if guarding against someone else instead of himself. He saw glimpses of Anne, wearing that same clingy dressing gown. The last time the door opened, steam was rising around her as she bent over the tub. She looked up and saw him, and the moment hung between them, fraught with a tension that burned in his blood, raised to even higher levels by the kiss they'd shared. He was aroused and frustrated and angry with himself all at the same time. No woman had ever made him feel so desperate, or made him forget every other female even when they threw themselves in his lap.

Then Margaret closed the door behind her as she left Anne's room, smiling at him with absent satisfaction when she found her own door.

Philip was left to stare at Anne's closed door and imagine her inside. Thoughts of her in the tub were haunting him, and he could not even put them aside for this mission he'd vowed to complete. Was she, too, distracted by the knowledge that he was just outside, so close?

He paced the corridor and forced his mind to consider ways to help the king. Success would bring him the attention of the female members of the court. A good marriage should be his only goal, his obligation to the memory of his family.

But there was Anne, so close, a woman he'd pushed away. A woman who had found something else to focus on instead of regret.

At the morning meal, when Anne next saw Philip, her regrets and her anger mingled. There had been nothing between them but "helpfulness," according to him. And kisses they couldn't seem to stop. She wanted to groan aloud. At least she knew where she stood with him. She'd been a dalliance, a maidservant near at hand. She would not forget.

But oh, her body wanted more.

Sir Walter was his usual impassive self, and she kept glancing at him, wondering if he'd overheard exactly what had happened with Lord Milforth.

An hour later, when it was time for them to depart Birkin Castle, she thanked the baron for his hospitality, ignoring his look of embarrassment. He'd had too much to drink, he assured her, and she forced herself to smile stiffly. To her dismay, she saw that Philip had overheard, and now he'd be curious.

At last they were on the road again, and the open sky and rolling countryside, once so peaceful, now seemed too vast. The castle with its shouts of farewell faded into the distance behind them. Though she was relieved that her masquerade had remained successful, those feelings didn't last long. The road harbored danger, and she slipped the gauze veil down, covering her whole face. If they were seen, she did not want another man realizing she wasn't Lady Rosamond.

She trusted the Bladesmen, knew that once again last night they had left the security of the castle to ensure her safety this morn, but they could not know what they would meet down the road. Her knights formed a square around Margaret and her, their gazes seeing far into the distance.

Throughout the morning, overcast and misty with patches of rain, Anne noticed that Philip occasionally broke the monotony by trying to converse with one of the knights, but got nowhere in his quest to learn more about them. She could have told him they would never speak of their personal lives. Bladesmen took an oath of secrecy, so she was told, and guarded their privacy vehemently. After all, they had lives to return to. She didn't even know if any of them were married or had children, or were noblemen or simple knights.

Yet never once did she hear Philip discussing the League itself.

Elizabeth had told her that Philip knew every story

of the League, had even mapped out where each event had occurred, as if he would be able to figure out where their command was located. Anne had just assumed he would want to be here, in close proximity to the Bladesmen, so that he could discover even more about them.

But had Sir Walter's invitation to join her retinue done him an injustice, rather than a favor? If he truly had decided he would no longer pursue membership, she'd taken him away from the path he'd chosen for his life.

Yet last night he'd said he would find a way to be noticed. What better way than aiding the kingdom? King Henry would probably be so grateful, that he'd offer Philip his choice of wellborn young ladies with ample . . . dowries.

Anne sighed, and Margaret, riding at her side, gave her a nervous glance, but asked no questions. Of course not—no one could ask about Anne's personal life; she was Lady Rosamond Wolsingham.

Who should not be thinking about one of her guards.

Chapter 7

As the morning progressed and they journeyed ever southward, Anne's head began to ache from searching the countryside for attackers. How did the Bladesmen remain so calm? They seemed to behave no differently. But of course, their lives were full of adventure. If she wanted the same for herself, she would have to become used to being alert and wary.

She had to endure Philip's obvious suspicion about what had happened with Lord Milforth, but he didn't ask her questions in front of the other knights.

They scouted for a well-protected area before breaking for the midday meal. Anne stiffly dismounted and gave a soft groan as she stretched her legs. She had never ridden this much in her life.

"Sir Philip?" Sir Walter called. "I feel the need for fresh meat this day. Do you consider yourself up to the task of hunting?"

"Of course," Philip said, patting the dagger at his waist.

His face was impassive when he turned away from

Sir Walter, but Anne saw Philip's expression change to curiosity, and she silently admitted to the same.

When he had gone, all three knights turned to face Anne, and she tensed in surprise.

"Is something wrong?" she asked.

"I overheard Lord Milforth's advances upon you," Sir Walter said.

Though she tried not to blush, she felt her cheeks heat in embarrassment. "And I was able to fend him off easily; he'd had too much to drink."

"I regret that I was not able to rescue you."

"That is kind of you, but unnecessary. Lady Rosamond should know how to deal with amorous men."

"But that is the problem."

To her surprise, he rocked once on his feet as if he were nervous, then glanced at his fellow Bladesmen. The other two looked at the ground.

"Just speak, Sir Walter." Anne couldn't imagine anything being worse than all this awkwardness.

He took a deep breath. "You are an innocent maiden, but Lady Rosamond is not. She would know just how to kiss such a man."

So he'd overheard Lord Milforth's remark, Anne thought, wincing. She could not confess that she'd been trying to dissuade him, that she already knew how to kiss—and more. Then they would know that she was not the innocent maiden they thought she was. Though she did not have much respect as a lady's maid, she valued the little she had.

"I promise that I will do better if it should happen

again," she said, forcing herself to meet their gazes.

After a wide-eyed look, Margaret busied herself at the fire.

"I think you need to be educated in such things," Sir Walter continued. "Lady Rosamond is a woman known to be open about intimacy. A kiss might happen again, and we cannot afford to have people suspicious."

She gaped at him—did he mean to teach her such a thing? He was of the age of her father.

Sir Walter pushed Sir Joseph toward her. The poor knight stumbled, his handsome face flushing red.

Sir Walter cleared his throat. "We thought he might be easier to kiss, because his height is not so much greater than yours."

How could she kiss Sir Joseph and still face him every day?

"I do not wish to offend any of you," Anne began haltingly, "but I cannot—it would be unseemly to. Cannot you just . . . describe it?"

A bolder woman would know how to deal with this, but she just stood there helplessly.

Suddenly, Philip came out of the woods, holding a dead rabbit by the ears. She was so relieved she could have wilted.

"That was quick," Sir Walter said.

Philip looked at them all, and she prayed he had not heard what they were discussing.

"'Tis a good thing I'm a fast hunter," Philip said mildly. "I would have missed this amusing discussion."

Anne groaned and turned away. She wished she

could glare at Sir Walter, but it wasn't his fault that she was too embarrassed to tell him the truth.

"Sir Joseph," Philip continued, "by your blush, I think you're a married man."

Anne peeked at the Bladesman, but he said nothing.

"And the rest of you are too old to be kissing such a pretty young maiden." He handed the rabbit to Sir Walter. "I will do the honors."

Philip understood her dilemma, Anne thought with relief. He was rescuing her, saving her from embarrassment. She kept a frown on her face just the same.

Sir Walter handed the rabbit to Sir David, and then turned back to Philip. "I do not think this wise. Sir Joseph would be able to control himself—"

"Because he is married?" Philip said. "You wish to make him feel he is betraying his wife?"

"I would not be betraying my wife," Sir Joseph said hotly.

"So you *are* married," Philip said with satisfaction. "That rules you out. Sir David, are you going to demand the honors?"

Sir David, towering above them all, hunched his shoulders and looked like he wanted to sink into the dirt of the forest. He opened his mouth, but nothing came out.

Anne was beginning to feel a bit rejected.

"Then it is up to me," Philip said, taking her hand. "Let's go, Lady Rosamond."

"Where do you think you're taking her?" Sir Walter demanded before they could turn away.

"Someplace private," Philip responded. "An innocent maiden cannot learn to kiss in front of a group of men. And since I have already walked through the area, I can guarantee that 'tis safe."

Sir Walter looked like he wanted to object, but all he said was, "Very well. Do not go far."

"Just on the other side of this copse here," Philip said, pointing to the trees behind him.

"And be quick," Sir Walter added. "And nothing more than kissing. Brief kissing."

Philip put a hand to his chest in mock horror, and Anne struggled not to laugh.

"Do you think I would take advantage of this situation?" he demanded.

"I'm never sure what you're going to do," Sir Walter said dryly.

Anne pulled on Philip's hand. "Please let us just finish this."

Philip joined her and moved ahead, leading the way. He held branches aside for her and pointed out mud to avoid. He behaved so normally, that by the time they reached a little clearing, where a stream splashed over rocks nearby, Anne was feeling calm, even though she kept looking over her shoulder, as if someone was hiding amongst the trees.

When he came to a stop and turned to face her, she nodded to him. "You have my gratitude for the rescue. I know I should have just told them I knew how to kiss, but I didn't want them to know—to think—"

To her surprise, he put a finger to her lips. The shock of his touch made every word dry up in her mouth.

"Shh," he murmured.

He stood far too close. Their clothing brushed, and her skin seemed to jump with awareness. His warm hands suddenly cupped her face, touching her as if she were the gentlest new flower bud on a stem.

"Philip?" she whispered, her mouth so dry she had to lick her lips. "What are you doing? We're going to pretend!"

"Perhaps you meant to," he whispered.

His thumbs traced her lips and she found herself swaying. "We've done this too much already!"

"Then think of me."

He kissed her brow, and the faint stubble on his chin teased her nose.

"I am a young man," he continued, sounding so reasonable. "I have to appear suitably flustered after having the opportunity to kiss such a beautiful woman as yourself."

Her will to remain unaffected was greatly hampered when he kissed the tip of her nose. "But—surely you are talented enough to pretend."

His mouth was so close to hers that she felt the warmth of his breath. She knew she could have pushed him away, for he only restrained her lightly with his hands on her face, but . . . her will was no longer her own. It was ensnared with his, as she remembered the stolen moments they'd shared in dark corners of Castle

Alderley, the tender kiss of comfort he'd given just two nights ago. The sun may have been shining, filtering down between the trees, but the size of him blocked out everything beyond his face, his body that she yearned to press closer to. Beneath half-closed lids, his eyes stared into hers with an intensity that banished the last of her very reasonable doubts.

"I cannot just pretend to kiss you," he murmured.

When his lips lightly brushed hers as he spoke, she gave a small, revealing moan.

"I am not so great an actor as you," he added.

With those words, he kissed her. And she kissed him back, soft searching kisses that explored his parted lips. She relived the taste of him, the smell of him, slid her arms about his waist and pressed herself against him, trying desperately to ease the ache in her breasts and loins that she'd only ever experienced with him.

Into her mouth, he murmured, "Anne," and a deep part of her was so very grateful. It had been the first time anyone had called her by her own name in days.

When he deepened the kiss, she could not mount a protest. She wanted the hot invasion of his tongue, the way he explored her mouth as if he might never stop. She felt his hands sweep her back, molding her to him. When she met his tongue with her own, they shared a groan.

Chapter 8

Philip forgot what it was like to be alone, so lost was he in Anne's embrace. She was warm and soft, and the curves of her body melted into his. He didn't think about his future or his past, only Anne and how she made him feel as if there were not enough moments under the heavens to go on kissing her.

He wanted more; his body craved hers with a hunger that seemed foreign to him in its desperation. He let his hands roam down her back, feeling the sweet shape of her, the firm muscle and bone of Anne beneath her garments. He didn't stop there; his hands drifted lower, until he cupped her ass and pulled her onto her toes, the better to feel her hips cradling his erection.

Anne gave a gasp, and suddenly the hands that had been pulling him close now pushed against his chest. He let her go immediately, and she stumbled back, staring up at him in dismay.

But her lips were moist from their kiss, and her black hair, once pulled back and covered by her hood, now escaped in tiny curls. She looked like a woman ready to tumble into bed.

But she was supposed to be Lady Rosamond, the woman he was guarding. And she was Anne, the woman he'd hurt by dallying with her once before without consequence.

With a groan, she turned away and started walking.

"Anne— Lady Rosamond," he amended when she didn't turn around.

She stopped, keeping her back to him.

"Think of this as another lesson, one you passed. You're going to be kissed by men whether you like it or not. Lady Rosamond is a widow, accustomed to such things. I thought you enjoyed being her."

He heard her sigh, but she only continued to walk.

"Women," he muttered, as he followed her back through the trees.

He adjusted the bottom of his jerkin, glad it hung to his thighs to cover what his woolen breeches probably did not. He still desired her with an ache that was fierce.

He told himself he wanted his future more—the chance to better himself, to increase the stature of his family. If he could not be a member of the League, he owed his mother that. She'd had dreams for him, dreams he'd taken on himself. He could not let his weakness for Anne interfere with that.

When he emerged back into the clearing just behind her, every eye turned toward them. The skinned rabbit was sizzling on a spit over a fire while Margaret tended to it. The expression she turned on them was so impassive as to be blank. The knights shuffled with obvious discomfort, but Walter only put his hands on his hips and glared at them.

"Well?" he demanded. "What did your need for privacy give you?"

"An ache in the gut," Philip said, rubbing his stomach.

Anne turned to face him with a questioning look.

He spoke quickly to forestall her. "She said I enjoyed myself a bit too much at her expense, so she gave an elbow to remind me of my manners."

Walter's jaw looked clenched, but he finally turned his imposing stare on Anne. "He did not take advantage of you?"

"Nay, he gave me complete control," she said firmly. "And I used it when it began to seem he'd forget himself."

"Good," Walter said, not bothering to hide his relief. "Our meal will be ready soon, and then we journey on."

"Will we arrive at the home of Lord Egmanton by tonight?" Anne asked.

Philip wondered darkly if she had the entire list memorized, one lord after another all anxious to please and entertain her.

Walter shook his head. "We shall stay at an inn tonight on the outskirts of Doncaster. It is too large a town to risk being seen at the best inns."

She nodded and sat down beside the fire on a spread cloth next to Margaret.

The meal was awkward and conversation forced. It wasn't until they were journeying again that everyone made an attempt to converse normally. Philip knew that they did it by unspoken agreement, to distract Margaret and Anne from the thought of being followed. Joseph reined in his horse to walk beside Anne. Philip, in the rear, rode a little closer to hear what was going on.

Joseph took a deep breath, as if speaking did not come easily to him. And why should it, Philip thought, when he had a face that, all by itself, made women stare at him?

"Lady Rosamond," Joseph said, "there are things you should know about noblemen."

Philip, so close behind her, saw her face in profile when she smiled at the knight, and his gut seemed to twist in jealousy. She never smiled at Philip like that anymore, although she kissed him readily enough.

"And what don't I know?" she asked merrily. "I have lived with them much of my life."

"Noblemen who want to seduce you will do more than kiss you." Joseph sent a skeptical glance at Philip. "Unless Sir Philip has already mentioned these things."

"Nay," Philip called, "I was too busy trying to remember to breathe from the force of her rejection."

He caught David's grin, and even Walter wore a faint smile.

"So what should I know?" Anne asked.

"A man will naturally want to embrace you," Joseph continued.

"The better for you not to get away," David said over his shoulder.

When Anne laughed, Philip wondered sourly if she believed that of him.

Joseph cleared his throat, as if to remind them all that he was serious. "He will make free with his hands on your body."

"And I should discourage this," she said, giving him another smile.

"Oh, by all means, my lady. A man will be far too encouraged if you do not. And you yourself might become . . . too involved."

Philip noticed that instead of joining in the merriment, Margaret rode slumped in the saddle, looking down rather than taking in the view of the Don River valley. Could a man be the reason she seemed so distant from them all? Did this mission take her away from him?

Or was she only worrying about the next attack?

"This cannot only pertain to noblemen," Anne said. "It would seem to me that every man takes what he can get from women."

Philip knew who that barb was aimed at.

Walter frowned. "Not every man."

Philip glanced at him. "Are you saying you should not be included with the rest of us humble men?"

"I did not say that. But many men treat women with respect."

"As you do," Philip said.

"I try."

"I think this is awkward for you because perhaps you have daughters of Lady Rosamond's age."

Walter only gave him an impassive look. "You may assume what you'd like. But my personal life does not matter here. Lady Rosamond's does."

"It must be difficult to give advice when you can't reference your own life." Philip gave an exaggerated sigh. "Ah, the price of being a member of the League."

"Anonymity can be a good thing," Walter said slowly. "No one forces you to take sides."

"Although they do try to sway you," David called back from the front of the party.

Walter shrugged. "Such entreaties are relatively easy to resist."

"Because you are a Bladesman, and must hold yourself above the rest," Anne said.

"Because we have a sworn duty," Joseph said. "And it is of a short duration, so we know we will only be in a situation for so long."

Philip smiled. "And then you can go home, and become a mortal man once again?"

Joseph laughed, and it was the first time Philip had heard such an expression of emotion from the Bladesmen. Maybe they were human after all.

"If each of your missions is so secret," Anne said, "do your families know where you are?"

Both Joseph and David glanced back at Walter, who rode at the rear with Philip. They were going to allow him to decide what to answer.

Walter hesitated. "Nay, but should something happen to us, messages prepared by each of us will be sent to them."

Those words were like an icy breeze sweeping between them all. If the traitors knew someone had overheard them discussing their plot against the king, and it now seemed likely, the chance of danger and injury would always be with them.

Philip cocked his head, determined not to shy away from the subject. "So you prepare to leave as if you might not come back."

Margaret gave a loud sigh, and although Walter bowed his head to her in understanding, he still answered.

"We take all precautions," Walter said impassively. "But did you not, Sir Philip, when you went to France?"

"I had no living family when I left," Philip said. He felt a pang of old sorrow, but he realized that Anne was watching him closely, and he made himself forget the past.

"But surely you had belongings or property you would have wanted taken care of," Walter continued.

Philip shook his head. "Not before I left for France. I was a poor, simple soldier."

"And since then? I have heard you were quite capable at tournaments."

"Quite capable? What a compliment, coming from you, Sir Walter."

Anne smiled, and the other two knights exchanged a look that could only be agreement.

"And since then," Philip continued, "my friend Lord Alderley holds my possessions for me."

"He cannot know where you are at all times," Walter said. "What if something happens to you?"

Philip didn't look at Anne, but out of the corner of his eye, he saw her bow her head.

"My reputation always precedes me. Fear not, someone will know where to send my body."

He heard Anne's soft gasp. At least she didn't like to imagine him dead. He glanced into her eyes, the color of obsidian, so mysterious, and he could have gladly stayed there, trying to understand her. He looked away quickly.

"Nothing is going to happen to any of us," Philip added. "Our visible mission is innocent enough, and it seems that the men who once followed us have scurried away. Perhaps they don't want to interfere with a countess's right to marry."

There were fake smiles and nods all around, but an uneasy silence settled over them once again.

The sun was near to setting when Anne and her party rode into the stable yard of the Trout and Goose Inn on the bank of the Don River, just on the far side of an arched stone bridge that looked as if the Romans could have built it. She sighed in relief, for the last few hours had been tense as more and more travelers joined them. She had found herself flinching every time someone rode by, and her knights received several ugly stares when they reacted so protectively, more than once unsheathing a sword. Then people had scattered out of their way, clutching children who rode pillion on their horses' haunches, putting arms around their wives. Anne had felt a little embarrassed, but knew their caution was necessary.

Most of these other travelers had continued farther into Doncaster, which made Anne feel better. It was easy to see why the Trout and Goose Inn would be avoided. Though it was several stories tall, Anne could swear that the second floor sagged over the first. Geese roamed the courtyard and honked whenever someone got in their way. The grooms were slow to leave the stables, and simply looked at the travelers with boredom rather than offer to help with the horses.

"Is this safe?" she asked quietly.

Sir Walter studied the building. "'Tis been here as long as I can remember. It will do for a night. You are not afraid of rats, are you, my lady?"

When her eyes went wide, he gave that faint smile, the only sign of his amusement, and dismounted.

To his men, he said, "We will have to see to the horses. I have little trust in the grooms here." He glanced at Philip and Margaret. "Wait with Lady Rosamond."

"You trust *me*?" Philip said with a laugh.

"I won't be far away," Sir Walter said, glowering at him.

Philip held out his arm to Anne. "Come, my lady, there is a bench beneath an apple tree in the courtyard that doesn't look as if it will collapse."

Anne caught a glimpse of movement out of the corner of her eye. Though she told herself to ignore Sir Walter's jesting, she was still thinking about the rats. But when she turned, she saw only an undisturbed water trough.

"Is something wrong?" Philip asked.

His voice had gone softer, deeper, and his hand rested on the hilt of his sword. Margaret turned about in a circle, her fingers twisting and untwisting, as if their attackers would appear in broad daylight.

"Nay, 'tis nothing," Anne said doubtfully.

"Then you don't trust me enough to touch my arm while I escort you?"

He held it out to her once more, his expression knowing. Did he realize how much his kisses had made her think of him all afternoon, had rekindled every unwanted feeling she'd struggled for weeks to forget? She was angry with him for making her remember, angry with herself for being so easily swayed by him—and yet, somehow relieved, too, just as she'd been weeks ago, when she'd worried that a man's kiss would forever remind her of another man trying to force his will upon her. She reminded herself that in the League, she would have to become used to men who would try to cow her.

But Philip wasn't one of those. She reluctantly put her hand on his arm and told herself he was just a man. But his body was warm, and immediately she was back in her memory, held against him, feeling him from her lips to her toes. Lord Milforth's kiss had certainly not made her feel that.

Those green eyes smiled down at her just as surely as his mouth. Then he glanced over her head. She turned to see what he was looking at, and this time, she saw, just peeking out from behind the trough, a tiny foot encased in a plain, cloth slipper.

"Ah," she murmured. "I knew I saw something."

"I'm sure the child is simply playing," Philip said. "Leave him be, and come sit."

"I'm too stiff to sit. I think we should walk a bit."

And walking would allow her to see the child. She strolled with Philip down the length of the courtyard and back. They could hear the voices of the Bladesmen inside the stable, and an occasional burst of laughter from the taproom of the inn. Margaret excused herself and walked swiftly behind the inn, looking for the privy. Anne was surprised she didn't ask for an escort, but perhaps Margaret's need made her feel too embarrassed.

Lulled by their lack of discovery, two children finally emerged from behind the water trough. Neither of them had much more than five years. The boy was dressed in a dusty shirt and breeches, and he carried two sticks tied together to resemble a sword. The girl's plain gown was belted at her waist with a braided rope, and she carried a cloth doll that appeared well loved.

To Anne's surprise, Philip looked away from them.

The two children seemed to argue, as they glanced or pointed at the inn.

"They are far too young to be alone," Anne said softly.

"I used to have the run of the castle when I was a boy. I was just fine."

She glanced up at him, intrigued that he'd referred to his childhood twice in one day. Whenever he looked at the children, he looked away almost too quickly.

"You were with people who knew you," she said. "This is a public inn, and not of the best quality. No one has come for them yet. I'm going to talk to them."

"Countess—" Philip began.

Ignoring him, she walked toward the children, who hovered near the bench Philip had first offered to her. When the children tensed as if to flee, she held up a hand.

"I shan't hurt you. Don't run away."

They clutched each other's hands and watched her warily. She wondered if Philip's sheer size was frightening them, but when she looked over her shoulder, he was still standing where she'd left him, watching impassively. Maybe he had realized he might frighten them . . . but somehow she didn't think so.

"Where are your mother and father?" she asked.

"Got no father," the boy mumbled, looking mutinous.

The little girl simply pointed at the inn.

"Your mother is inside?" Anne asked.

The little boy frowned at the girl. "Don't tell her nothin'. She don't know us."

"Would you like me to go find your mother?"

The little girl nodded, her blues eyes wide over the head of the doll, which she held against her mouth.

The boy groaned. "She'll be mad, Lise, ye know that."

"Why would she be mad at you?" Anne asked, suddenly worried about how these children lived.

The girl lowered the doll. "We mustn't be here. She's workin'."

"Ah," Anne said, feeling relieved. "And you're supposed to be at home?"

His voice still reluctant, the boy said, "With me aunt."

"You shouldn't go back alone. Wait here with my friend"—she pointed at Philip—"and I'll bring your mother to you."

The little girl's eyes went wide, and she stepped behind her brother. Anne looked over her shoulder and realized that Philip had finally begun to approach.

He wore an expression she'd never seen on his face, and it took her a moment to place it—awkwardness.

"Countess?" he said.

She wanted to ask him what was going on, but the children mattered the most. "Philip, could you remain here with the children while I fetch their mother?"

"You cannot go in there alone. I'll come with you."

She frowned at him, but didn't want to point out the obvious flaw—she didn't want to leave the children alone. They might flee, and then who would help them? She looked about and spotted Sir Walter emerging alone from the stables.

She lowered her voice. "I'll have Sir Walter escort me inside. Their mother might respond better to me than to you." To the children, she said, "Wait right here, will you?"

They both nodded, but they looked at Philip with mistrust, and she thought he might be feeling the same thing. How strange.

She hailed Sir Walter and hurried to his side, sending one last look over her shoulder. Philip had sat down on the bench, and he and the children were just staring at each other. At least Lise had emerged from behind her brother.

Finding the children's mother, a maidservant who cleaned the chambers, proved easy enough, once Anne described the children to the innkeeper. Anne hoped it was not merely her presence that made the man speak kindly to the woman. She was given leave to take her children home.

Anne and Sir Walter accompanied the maidservant out into the courtyard, where they all came to a stop. Philip was seated on the bench, the little girl curled in his lap with her doll. The boy leaned against Philip's legs as Philip showed him a parrying move with the stick sword.

A strange softness stole over Anne as she watched the large knight suddenly so at ease with little children. Why had he been so hesitant, when it seemed that he knew just how to make them feel comfortable?

Chapter 9

For the rest of the evening, Philip felt like England's biggest fool. He'd seen the way Anne had looked at him when she'd come out of the inn, as if she couldn't believe he was capable of settling down into a truce with the children. So . . . he'd been worried about it himself. He'd made a concerted effort the last six years to avoid children. The girl had finally stopped looking at him like she was about to burst into tears. The boy had been in awe of a real sword, which became an easy topic for discussion. Philip had been rather stunned when the girl had crawled into his lap, as if she was going to fall asleep. Thank God their mother had come before that had happened.

Their party had supper in the private dining room that was reserved for the upper classes. It was good to relax while they ate, rather than worry about the motives of people walking too close to Anne. But she would not stop staring at him.

To distract her, he had tried to question the knights about the League. But they'd gone back to their usual taciturn selves, and she had only stared at him with narrowed eyes. He was glad when she retired to her bedchamber.

Joseph was assigned first shift outside her door, and they all realized that in so public a place, they had to be even more vigilant.

As the knights climbed the stairs, Philip remained standing at the bottom. "Sir Walter, I will join you soon. An ale in the taproom sounds appealing." He hoped Walter realized that Philip could listen in on private conversations, hear what various travelers were up to.

The older knight turned about on the narrow stairway. He studied Philip with those eyes that seemed to understand everything.

"Your shift is only a few hours away," Walter said at last. "Do not forget that."

"I won't."

And with that, Philip was relieved of duty.

In the taproom, the innkeeper brought a tankard of ale to Philip's table. "My best," he said proudly.

"You brew it here?"

"My wife does."

Philip tasted it, and then hefted the tankard in a salute. "Send her my compliments."

By his second ale, Philip was feeling more relaxed, grateful to have no Bladesmen grading his every move. The taproom was slow this night, and the few people there were as solitary and quiet as he was. But when the hair on the back of his neck rose, he sensed that he was being watched by a man seated at a table near the hearth.

When they'd traded gazes for several minutes, Philip finally called, "Do I know you, sir?"

That seemed to be enough of an invitation, because the man ambled over with his tankard, straddled a stool and sat down. Philip had his dagger out beneath the table, but he was getting no impression of danger. The man was broad through his face and body, and he already had a flush of drunkenness. His tunic and hose were finer than the Trout and Goose Inn must usually see.

"You do not know me," the man said thoughtfully, leaning forward to prop himself on his elbows, "but the innkeeper mentioned that your mistress is Lady Rosamond Wolsingham. Be that true?"

Philip was judging whether he should go for his sword rather than use the dagger. "Why do you wish to know?"

"Because I know her!" he said, smiling.

Philip could not imagine that a true enemy would announce himself, but he did not sheathe the dagger.

"Although I admit I am surprised that one such as her is staying at the old Trout and Goose, but mayhap she wants to keep her identity a secret."

Not with such a talkative innkeeper, Philip thought dourly. "How do you know such a fine lady?"

The stranger chuckled and tapped Philip's arm knowingly. "I collected taxes for her father, the old duke. I be Lionel Fitzhugh. Sorry I am to hear about her husband dying, leaving such a young widow."

After putting the dagger away, Philip signaled for more ale. "Allow me to buy you another drink, Master Fitzhugh."

For another hour, he listened to the man, encouraging him to both talk and drink, without confirming Lady Rosamond's identity. When at last Fitzhugh almost sank under the table, Philip helped him up the treacherously narrow stairs and to his room, needing to know if the man truly traveled alone. But there was no one in the cramped chamber, and only one saddlebag rested on the table. Fitzhugh fell onto his bed sound asleep, and Philip hoped he would sleep the morning away, missing their departure completely.

He trudged down the corridor to Anne's door, where Joseph studied him with narrowed eyes.

"I have to speak to Lady R-Rosamond," Philip said. For some reason, it was difficult to pronounce her name.

"She is abed," the Bladesman replied. "And you must sorely need yours."

The door suddenly opened and Anne stood there, clothed in that same thin dressing gown which curved to every part of her body and made Philip sleepless remembering what was beneath.

"Sir Philip, what is wrong?" she asked.

Joseph sighed. "I think he's had too much—"

"I am not drunk," Philip said. He frowned at how loud his voice sounded, and carefully lowered it. "But I met someone in the taproom who knows our lady, and I did need to make sure he was too drunk to wake up early in the morning."

When Joseph put a hand on his sword, Philip waved at him. "Nay, it is not like that. Everything is as it should be."

Anne felt a shudder of worry move through her, and she exchanged a glance with Sir Joseph. Philip seemed slightly the worse for wear, but not incoherent. He wasn't even swaying, but he was wearing a slightly silly grin.

She wanted to stay angry with him. After all, he kept using her for his pleasure as he would any other serving girl. But maybe she needed the occasional reminder of the kind of woman she really was. After all, if he could tell she enjoyed being Lady Rosamond, she was showing it too much. Or maybe he noticed, because *he* liked her more as Lady Rosamond.

She watched Sir Joseph point the way to the bedchamber Philip shared with Sir Walter, but Philip only leaned back against the wall, looking proud of himself. He jauntily arched an eyebrow at her as if he expected more praise.

Anne found herself glancing down the corridor, trying to be inconspicuous. She was hoping Philip would leave quickly, so she only had to deal with Sir Joseph when—

Margaret appeared at the top of the stairs, pushing her hood back from her head.

Anne winced. She had allowed Margaret to ensnare

her in a minor deception, all because she wanted the maid's friendship—or at least her respect. She had seen Margaret's cool reaction to the "kissing" exercise earlier in the day, making her feel unworthy to be Margaret's mistress. They would be traveling together for many days yet, and Anne wanted to feel at ease with the only other woman in the party. And the fact that Margaret dared to leave the inn, even if only for the nearby courtyard, made Anne realize how much it meant to the girl.

"Margaret?" Sir Joseph said with a frown. "I thought you had gone to your bed. Surely you know how dangerous it is to leave us."

"I had to use . . ." Her voice died away as she blushed.

Sir Joseph cleared his throat. "Of course, but I never saw you go. And you have your cloak."

"I feared it might be rainin'."

Anne stepped back into her doorway. "Margaret, could you please assist me?"

The maid hurried past her, and Anne simply smiled at the two bemused knights. "Good night, gentlemen."

She shut the door. When she turned to face Margaret, the maid was removing her cloak before the hearth. Margaret glanced at Anne, and her face relaxed into the first true smile Anne had ever seen from her.

"Milady, I cannot thank you enough," Margaret said.

Anne hurried toward her, speaking softly. "I had

great regrets about allowing you to meet your friend. I was so worried!"

Margaret briefly squeezed her hand. "I told ye I grew up near here. Doncaster holds no secrets for me. And surely ye don't think Sir Walter would let us stay here if he had any worries?"

Anne didn't think the Bladesman as infallible as that. "But you should have taken one of the knights with you."

"But *he* was with me, milady, protectin' me, do ye not see?"

Margaret hugged herself, looking so happy. There was a radiance about her that Anne envied.

"Stephen met me in the courtyard. 'Twas so many weeks since I last saw him!"

"And how did he know that we had arrived?"

Margaret blushed. "I told him we would be passin' through Doncaster. This afternoon, I paid a groom to take a message to the inn Stephen told me he would be stayin' at." As if she couldn't remain still, she almost danced to the window and threw back the shutters. "Tonight when he met me, he took me walkin' by the river, and we talked and talked."

Anne sank down on the edge of the bed. "Margaret, you did not discuss me, did you?"

Her eyes flew wide. "O' course not, milady. He thinks I'm travelin' with Lady Rosamond. I would never risk her life—or yours."

Anne smiled with relief. "Thank you."

"Now that we've seen each other again, and the feelin's are as strong as ever, he promised that he'll ask his lord if he can marry me, and bring me to live with them."

Anne was still rather amazed at how much Margaret was telling her. It was as if, now that Anne had proven herself by helping her, Margaret considered her a friend.

"I hope everything works out for you, Margaret."

The maid nodded, clasping her hands together and looking out the window, as if she could see her whole future before her.

Anne felt a little envious, a little sad. By placing her lot with the League, she thought she would never marry. Philip's face appeared in her mind, but she immediately banished it. They wanted different things from life, and she did not believe she was the sort of woman who could give herself to a man with no thought to the future.

Before dawn, Philip ended his shift at Anne's door and escorted her downstairs to the private dining room where they would all break their fast. Bells from a nearby church tolled the hour, but they would miss mass this day in the interest of safety. God forbid Lionel Fitzhugh decide to come see his old duke's daughter.

Anne patted her mouth with her napkin and turned to Walter. "What time will we arrive at Lord Egmanton's?"

"Late in the day."

"And are we staying one night or two?"

"We were asked to only stay one, but I explained that since we would be arriving late, you would have little time tonight to converse with Lord Egmanton."

She frowned. "Why were they requesting only one night? I've never heard of such inhospitality."

Walter put down his spoon next to his porridge bowl with his usual precision. "My lady, Lord Egmanton is younger than you, and this request actually came from his mother."

Philip choked on his buttered bread.

Anne shot him a glare, but all she said was, "I guess having an older widow for a new daughter is not her preference."

Margaret and Anne glanced at each other, and an unspoken sympathy passed between them, a new ease that had not been there the day before.

Until last night, Philip thought with suspicion.

When the knights rose to go finish packing, Philip whispered to Anne, "Tell them you're not done. I wish to speak with you."

She frowned at him, opened her mouth, and then seemed to think better of it. "Sir Walter, I would like another cup of cider. Sir Philip will wait with me. Margaret is so efficient, that she has everything ready for the journey."

Margaret flashed her a smile so brilliant, Philip wanted to tell her that she was making everyone curious.

When they'd all gone, Philip frowned across the

table at Anne. "Think not that I was too drunk to know something was going on last night. Where had Margaret gone and why did you help her, when being alone outside might have gotten her captured or killed?"

Anne winced. "Philip, she didn't leave the courtyard. I'm finally earning her trust. Do not make me—"

"You already have *my* trust. I don't wish to regret it."

"'Tis nothing important, really, just a matter of a woman's heart."

"So she met someone."

"Not here—I mean not originally."

"Just tell me, my lady," he murmured. "I need to know, and I will not tell anyone else."

With a sigh, she quickly told him about Margaret's suitor.

He sat back in his chair. "I understand that it is difficult to see one another when two people are servants in different households, but it seems to me that this Stephen put her in danger by having her go out in the evening unaccompanied."

"He was with her."

"Tell me that you were not foolish enough to meet this man."

"I did not."

"I wouldn't have been surprised if you volunteered to go with her."

When she hesitated, he groaned.

"Philip, you must understand that I am not used to anyone caring about my reputation or my safety." She lowered her voice. "I am but a maidservant, just like Margaret."

"And you're also Lady Rosamond, who far too many men are interested in—and not just for romantic reasons. As for Margaret, your behavior suggests that you wanted to be her friend, instead of her mistress."

She sighed.

"Promise you will tell me when Margaret feels the need to sneak off again. It is too dangerous for both of you."

"I promise."

"I care about your safety." He wanted to reach for her hand, but thought better of it. The touch of her tended to make him forget words. "And I'm sure Lady Elizabeth has always cared, too."

At the mention of her friend, Anne stiffened and turned away from him.

"I miss her," she whispered. "I always had her to talk to, to confide in, to—" She broke off, giving him an annoyed look, as if she regretted revealing so much of herself.

"And now you're trying to fill her place with Margaret."

"Nay, I know it could never be the same. My friendship with Elizabeth took a lifetime to form. But I just want things to be . . . easier with Margaret."

"It seems you have your wish." He stood up, tossing his napkin onto the table. "Shall we go? I fear any more togetherness will fuel Walter's suspicions."

As she preceded him to the door, she glanced at him over her shoulder. "Why should he be suspicious?"

It was his turn to sigh. "I don't know—perhaps because I offered to kiss you yesterday? And we are alone right now?"

Saying the words aloud seemed to rekindle the tension that always hummed between them. She looked up into his face, and without conscious decision, he lifted his hand as if he meant to touch her cheek. He wanted to feel such softness again, to explore the way her pulse pounded beneath the curve of her ear. Her breasts rose and fell with her quick breaths, and the urge to cup them was so strong—

But outside the door, the stairs shook as guests came pounding down them.

Anne backed away and grabbed for the door handle.

Philip closed his eyes and shook his head. So much for keeping his thoughts to himself. He almost felt like a boy unused to being around women—yet he had had the best tutor in the ways of noble ladies, his first master's daughter. She had taught him to read, to dance, and most importantly what to say to women. But the memory was a sad one, and didn't bear dwelling on, he thought as he followed Anne out of the dining room. With Anne, every lesson in propriety seemed to be for naught.

When they were waiting for the horses to be brought from the stables, Philip managed to speak privately to Margaret.

She stared at him nervously. "Aye, Sir Philip?"

"Margaret, I confronted Lady Rosamond about your absence from the inn."

"Oh, 'twas not her fault!" she hastened to say.

"I know, and she didn't reveal much to me, but I just need to know if your suitor is still here. I should talk to him."

"Heavens, no, sir! He has already left Doncaster. 'Twas why we could only meet last night."

Though her eyes lowered subserviently, and Philip accepted her words, he felt . . . uneasy. Something wasn't right. But Margaret had followed her own mother into service for Lady Rosamond, and deserved the benefit of the doubt. But he would keep her under closer surveillance from now on. He didn't like that a strange man had come so close to one of their retinue.

Anne watched Philip and Margaret, and knew with a feeling of guilt what they were discussing. Of course Philip had every right to be concerned, and she had probably made a mistake allowing Margaret her freedom. But nothing terrible had come of it. When Margaret glanced at her, Anne widened her eyes, but all the maid did was smile and shrug. Relief swept through Anne.

When they were all mounted, Sir Walter looked back at them and said, "I must make one stop at a nearby merchant's shop."

Sir David and Sir Joseph did not even glance at each other, as if they understood. Yet Philip looked curious, so she wasn't the only one ignorant of a change in plans. They walked their horses through the narrow streets of Doncaster until Sir Walter stopped beneath a sign with the crude image of a hat. Through an open window, they could see several people being waited on by the haberdasher.

Sir Walter dismounted, staring within the shop, then glanced at Anne. "Lady Rosamond, I could use your assistance. The rest of you can wait here. This will not take long."

Sir Walter came to help her dismount, even holding her briefly to set her down where the ground was not muddy.

She put her hand on his arm as they walked slowly to the shop. "I assume I am functioning as your noble lady?"

He gave her a faint smile. "You will be my distraction, Lady Rosamond. Exclaim over the hats and draw the shopkeeper and the other customers to you at the front of the shop."

"And you don't care how I do it?" she asked, nervous and excited as she warmed to her part. *He trusts me!*

He shook his head, and then went through the door first, hands on his hips, inspecting the establishment as if the king himself needed the security. Peeking past his shoulder, Anne could see a neatly dressed man, standing with three other customers, give Sir Walter a curious frown.

She took that as her cue, raising her veil so that her face was visible, and sweeping past her knight. "Come, man, move aside. There are hardly men waiting to attack me amidst the hats."

At the sight of Anne in her fine garments, the haberdasher's eyes went wide, and he swept forward through his customers, scattering them like a flock of startled birds. "My lady," he said with emphasis, "do come in. How may I help you?"

"I have heard of your fine hats for gentlemen, good sir," she said, "and I admired the beaver hat with the feather in your display. Do show it to me." As he came toward her, she lowered her voice a bit, saying, "But I would want to be the only one who owns such a design."

And with those words, she felt the other customers crowding around her for a better look. While the haberdasher held up the hat for her, embellishing its merits, Anne was able to glance over his shoulder several times at Sir Walter. The commotion had drawn another man from the rear of the shop, an apprentice by the plain cut of his wool garments. When he saw Sir Walter, his eyes went wide for only the briefest moment. Sir Walter put something on the counter—Anne could not see what it was—and the apprentice took it wordlessly, only giving a nod.

And then Sir Walter approached her, bodily pushing people away as they came too close to her. "You heard my lady!" he said. "Aside, aside, I say!"

In a huff, Anne sailed to the doorway. "I cannot buy such a thing if everyone will have it," she said crossly. "I will return, sir, at a quieter time."

She felt a twinge of guilt at the haberdasher's crestfallen expression, but Sir Walter had his hand under her elbow, guiding her firmly through the door and to her horse. After she was mounted, she pulled her veil over her face, and allowed her horse to pick its way through the holes in the street, back past the Trout and Goose, and into the countryside. As a light rain started to fall, she maneuvered until she was riding beside Sir Walter. Philip was right behind, and she allowed it, knowing he was just as curious as she.

"I saw you make contact with the haberdasher's apprentice," Anne said. "Does he work for the League?"

Sir Walter nodded.

"And you knew of him?"

He shook his head. "I do not know everyone, but there are places and ways to make contact. I discovered that no one from the League has sent us a message, but I sent one of my own, detailing the attack and our suspicions."

"What if someone intercepts it?" Philip asked.

"They'll read a missive to my mother, concerning a bout of the flu I'm suffering."

"A secret code," Anne said with admiration. "And how will you hear back?"

Sir Walter only shrugged, and Anne thought he almost seemed amused at keeping them in such suspense. But then he looked back at the town, his frown growing.

"Last night we moved through Doncaster and the surrounding countryside, and still we have seen no evidence of being watched. The quiet disturbs me."

"As if they're preparing for an attack?" Anne said,

looking at the foggy fields patchworked with long fences of stone.

"I know not. But we can only keep going."

Through the rest of the day, as they left Yorkshire and entered Nottinghamshire, the trees of Sherwood Forest gradually dominated the west, and to the east the flat plains ran into the marshes of Lincolnshire—or so Sir Walter said, as he was obviously attempting to distract Anne with a lesson in geography. Rain drizzled on and off all day, and she huddled miserably in her cloak, swaying side to side as her horse walked. She kept imagining approaching riders coming at her through the fog, and she felt tense all day, even though her knights took turns scouting the area. When Markham Keep rose like a craggy mountain near the forest, she was looking forward to being warm, and didn't care that they would have to be wary.

But there were no welcoming crowds, no one to greet them at all. Sir David had gone ahead to announce their presence—had he gotten lost? Or attacked? She looked back down the road, wondering in sudden fear if he had even made it here at all. Soldiers manning the battlements and gatehouse allowed them in. When Sir Walter questioned them, they said that Sir David had been admitted not an hour before. Anne took a deep, shaky breath.

The keep was ancient, with no windows cut into the building itself, as was now happening to more and more castles. It looked gloomy and old and Anne's spirits sank. Rain dotted in puddles in the inner ward, and the party sat on their horses, staring at each other in disbelief.

Several grooms, hunched against the rain, finally came out to take their horses. Her slippers, already wet before, were now soaked and filled with mud. She noticed that Margaret, so small and slight, was shivering uncontrollably. Anne put an arm around her, and the maid gave her a grateful smile.

Sir Walter took Anne's other arm. He looked up at the keep, rain dripping from his gray eyebrows and splashing his cheeks. "My lady, allow me to help you inside. I cannot believe the ignorance of these people."

"We already know that Lord Egmanton's mother isn't all that excited by my visit," she said ruefully, between chattering teeth.

He gave a grim nod, and together, all three of them climbed up the stairs to the great hall on the first floor. Anne glanced over her shoulder and saw Philip and Sir Joseph fall into line behind. Philip gave her a grim smile, and she quickly looked away. She dwelled too much today on that one moment in the dining room when he'd stood so close and looked as if he wanted to touch her, perhaps to kiss her. And she would have let him—again. Even though she knew he but used her for a moment's pleasure, she couldn't make herself stop wanting to lose herself in his arms.

The great double doors of the hall slowly opened wide, and a welcome current of heat engulfed them.

Anne sighed with pleasure. Tallow candles lit the gloomy afternoon and fires burned in hearths at both ends of the hall. She savored the delicious smell of roasted meat. They had had no hot food since breaking their fast, and her insides were as cold as her outside.

But to her dismay, the trestle tables were being taken down from the midday meal. A dozen servants were busy at tasks, and many gave them curious looks but did not come forward to greet them.

Philip stopped at her side, hands on his hips. "Shall I give a shout, then? Mayhap someone with authority might care."

"Where is Sir David?" Anne asked.

At last a man came toward them from an arched doorway across the hall, and in his wake strode Sir David, looking grim as he towered high above the other man.

The man bowed to her. "Lady Rosamond, please forgive this rude greeting. I am Sir Daniel, Lord Egmanton's steward. I could not meet with Sir David early enough—"

"I was made to wait an hour," the knight said in a gravelly voice that betrayed his anger.

Sir Daniel bobbed his head in agreement. "It is regrettable. We were told you would not be arriving until late in the evening. The baroness is unavailable at the moment—"

"And where is Lord Egmanton?" Anne interrupted, stepping forward as she dropped her sodden hood to her shoulders.

Sir Daniel gaped up at her—he was several inches shorter. "He is detained in the village due to the weather. But both will be at supper. Might I show you to your chambers? I can have hot baths prepared, and if your clothing is not dry, I can provide you with what you need."

Somewhat mollified, Anne said, "You have my thanks."

In their chambers, they discovered that no one had prepared for them. Anne herself would have just made due, but she was Lady Rosamond now. She demanded Sir Daniel's presence, and showed him the bedchambers assigned to her and her retinue. He looked embarrassed, but not all that surprised.

Anne turned to her men and her maid. "I see no reason to be insulted. Who is next on my list?"

Sir Walter began to rummage in his saddle bag.

"My lady, please!" Sir Daniel said, raising both hands to halt her. "Lord Egmanton desperately wishes to meet you." Wincing, he added, "But he is not in charge of the household."

"Ah, I see. Lady Egmanton is behind this."

Sir Daniel looked terrorized. "My lady, I never said—"

Anne gave him her most brilliant smile. "Fear not, Sir Daniel. There is no reason to mention your name to her ladyship. I will deal with her."

He bowed himself out, bobbing up and down in his gratitude.

When he was gone, Sir Walter watched her carefully. "My lady, what do you mean to do?"

"Greet our hostess, of course," Anne said. "Obviously she does not care much for this match—her young son and a scandalous widow."

Philip folded his arms across his chest and looked approving. "And you mean to . . . ?"

"Thoroughly impress upon her son that I am the wife for him. Do you not think his mother will like that?"

"Remain alert more than angry, my lady," Walter cautioned. "Perhaps the Egmantons don't want you here for a more sinister reason."

Anne felt her anger fade as she remembered her determination to discover if one of the noblemen on her list could be a traitor.

"Isn't he rather young to already be against the king?" Philip asked.

"Sir Walter is right," Anne said. "I promise to be cautious."

She tried to keep her expression serene, but Philip was looking at her with suspicion.

Chapter 10

Philip could see how the baroness had meant supper to go. He and his fellow knights sat at their assigned table, well below the salt cellar with the servants, a deliberate slap at Lady Rosamond. But however the hall was designed, he was still able to hear Lady Egmanton. Perhaps her booming voice carried naturally. She had a large bosom, broad hips, and when she entered the room, she was like the lead sailing ship, with her attendants trailing in her wake and her headdress fluttering as sails on a mast.

Her eldest son, with but twenty years, Philip had heard, greeted her with a kiss to the cheek. He was rather on the thin side, as if training on the tiltyard was not something he valued. He didn't look like a man with the fortitude to go against his king. His twin sisters, of marriageable age but still young, were healthy, handsome girls who would obviously have to be careful if they wished to avoid their mother's fuller shape.

Lady Egmanton looked about the hall, her nose in the air. When she realized that Lady Rosamond had not yet appeared, Philip could see the anger she didn't bother to conceal. She had obviously wanted to make the final grand entrance of the evening, and wasn't used to being crossed in her own little kingdom. She seated herself at the head table. She glared at her son as if it were his fault that her meal would be delayed. He only shrugged and signaled a maidservant. She brought him a goblet, and Philip noticed how carefully the girl remained as far away as she could. When Egmanton let her go with a nod of thanks, the relief on her face when she turned away worried Philip.

At last, at the head of the stairs leading up to the second floor, David appeared. Though he was tall, he seemed abnormally so at the top of the great hall. When he raised a hand, the entire chamber went silent. Lady Egmanton frowned.

David began to speak in ringing tones. "Lady Rosamond Wolsingham, daughter of the duke of Morley, widow of the earl of Wolsingham."

When Anne appeared at the head of the stairs, a round of cheering broke out. Philip almost joined, so impressive and tempting did she look. She wore a wine red gown that made her skin shimmer pale and flawless, down to the pointed bodice that just hinted at deep cleavage. No embroidery or pattern detracted from the sheer beauty of her shape in the gown. The tight sleeves showed her lithe arms, and on her head perched the smallest headdress with a veil attached. Once again she had chosen to display her black hair, though it was pulled up off her neck. Brilliant emeralds hung from her ears and decorated her neck. She appeared every inch a noblewoman.

Anne unnecessarily lifted her skirts to display matching red slippers and delicate ankles as she glided down the stairs. When she reached the bottom, she released her skirts and looked about, wearing a pleased expression. "Good evening to the residents of Markham Keep!"

There was more cheering, and she clasped her hands together and bowed her head repeatedly toward each group of tables in the hall. Philip rose to continue his part in the play. He escorted Anne to the head table, where Lady Egmanton remained stiffly seated. Her son had already risen to his feet, and now came around the table. Anne dropped into a deep, graceful curtsy.

Egmanton took both her hands and raised her to her feet. "Lady Rosamond, it is such a pleasure to meet you at last. Do forgive me my absence this afternoon."

Anne waved a hand. "We traveled faster than we expected to, my lord. Now I am here, and so eager to make your acquaintance."

She subtly emphasized the word "eager" as if it were foreplay. Philip, who had kissed those red lips and craved more, felt a shiver of desire move through him. The young baron flushed red and cast a guilty look at his mother.

The baroness's eyes glittered with her anger, but all she said was "We are glad to give your marital state our consideration," using the royal "we" like a queen.

Anne laughed in that husky way she used as Lady

Rosamond. "Lady Egmanton, my marital state is . . ."—she demurely glanced at the woman's son—"open to evaluation."

"Then sit down so that we can be served," the woman snapped.

Philip held Anne's chair until she was seated, then stepped back off the raised dais and stationed himself behind her. He had not been told to do so, but the people at Markham Keep made him uneasy, and he had learned never to doubt his instincts. He didn't want to be across the hall from Anne should she need him.

With Philip at her back, and her entrance a success, Anne felt a powerful confidence that was rare for a woman of her station. She would not go too far angering the baroness, but surely the woman deserved some taunting. And Anne had to be subtle and casual if she was going to discover if Lord Egmanton had a secret agenda.

She felt more wary of the mother than the son, for he was unfailingly polite throughout the meal and allowed his mother to steer the conversation. He seemed very young, but very interested in her. Surely she was unlike the innocent young girls usually paraded before someone like him. Anne glanced at his sisters, both seated on the far side of their mother as if they had to be protected. They were almost perfectly alike in looks, although they wore different color gowns. They watched Anne with awe, which couldn't be helping Anne's case with Lady Egmanton.

The baroness sucked the last meat from the starling

bones and said, "How old are you, Lady Rosamond?"

"I have twenty-five years, my lady." Three years older than Anne's real age.

Anne glanced at Lord Egmanton, smiling with her eyes, hoping he understood that being with an older woman could be a good thing. She must have succeeded, for he couldn't take his gaze off her. Lady Egmanton's face flushed purple. He seemed easily led.

"You are very old to be a young man's bride," the baroness said coldly.

Anne was so tempted to say that experience could be pleasurable, but restrained herself. She didn't want the old woman to have apoplexy.

"I do not consider myself old, my lady," Anne said with a smile.

"But you are old to have not borne children."

Anne heard the two sisters gasp, and on her left Lord Egmanton stiffened. On her right Lady Egmanton continued eating the gravy-sopped bread trencher, as if she had not spoken cruelly. She seemed desperate to make Lady Rosamond take her son off the list.

"Lady Rosamond?" One of the twins had gathered her courage to speak. "Have you been to court?"

Anne smiled at the girl, but before she could respond, the baroness interrupted.

"Appearance at court matters not at all. Suitability to be a wife and mother are the first requirements."

"Not a dowry, my lady?" Anne said, blinking innocently. She saw how the reminder of her wealth affected each of them, from the twins' innocent envy to Lord Egmanton's satisfaction to his mother's disappointment. Of course Lady Rosamond's wealth mattered greatly. Anne went back to cheerfully eating, while the rest of them locked gazes with each other in silence.

Philip quickly ate his own meal, keeping Anne in his sights. Her flirtatious manner bothered him, and she seemed in a dangerous mood this evening. As she walked about the hall with Egmanton, she stopped by their table and smiled at them.

"Lord Egmanton is taking me on a tour of the castle grounds," she said, patting the young man's arm. "He says the sun sets most beautifully here in Nottinghamshire."

He gazed at her worshipfully, blushing.

"My lady—" Philip began, rising to his feet.

"Nay, sit, finish your meal," Anne said. "There are soldiers everywhere. Certainly my lord will keep me safe."

Her use of the possessive made Egmanton blush even more furiously. At the head table, his mother glowered, but remained silent, as if she'd done all she could.

Philip had not. When Anne and Egmanton left through the great double doors, he followed them after receiving Walter's approving nod.

Once in the inner ward, it was easy enough to stay out of Anne's way. The sun, which had come out only *after* they'd ended their journey, was already below the

curtain walls, casting long shadows over everything.
Servants went about their business preparing the castle
for the coming night, lighting torches and lowering the
portcullis to guard the gatehouse. While Philip waited
beside the stable for Anne to move farther away, she
bent her head flirtatiously toward the young lord, and
then laughed at something he said.

Philip walked swiftly to the dovecote, where the
birds fluttered as they sensed him just outside. When a
soldier frowned at him, Philip made a show of examining the structure with impressed curiosity. By the time
the soldier finally left, Philip turned back toward the
courtyard, but could no longer see Anne.

Where was she taking the boy, and what did she
think she was proving? If Egmanton were the traitor, if
he knew something about Lady Rosamond, she could
be in danger.

He walked swiftly the way he'd last seen them,
turned a corner of the castle, and saw the dark shadows
of the lady's garden before him.

He swore silently to himself, then slipped over the
low half-wall and slid into the darkness among the
shrubbery and fruit trees. After hearing Anne's laughter, some of his fear eased. He crouched low to the
ground and parted the fronds of a fern to see the young
couple.

Anne was leaning up against the wall of the castle
itself, looking beautiful in the soft glow of the evening
twilight. She was smiling at Egmanton, who stood too
close to her. Beside them, recessed in the wall, was a

statue of a woman with a raised hand, gently holding a bird.

"My mother says you are far too experienced for me," Egmanton said.

Anne tilted her head. "Am I?"

And then Egmanton leaned in and kissed her. Philip kept waiting for Anne to push the boy away, but she didn't. Philip told himself she was playing a part, but he could not explain away his own jealousy and confusion.

Egmanton leaned into her, and with his other hand began to draw up her skirts.

Everything inside Philip protested, but he reined in an explosion of anger. When Anne pushed Egmanton's hand back down, Philip knew that at least she was being sensible about how far she would take Lady Rosamond's boldness. But her skirts began to inch up again.

Philip crawled backward for several yards, then stood up and turned his head away to muffle his voice. As he brushed at the dirt on his knees, he called out, "Lord Egmanton went this way. Does his mother wish his presence?"

Making a lot of noise, Philip stomped through the garden until he came upon them, both facing him, wearing innocent expressions.

Philip bowed and spoke humbly. "My lord, you are wanted in the great hall."

The young man took Anne's hand and kissed it. "Shall we return?"

But Anne glanced at Philip and shook her head. "You go, my lord. I wish for a moment's respite from the heat and noise of the hall. My knight will guard me."

Lord Egmanton bowed and swept past Philip.

Philip crossed his arms over his chest and looked at her.

She made the same gesture and inclined her head at him. She was daring him to protest, and he admitted that her very boldness heated his blood.

"What was the point of this scene?" he asked softly.

"And did you see more than us standing here conversing?"

"I did. Someone has to keep an eye on you, and who better than one of your bodyguards."

"I have to know if a man with so few years can be capable of being my husband."

She was speaking in the bold voice of Lady Rosamond. Was she behaving like this in case someone watched them?

"And you were going to test that?"

She laughed, and he found himself moving toward her slowly.

"With a kiss, aye," she said. "But it seems that Lady Egmanton does not know her son as well as she thought. He was quite experienced. But I can manage him."

"Like you managed the last lord?" he asked, trying to quell the anger that simmered inside him. It wasn't his place to feel this way, all tight and hot at the thought of her in the hands of one man after another. He had no claim on her—he told himself that he wanted no claim.

Her smile faded. "I took care of myself well."

"You're pushing this too far."

He was close now, within a few feet of her. Above them, the statue watched silently.

"There will be men you can't handle so easily, men who will take your playfulness as assent."

"Then I will disabuse them of that notion, as I did Lord Egmanton." She cocked her head, hands on her hips. "Isn't this the kind of woman I'm supposed to be, the kind of woman you like, the kind of woman who would boldly kiss you just because she could?"

He tensed, feeling aroused and confused. Then she took his jerkin in both hands and turned him about. He let her handle him, let her push him against the wall, where the statue loomed above them, sheltered them. He wanted to understand her strange mood—but he also recognized the darkness within himself, the lusting part that wanted not to understand, only to feel.

She put her hands around him, grabbed his ass and held him to her. His cock was hard between them.

"This is what the Lady Rosamonds of the world know all about," she whispered, her face below his. "I'm just beginning to learn."

"If that's what you want," he said in a low growl, "then let me teach you more."

He turned her about and pressed her into the ivy-covered stone wall, feeling every soft inch of her body along his. He took her mouth in a kiss, arching her head back so that she had no choice but to succumb to him. But he didn't need to seduce her compliance. Her hands clutched at his back, she moaned beneath his mouth, and met his tongue with eager passion.

"Did that boy kiss you like this?" he asked against her lips.

Her tongue teased him. "He did. Do you want to hear how you compare?"

He gave a harsh laugh. "I don't need to."

He possessed her mouth again, losing himself in her passion. Nothing existed but the heat between them, and the clothes that kept them apart. He ran his hands up her arms and across her shoulders, then traced the neckline of her gown down to where it met in a point. His fingers dipped into the warm, damp hollow between her breasts, and she moved restlessly against him. He could not resist. He smoothed one hand over her breast, letting his thumb brush her nipple last. Beneath his touch, it rose up until it was outlined in silk. He caught her cry within his own mouth, felt her tremble with the sensations.

He knew he'd been the first to touch her like this, the only one to awaken her sensuality. The darkness of night settled over them, and he wanted to hide her away, to keep her with him, to do things to her—

But he wouldn't abuse her trust. With both hands he held her breasts, stroked and petted them, while he worshiped her mouth with his. She made the most tempting sounds deep in her throat, as she restlessly moved her hips against his.

Anne was lost in a world of heat and temptation, and Philip was the center of it all. She was overcome by her desire for him, thrilled to know he shared it. She cared not where it led her, only that he go with her.

His hands on her breasts stroked a fire inside her that spread into the depths of her stomach, and even lower, until between her thighs grew a fierce ache that she did not know how to appease. He had brought her here before, to this place of hunger, and she'd never seen how it could end. His mouth left hers and he pressed a kiss behind her ear, and another where her neck and shoulder met. One of his hands skimmed down her waist and over her hip. With a tug he lifted her thigh. Though her skirts pulled tight, restricting him, she felt him press between her legs, a roll of his hips that made her groan her approval. She wanted him to stroke her there, to quench this fire.

But he suddenly lifted his head, his face harsh with passion in the growing darkness. "This isn't what you want," he said, breathing heavily.

Anger stormed over her, and she pulled her leg from his grasp. "You don't know what I want. You never did."

To her shock, her plans to find a way into the League almost spilled from her lips. Why would she think she could confide in him?

He slid his arms around her back and held her

loosely, with no threat, no promise of more. "You won't believe me," he said, "but I didn't mean this to happen again. I came here to protect you, and instead I continued where that foolish boy left off."

She stepped away from him, away from the statue that rose over them so impassively. It did not condemn her, and she couldn't condemn herself. She wanted membership in the League, but what else did she want?

To be like Lady Rosamond? To be the woman men were attracted so desperately to, and to know she could return their passion with her own? She had never known the power of wealth and beauty, and how easily it could change a woman's life.

Maybe she was changing too much. Did she want to be like Lady Rosamond for herself—or for Philip? Or for her parents, who'd taken advantage of her? Did her motives even matter? She was changing so much, doing things she would never have imagined just a few short months ago.

"Talk to me, Countess," he whispered.

Was she testing him? Using him to see if Lady Rosamond was the sort of woman she should become? She had no one but herself to please, no future except what she could fashion for herself, here with the League. She wanted their excitement and danger, to know she was helping an important endeavor. She wanted them to keep needing her help—and if that meant becoming as bold as Lady Rosamond, then she would do so.

With a sigh, she faced Philip, who waited quietly, watching her. Was he expecting a transformation?

Though she'd decided to change, somehow his wanting it hurt her.

"I do not know what the moonlight has done to me tonight," she said lightly. "We should return to the party in my honor."

He opened his mouth, and then seemed to rethink whatever he had first meant to say. "It is only the moon affecting you?"

She gave a throaty laugh, stared at him out of the corner of her eye. "But you want it to be only you?"

He studied her as if she puzzled him, and suddenly she didn't want the scrutiny. She turned her back and began to wind her way through the garden, knowing he followed. Would he keep following wherever she led, whatever she did?

And follow her he did, even though she thought she could escape. When she returned to the great hall, she saw Lord Egmanton talking to his steward, Sir Daniel, and then the two of them ducked down a corridor. What was he up to at this time of night? Surely the castle business was through for the day.

Anne glanced behind her to see that Philip had stopped to talk to the other Bladesmen. She was still on the fringe of the castle residents, who milled about the hall as the trestle tables were taken down. It didn't take much for her to slip amongst them, hiding herself in plain sight, and then follow Lord Egmanton. This was another opportunity for her to prove herself to Sir Walter.

The corridor was dark, but for the occasional pool

of torchlight. As the music and voices faded behind her, she could hear the echoing steps of the men ahead of her, so it was not difficult to follow them. But she couldn't quite hear what they said. She was grateful that her own slippers allowed her to walk softly, undetected.

Ahead of her, Lord Egmanton and his steward reached a corner and turned. She stopped, peeking around the rough, damp edge of the stone wall, and saw the two of them open a door. They stepped through, but she thought they did not quite close it behind them. She'd probably be able to hear them if she—

From behind, a man clasped his arm around her waist, pinning her arms against her as he covered her mouth. He propelled her forward, across the corridor and into the darkness of the circular stairwell.

"Be quiet," he hissed into her ear.

She recognized Philip almost immediately, but still her heart raced, and she breathed frantically through her nose. He didn't let her go, only leaned against the wall and pulled her back to his chest.

She heard Lord Egmanton's voice growing louder as he came back down the corridor, and she stopped struggling. If Philip hadn't gotten her out of the way, she'd have been discovered. But what if he came into the stairwell?

"Mother is impossible!" Lord Egmanton said with fury. "She even called me in to the great hall just now, and then denied doing it! She is determined that I not marry Lady Rosamond."

By the end of his speech, Anne could hear his voice quite clearly. He must have stopped right next to the stairwell.

"My lord, she is only looking out for your interests," said Sir Daniel.

Philip's arm around her waist felt warm and hard, so powerful that he could easily hold her immobile. His strength made her feel languid and hot, burning away her resistance. His hand on her mouth was so large he could have spanned her face. With her backside pressed against his hips, she grew even more heated, feeling the long, hard evidence of his erection nestled between her cheeks. Her garments were fine and thin, not much protection between them. She felt his breath, hot against her neck.

"I was alone with Lady Rosamond," Lord Egmanton whined. "Somehow I have to manage it again."

Philip held her trapped, and she should have felt frustrated and angry; instead a rush of excitement swept through her. They might be discovered at any moment, and the danger only seemed to make her fearless and wild. She couldn't move her arms, but she could move her hips. She rubbed against him, and heard his breathing cut off in a gasp. What they had started in the garden hadn't gone away, had only slumbered, waiting for fuel to toss on the flames.

Sir Daniel said, "What if you take her on a hunting trip tomorrow? You know your mother would never attend that."

She felt Philip's open mouth on her neck, even as he

rubbed against her, hard. She bit back a moan, closing her eyes, then shuddered as she felt his teeth scrape her skin. His hand left her mouth and slid downward, and then the other joined it, cupping her breasts. She leaned into his hands, which only pushed her hips harder into his. He rocked into her, playing with her nipples, shooting arrows of desire through her body with each stroke. In the heat of passion, she was losing herself in Lady Rosamond's boldness, and needed more from him. She took one of his hands and slid it down her body.

"A hunting party!" Lord Egmanton said, sounding like a little boy at Christmas. "Perfect!"

Their footsteps faded away, but Anne didn't care. Through her skirts, Philip cupped between her thighs, and a weak groan escaped her. His fingers slid slowly against her, pressing and circling, while his hand on her breast did the same. Inside her the fever writhed and fed on her helplessness. She was shuddering in his arms, and could not control the sounds she was making. That made her realize that she could not allow herself to be caught like this. She flung herself away from him, falling against the curving stairs, trying to find the breath that heaved in her chest.

He caught her arm, pressed his mouth against her ear, and whispered, "Do you want to find your chamber and finish this once and for all?"

She turned onto her back, the stairs digging into her spine. Philip leaned over her, his expression harsh, but she knew it wasn't anger, only the same desperation for completion that she felt.

With a groan she staggered to her feet and pushed past him, halting in the entrance to the stairwell to make sure no one had come down the corridor. Over her shoulder, she said, "I didn't want you on this journey in the first place. I knew you would be such a distraction!"

There was a pause where she wondered if she had wounded him.

"A distraction from what?" he demanded. "What did you think you were doing?"

"Seeing if Lord Egmanton was more than he seemed!"

"He seemed like a boy tied to his domineering mother, and that little speech proved it. You don't think the Bladesmen can figure this out for themselves, without your help?"

Chapter 11

Philip accepted her glare, because he knew she was defending herself against him, against the passion that erupted between them every time they were alone. A distraction, was he? She was the one who'd boldly rubbed against him. But it wouldn't be wise to say so, not if he ever hoped to enjoy such a surprise again.

For she surprised him in so many ways, and he wanted more. His body ached with need, and he could barely keep himself from pulling her back against him.

When she would have headed back for the great hall, he caught her arm and dragged her the other way. "You shouldn't go back there—it might look as if we deliberately wanted to be alone together. Before supper, I explored the castle. This way."

As he pulled her, she looked back over her shoulder. "But Sir Walter—"

"If you cared what he thought, you wouldn't have tried to escape him to follow Egmanton."

"I was trying to help!"

"And I told him I thought that was your motive. I said I'd find you and make sure you avoided trouble."

"You *are* trouble!"

"So are you, and you'll be less so in your bedchamber. Now stop fighting me, before someone thinks I'm dragging you off to be seduced, instead of the other way around."

"Ooh!"

But she didn't get the chance to speak, because he was forced to release her as two pages carrying buckets of water came down the corridor toward them. Philip glanced over his shoulder to find her walking serenely behind him. He ignored the pages, but they smiled, bobbing their heads at her.

He led her up a floor in another wing of the castle, and to her door. When she was safely inside—she'd clearly wanted to slam the door in his face, but had thought better of it—he went next door to the bedchamber he shared with Walter. He saw that the knights were there, preparing for the evening's activities, which they still hadn't invited him to attend yet. They were dressed in black, wearing mysterious pouches at their waists. He understood; he didn't know their secret methods, and unless he was a member, they weren't about to show him. Though he didn't care about joining their League, he would always be curious about the skills they were trained in.

"We will return within two hours," Walter said. "Can you take a long shift, if need be?"

"Of course, but why are you leaving now, so early?"

"The soldiers will be distracted with people finding their beds. It will be easier to slip by them."

"Through a closed gatehouse?" Philip said, smiling.

Walter only arched a brow and said nothing.

As Philip backed out the door so they could pass, he sensed someone at Anne's door. He thought at first that it was Margaret, but the maid wouldn't be trying to be so inconspicuous. While the Bladesmen left him one way, he knew behind him that Anne was leaving the other.

When the knights had turned a corner, Philip darted back the other way, chasing her. What was she thinking? She disappeared within the stairwell, and as he turned in, he saw the last of her skirts as she went up.

Was she following the Bladesmen now?

At the top of the keep itself, she went outside, to where wooden walkways linked the keep to the curtain wall. There were no torches, no soldiers at all, as far as Philip could see. Like many castles, they'd given up the strict need to be defensive.

But the moon was full, lighting the night well enough for him to catch up to Anne where she hid within the shadow cast by a half-wall. When she saw him, she didn't even seem surprised.

He pressed his back against the wall beside her and whispered, "How many times must I follow you tonight?"

She lifted her chin. "You're just as curious as I am

about how they're leaving the castle. Now be quiet. I think they are on the far walkway."

Gritting his teeth, Philip sighted along the arm she pointed and saw figures in black as they crossed onto the battlements. Her eyesight was excellent; he might not have noticed them, so stealthily did they move, keeping to the shadows. The Bladesmen had chosen a rear corner of the curtain wall, out of sightline of either the main or postern gatehouse. Philip allowed Anne to creep closer, staying near in case she needed to be rescued from herself.

It was plain they affixed ropes to a merlon, the high point between the lower embrasures, that rose in regular intervals along the battlements. Then one by one they went over the side of the wall and disappeared from sight.

Climbing ropes. Hell, he could do that. He was almost disappointed.

But Anne ran swiftly across the walkway, her skirts flying behind her. Philip followed, and joined her as she put her back against the merlon and looked at him with excitement, the moon sparkling in her eyes.

"Do you think I can peer over now?" she asked.

He crossed his arms over his chest. "Give them a while longer. The wall is high, and you don't want them to see you before they reach the ground."

She breathed as swiftly as she did when she was moaning with passion in his arms. Feeling irritated, he said, "Why are you doing this? What does it matter how they protect you? Why follow Egmanton? Does it all tie together?"

Ignoring him, she touched the rope behind her back. "The vibration is gone. The last one must be down."

With a jump, she landed chest-first across the embrasure, then wriggled forward over the thickness of the wall until she could just peer over the edge. Philip put a hand on her hip, feeling rather dizzy with her so close, and the wind picking up. It never bothered him when a fellow knight stood like this, ready to drop boiling oil on besiegers below.

"What do you see?" he asked.

"Nothing," she said, disappointment obvious in her voice.

"They're dressed in black."

She wriggled backward until she could drop back to her feet. With her hands on her hips, she frowned at him. "You don't need to patronize me."

Under the moonlight, her eyes were dark shadows.

"Then answer my questions," he said. "What are you planning?"

"To be invited to join the League permanently."

His eyes widened, and he saw her wince, as if she had not meant to tell him the truth.

She held up a hand before he could speak. "You don't have to tell me that there's never been a Bladeswoman. Neither of us can know that for certain. But I'm good at this, Philip. I want to do this."

"And you think just proving your commitment is enough to these men?"

Softly, she said, "I know it is not, or you would have been asked before now. But Philip, look how much you've helped them. Surely they will ask you now. Maybe they'll ask us both."

He hesitated. "The League's view of me no longer matters," he finally said, his tone mild.

She looked confused. "At Alderley, you spoke of the League as if they were the pinnacle of knightly success. Elizabeth said you weren't asked to join—"

"So you thought you could drag me along with you, take up the cause?" He found himself amused rather than upset. "I have other things I'd rather do now, Lady Rosamond. Do not concern yourself with me. If you're asked to join the League, think of the dangers you will face."

"Only once a year, for several weeks at a time," she recited primly. "But I hope to convince them that I would gladly serve more."

"And what will you tell your husband?" He had a sudden image of her in another man's arms, and he felt angry and jealous, two emotions he had no right to feel.

"I'm not going to marry. I have more important things to do."

He gaped at her. "What woman doesn't want to marry?"

"A Bladeswoman."

How could he tell her that she'd fixated on something that probably wouldn't happen? But it was not up to him to decide her life for her.

Side by side, they looked out over the dark countryside. She had left her headdress in her bedchamber. He
glanced at her, seeing her hair catch in the wind, dancing around her face. He would wait with her as long as
she wanted, because he liked being alone with *Anne*, not
Lady Rosamond. He turned back to the Nottinghamshire countryside, looking at trees touched by moonlight and the glistening of a stream in the distance.

Suddenly she stiffened. "The rope is going taut."

They both backed away, sliding into the shadows
cast by the moon. In a few minutes, David pulled himself up into the embrasure and dropped to the battle-
ment walkway. The look on his face was so intense
that Philip put a hand on Anne's shoulder before she
could speak. After David rummaged for something in
the pouch at his waist, he pulled up the rope swiftly.
With his back to them, they could not see what he was
doing, but at last he dropped the rope back over the
edge, then looked over for several moments. Then he
climbed back up into the embrasure, held on to the
rope, and seemed to drop from sight.

Anne gasped and raced forward with Philip. While
she boosted herself up to look over the edge, he studied
the top of the rope.

"He's going down so fast," she said in amazement.
"And someone is coming up equally as fast!"

"It's a pulley system," Philip said with reluctant admiration. "I've never seen one so delicately made. David's weight is bringing up the next man. Why couldn't

he climb?" He glanced down at the rising figure. "Get back, Anne."

As she did, they heard a groan as someone reached the top with a quick stop. Philip leaned over to help and was met with the point of a dagger.

"Joseph, 'tis me," Philip said, hands held up unthreateningly.

Joseph grunted. "Then help me over."

Philip reached forward and Joseph took both his arms, detaching himself from a bar that had been attached to the rope.

"You couldn't climb?" Philip said.

Joseph dropped to the walkway and collapsed into a sitting position. "I hurt my ankle." Breathing heavily, he glanced at Philip, then seemed to notice Anne. "Following us?"

Philip shrugged.

"Then help me remove the pulleys so the others can climb up."

It wasn't long before David and Walter joined them at the top. Walter's expression was grave upon seeing them, and only now did Anne begin to look guilty.

David helped Joseph to his feet, and Philip took one of his arms across his shoulders. "Did you find anything?" Philip asked.

Walter glanced out over the dark countryside, the wind ruffling his hair, his expression troubled. "We covered the ground in ever widening circles from the castle. On our second pass, we found a campsite hastily dismantled, the embers still warm. Travelers so close to the castle could have come inside for the night. These men chose not to."

"We tracked them for a while," Joseph said, "and got close, but they were mounted, and eventually they reached open country and escaped. That was when I turned my ankle."

"They could have been poachers," David said objectively.

Walter narrowed his eyes. "My instincts say otherwise. We are still being watched, but someone doesn't seem to want to make the mistake of attacking us again."

"They still believe I'm Lady Rosamond," Anne said softly. "And they don't know if Lady Rosamond overheard them."

"Exactly," Walter said. "Our best defense is to keep these watchers from catching a good look at you."

After mass the next morning, Anne accompanied Lord Egmanton's twin sisters on a tour of the women's apartments of the castle, the sewing and weaving chambers. Lady Egmanton avoided them, and Anne could not be displeased.

At mid-morning, while Anne waited for Lord Egmanton to finish meeting with his steward, traveling minstrels arrived. Lady Egmanton interrogated them for the latest news. The lute player, who was tuning his instrument for the coming evening, was only too happy to bow to the baroness, where she sat before her hearth. After all, Lady Egmanton was the reason he would eat and be sheltered for however many nights the minstrels could continue to amuse her.

After teasing the baroness with several pieces of light gossip about royal flirting and noble betrothals, he finally met her gaze and allowed his cheerfulness to fade. "Milady, this last news be not so pleasant. There has been a terrible death, and it is proven no accident."

Anne exchanged a glance with Philip, who was nearby playing a game of Tables with Sir Walter.

"Someone was murdered?" Lady Egmanton asked with excited interest.

"Lady Staplehill was found dead in her bed not a fortnight ago," the lute player said, blessing himself.

Margaret, who had been bringing Anne a goblet of wine, gasped. Several drops of wine spilled into the rushes. But Anne could only stare at Margaret's face, which had gone pale.

"She did not die naturally?" Lady Egmanton asked her question with an eagerness that made Anne feel ill, especially when Margaret looked helpless and worried.

The lute player gravely said, "She was found with the dagger still in her fair bosom."

As several people murmured to each other, Anne experienced a moment of confusion—was Lady Rosamond supposed to know this woman? Was that why Margaret looked so ill?

As if she could read minds, Lady Egmanton suddenly turned to Anne. "Lady Rosamond, did you not know Lady Staplehill? She was not much older than you, and surely was at court when you were."

"I only met her in passing, my lady," Anne answered somberly. "It is such a tragedy." She turned quickly to the lute player. "Have they captured the terrible villain responsible?"

He shook his head. "Sadly, milady, they have not. But all wonder—who could have been in the lady's well-guarded chamber that she shared with her husband?"

"Do they not suspect her husband?" Lady Egmanton asked.

Anne saw Philip studying Sir Walter with suspicion. Both Sir David and Sir Joseph seemed unusually impassive where they stood watching the game board. What was going on? And how could she find out?

"Her husband is a grief-stricken man with two young children to raise," the lute player continued. "They say he has no reason."

"Could there be a lover?"

"Lady Egmanton." Anne rose to her feet, trying not to frown her displeasure. "Such sad tidings make me feel the need to refresh myself. Your son is still with his steward?"

The old woman smiled with satisfaction. "He'll be very busy for much of the day."

"Such a shame," Anne said, feeling relieved, hoping that the hunting trip idea had been declined. She turned to her knights. "Gentlemen, I feel the need to ride, to see the peace of the land after such sad news. Would you escort me?"

Though Margaret seemed most reluctant, Anne brought her along, too. While they waited in the courtyard for the men to saddle their mounts, Anne whispered to the maid that they would stay within shouting distance of the castle. The last thing Anne wanted to do was ride, especially with a "watcher" out there somewhere, but she saw no way to escape interested ears if they remained at the castle.

At last their horses trotted beneath the raised portcullis of the gatehouse, and they were free. Sherwood Forest stretched out beyond them, but Anne did not aim there, fearing that they would be too easily trapped. She tapped her horse's flanks and broke into a fast cantor, until at last they had put some distance between them and Markham Keep. The road leading into the castle was still dotted with the occasional cart or villagers coming for business. She felt safe enough from attack. Sheep grazed in the distance, and she pulled up and allowed the horse to walk, as if she wanted to watch the pastoral scene. At her side, Margaret sighed.

When all the knights had come up beside her, Philip spoke first. "What do you know about Lady Staplehill's murder?" he asked Sir Walter, a low hum of anger in his voice.

The older knight raised a gray eyebrow. "Know, Sir Philip? A woman is tragically dead."

Philip turned to Margaret. "So Lady Rosamond knew her?"

The maid lowered her gaze and nodded.

Anne was surprised when Sir Walter frowned.

"Sir Philip, this does not concern you."

"You know something about this murder," Philip said angrily. "You knew before you left on this mission."

"What does that matter?" Sir Walter asked. "It has nothing to do with us."

"Perhaps it does," Philip said, turning back to Margaret. "Please, tell us what you know, if not for our sake, then for your lady's."

Anne expected the Bladesmen to protest, but perhaps they realized that withholding the truth would make things worse.

The maid hugged herself. "I last saw Lady Staplehill at the Durham tournament."

Philip nodded. "The tournament where Lady Rosamond overheard the traitors."

Anne looked about in worry, but they were alone on the grassy knoll, the wind sweeping away their words, and sheep the closest company.

"There were many people at this tournament," Sir Walter said calmly. "No one was murdered there. This crime happened when the lady returned home."

"Where a young mother would be even less likely to be murdered in her bed," Philip shot back. "Does that not make it even more suspicious?"

Anne had never seen Sir Joseph and Sir David look so completely removed from emotion, as if this was none of their concern. Could this death really have something to do with Lady Rosamond?

"The League investigated," Sir Walter continued.

"Lady Staplehill's husband has enemies—and debts. The murderer was most likely looking to punish her husband."

"Most likely," Philip repeated. "This might have been more proof that the traitors know they are compromised."

"If that were true, my superiors thought that the traitors now believe they have killed the source that worried them."

"But now we've been attacked."

"And I put that in a missive," Sir Walter said calmly. "The traitors are nobility, with armies at their disposal. If they wanted Lady Rosamond dead, they would have sent someone far more efficient."

"Regardless of whether that is true," Philip said, "you withheld important information." He turned his smoldering eyes on Anne. "Did they tell you any of this?"

She shook her head. She didn't know how she felt about being misled, but surely Sir Walter thought it did not matter to them—or his superiors thought so, and he had no choice but to obey them.

"Sir Philip," Sir Walter said patiently, "I know much that is League business, much that most people are unaware of. Are you trying to tell me that I am supposed to confide everything I can think of in you?"

"Now you're twisting my words," Philip said. "Anne, I need to speak with you—alone."

Sir Walter frowned. "Philip, think about what you're doing."

His abandonment of Philip's title made Anne think the captain almost sounded desperate. She didn't want this to escalate into something ugly.

"I will speak with you, Philip," she said, forcing herself to sound calm and in control. "Sir Walter, would you and your knights take Margaret back toward Markham Keep? Of course you may keep us in sight."

The three Bladesmen wheeled their horses about and trotted back the way they'd come. Margaret looked small and deflated riding beside them.

Philip's gut twisted with worry and anger and confusion. How could the League have been deceitful? It went against everything he thought he knew about them.

"Even the maid is worried," Philip said when they were alone.

"Margaret is always worried about Lady Rosamond," Anne answered calmly. "It is a dangerous journey the lady has undertaken, and a risk that should be applauded for its bravery."

He leaned forward on his pommel, needing to make her understand. "And you, too, are risking your life. You've been lied to! Perhaps if we'd have known about Lady Staplehill's murder—"

"He did not tell me something that did not seem important to the League. Perhaps he even regretted it then, as well as now."

"Anne, you volunteered for this mission, believing it was necessary only as a precaution. We have more than enough proof now that the traitors discovered that *someone* identified them."

"They obviously don't know the person's identity."

"Do you want to be the next body? You should end this mission."

"Philip, do not ask such a thing of me. This is too important for the future of our kingdom. Would you listen to me if I asked you to abandon the king in battle?"

"'Tis not the same thing, and you know it."

"Nay, you are right, but for the wrong reasons. In battle, you are one of many—here, I might be all that confuses the enemy, all that allows Lady Rosamond to reach London. I've told you what it means to me to be with the League."

"At what price, Anne?" he asked.

The horse danced restlessly beneath him, and he flung himself from the saddle and lifted his hands up to her. She leaned toward him and allowed him to catch her and set her on the ground. Both horses lowered their heads to the grass.

He didn't remove his hands from her waist, only held her tighter.

Anne felt warmed by his concern. "There will be no price, Philip. I'm not vulnerable. Though you annoy me—"

She smiled tightly at him, but he didn't smile back.

"—I am grateful for your help. Perhaps even the League will be the same."

"My mother is the one who needed the League." He ran a hand through his hair and turned away from her.

Perplexed, she walked to his side and looked out at the horizon, as he was doing. There was still nothing but endless grass and sheep in this direction, and a shepherd far in the distance watching over them all. Yet to the west a wind picked up through the forest trees, and she shivered.

When he didn't seem inclined to continue, she softly said, "Your mother?"

He sighed.

At least he didn't look angry anymore, just resigned.

"Philip? I thought you said that your grandmother was saved by a Bladesman. Was your mother so grateful that she wanted you to be invited to join?"

"She had no hope that I'd be invited," he said softly. "She was but a seamstress for Lady Kelshall. She would never presume that the son of a servant could aspire so high." He gave a harsh laugh. "'Tis amazing how many memories are coming back to me, now that we're traveling closer to where I grew up."

Anne stared at him in surprise and disbelief. He was the child of a servant. She had thought him the younger son of a noble family, or at least a distant cousin. But he had been born and raised . . . just like her. In fact, her father, who owned his own farmland, would be considered higher in class. And she had thought she and Philip too far apart to ever be equals.

But they were very unequal, she reminded herself.

He had raised himself up to be a knight, making his family proud. It made so much more sense why he wanted a good marriage. It was a good thing she had realized that her goals would never include him.

"You must be disappointed in me," he said.

"Disappointed? How could you believe such a thing, after everything you've accomplished with your life?"

"After my grandmother was rescued—she was being robbed on an errand for her mistress—my mother developed this worship of the League that lasted her whole life. She collected stories of them and told them to me every night before I slept."

"Collected stories?"

"Aye, she may have been a simple seamstress, but she had once lived in London with Lady Kelshall, and knew much of the world. And she would listen to every traveler who passed by Kelshall Castle and glean even more."

That name was starting to sound familiar.

"She put into my head these dreams of knights and distant adventures that I could never have imagined myself," he said in a low voice. "She had a way with words that could make visions appear to me, as if I could aspire to such a world. It made me . . . different from the other boys, who only hoped for a plot of land and a decent wife. I found myself near the tilt-yard all the time, watching the training of the soldiers. I wanted to be one."

She could not believe he was confiding something

so personal to her. She was afraid to talk, afraid to even breathe, for fear of breaking this spell of intimacy his words wove between them.

At last she murmured, "Your mother wanted more for you, and you succeeded. You became a soldier, did you not?"

He nodded. "My lord noticed me; I traveled as his squire, and was knighted in France. My mother was long since dead, but still I was following the path she'd laid out for me."

His serious gaze turned back to her. "But it was not *my* path. I did not realize that until I met the Blades-men at Alderley, and understood that I no longer needed their approval. Yet now perhaps they think I am searching for it."

She saw the anger inside him. What else was he not telling her?

"Philip, if you still need my permission to go, know that you have it, because you owe me nothing. But I cannot leave. The king, though he knows it not, needs me."

A corner of his mouth curled in a smile. "Ah, you have such a destiny, Countess."

She shrugged and looked away.

"I will stay with you then, until the end."

"You make it sound so dramatic," she said dryly, trying to mask her relief. "But I am simply Lady Ros-amond, a noblewoman looking for a husband. And when this ends with only a king's gratitude, perhaps I will have won my own place in this world."

He caught her arm before she could turn away. "Anne, these men have lied to you, whether or not you want to believe their motives are noble. They are desperate to keep you right here with them. Do not forget that desperate men are capable of many things. To me, they have misled an innocent woman, something that should be beneath them."

She wanted to argue, but it had all been said before. "I will remember your words."

He helped her to mount, and together they rejoined the Bladesmen. Sir Walter's stare was unreadable.

"We are both staying," Philip said shortly. "But I will remember what you withheld, Walter."

Anne flinched when Philip no longer used the man's title. They all knew too many things about each other now. Walter, his expression unreadable, only nodded.

As they rode back to Markham Keep, Anne thought about what she'd learned of Philip's life. She understood now, after all he'd overcome, why it would be important for him to make a good marriage worthy of his knighthood. His mother wanted more for him, and Anne believed in it, too. He had his own destiny.

Yet that did not stop him from desiring her, and she him.

Chapter 12

That afternoon, Lord Egmanton invited Anne to accompany him on the hunt. So he had outmanipulated his mother, she thought. She was leery about traveling into the forest, but with such a large party, surely she would be safe. Over a dozen people traveled with them—her own four knights, Markham Keep's steward, several bailiffs and knights from neighboring manors, Lord Egmanton's guards as well as his sisters. They set off from the castle, the hounds kept well in hand by the huntsman. For a while, they galloped across the valley beneath the sun, and Anne enjoyed showing the twin sisters how easy it was to ride astride rather than sidesaddle.

They rode into the trees of Sherwood Forest, along ancient dirt paths that seemed well used for this purpose. At last the huntsman set loose the hounds, and Anne smiled as they streamed off into the forest, baying loudly, searching for hare, the quarry of the day. Then the chase was on, as the riders threaded their way through the trees, trying to keep up with the hounds.

Though Anne had tied back her hair, the streaming wind caught the curls as she leaned low over the horse's neck. She threw her head back and laughed in sheer exuberance, and found Philip riding nearby, watching her. As the horses dodged trees, Philip moved nearer and apart, and they were often separated by David or Joseph. It was a game, who could keep ahead of whom, and Anne almost forgot the hunt in the exuberance of racing against her knights.

At last a great cry went up from the riders in the lead, and as Anne slowed, she could hear the frantic baying of the hounds as they cornered their prey. Anne and the twins remained toward the rear of the party, not needing to see the bloody rituals of the hounds being awarded their share of the dead animal.

Philip rode back to them, and Anne noticed that the girls blushed and giggled when he smiled at them.

Philip noticed, too, because he leaned on his pommel and said, "Ladies, do you often hunt with your brother?"

They nodded vigorously.

Anne reminded herself that they were the sort of young women Philip should be pursuing in his own personal hunt. They were even of the right age, and she knew that she should not be jealous, not if she wished a better future for him.

But she *was* jealous. She was the one he could not keep his hands from; she was the one who could have him in her bed, if she wished. It would be easier for a Bladeswoman to experience pleasure, but not love.

Love would be too complicated in this life she planned to lead. As she watched Philip talk to the twins—and he wasn't even flirting, just being polite—she wondered if he thought about returning here someday, to woo and win the favor of the baron's sisters. They would not be too above the reach of a champion knight.

Besides Philip, David also remained nearby, as if it was his turn as her bodyguard. Joseph's ankle still pained him. She knew David, too, would keep her safe, but she wished Philip's words against the League hadn't put such doubts in her head.

They set off in a different direction for another hunt, and then at last, the hunters brought their spoils to a clearing in the forest, where a pavilion had been set up to eat out of doors. Cooks worked over a fire, and Anne watched Lord Egmanton formally present the hare carcasses to be roasted on a spit. There was cheering and laughter. Even the minstrels had arrived to lend music to the afternoon's entertainment. She made herself relax.

Lord Egmanton helped Anne dismount. "My lady, I am impressed with your horsemanship. Your father allowed you to ride astride like a man?"

"Aye, he did, my lord, and perhaps that was unwise of him. Many men have said it gave me unnatural ideas."

The other hunters laughed, the twins looked bemused, and Philip appeared resigned.

"Come walk with me, Lady Rosamond," the baron continued, smiling broadly. "There is a stream nearby that my sisters tell me is pretty enough for a painting."

Anne allowed Lord Egmanton to lead her by the hand. She saw one of his lordship's soldiers fall in behind them, and David did as well. She did not look back to see if Philip watched her. He could not always be with her—and there were young ladies he could flirt with.

The sunlight in the clearing was muted through the leafy branches of the oaks and hawthorns overhead. Lord Egmanton seemed unusually quiet, and his hand perspired in hers. But when she smiled at him, he smiled back with a boyish eagerness that amused her. She heard the stream before she saw it, and when they walked around an ancient oak, it spread out in dappled sunlight before her. The stream fell from boulder to rock, raising mist as it splashed. Pockets of yellow primroses and purple columbine grew near the rocks, wet with the stream's spray.

"How lovely," she said softly, as if her raised voice might disturb the beauty.

Lord Egmanton led her forward, and a bunny darted into the underbrush as they approached. Anne glanced back casually, and then did so again in surprise when she saw no one behind them.

"The soldiers are within hailing distance," Lord Egmanton said, as if reading her mind. "I didn't wish to be disturbed."

She felt uneasy, and she chastised herself silently. After all, a whole party of people relaxed nearby while the meal was being prepared. David was only a shout away. And she had already proven that she had Lord Egmanton well under control.

But in the lady's garden last evening, Philip's shout had interrupted them. Would the young baron have pressed her further without Philip's intervention? He led her toward a large boulder and leaned against it, smiling devilishly.

It seemed she was about to find out.

"How many noblemen have you visited so far, my lady?" he asked.

Anne walked to the water's edge, where she bent to pick a primrose. "You are the third, my lord."

"And are we all very different—or the same in our search for the proper bride?"

After smelling the flower, she laughed. "Different— and alike. Several of the men were far older than you, and searching for their second wife."

"Ah, then they already had an heir."

"Aye, they did."

"But of course, you realize I would need that from you."

When he grabbed her hand, he startled her so much that the flower fell to the grass. He pulled her closer, and her unease increased. He had allowed her to lead in the kiss the previous evening, but he was proving bolder today.

She put her hand on his chest and smiled firmly. "And I would be glad to give you an heir, my lord—if we marry."

"But there is so much we can do before that," he said, pulling her against him and pressing his mouth beneath her ear.

"Your youth is misleading, my lord."

She told herself to relax, allowed him to kiss her neck, to fondle her back. She could not help but realize how little he moved her, compared to even one caress from Philip.

Lord Egmanton slid his hand around her waist and then covered her breast.

She tried to rear back. "My lord, you must not touch what is not yours."

But instead of releasing her, he only pulled her tighter. When he fondled her, she squirmed with the discomfort of it.

"I have asked you to cease," she said firmly. "Forcing yourself on me will not make me choose you."

He grabbed her head and held her still for a quick, deep kiss that almost made her choke. Unease blossomed into worry, yet still she told herself to be calm. Help was nearby. And if she were to be a Bladeswoman, she would have to be able to handle such occasions herself.

Ending the kiss, he said, "Rosamond, I can make your choice easy. If you were to carry my child, then of course you would choose me."

She pushed hard against his chest, but he was stronger than his thin frame suggested. She hated the feel of his arousal pressed into her, especially when he continued rubbing against her.

"Cease now or I will scream," she commanded him. He suddenly seemed to have more hands than she did as she kept fending him off. She was overmatched.

Her worry was quickly escalating to fear. "David!" she suddenly shouted.

Lord Egmanton only smiled, then turned and pushed her back against the boulder. His hips pressed so hard into hers that her legs were forced apart.

Where was David? she thought frantically.

"He won't come," the baron said, his gentle words the opposite of his tight grip on her upper arms. "My man has been instructed that I wish to be alone with you."

She spoke as calmly as possible, hoping to reason with him. "My lord, your sisters are nearby. When they discover what you've done—"

"They won't discover, because if you tell anyone, then I will never marry you. You will be shamed before the court, and no man will want you."

If he thought that would be enough to calm her, then he was mistaken. She stomped hard on his foot, and though he winced, he forced a kiss on her. As she struggled, she found herself reliving another time when she was helpless, although that time she was but a maidservant in the same circumstance—with a man who felt he had the right to marry her. The sadness, fear and vulnerability from that time just months ago mixed in with her emotions now, until she couldn't remember which man she struggled against.

Philip barely kept himself from pacing after Anne left. He had tried to keep himself distracted by talking to the Egmanton twins, but they seemed so young and naive.

He kept remembering the soldier who'd followed Egmanton. Why would the baron need even more protection than David could provide? Who would attack such a large party?

Unless . . . the soldier was to keep David in line.

Philip glanced toward Walter and saw the older knight watching him. They had been awkward with each other since the morning's revelation, but now he seemed to know exactly what was on Philip's mind. Philip nodded his head in the direction Anne had gone. He waited for Walter's assent, praying he'd get it, because he did not think he could obey an order to remain here.

Though Walter's eyes narrowed, he gave a small nod.

Philip slipped among the trees and moved silently, swiftly. He had already asked one of the twins about the stream and knew the general direction. But before he reached it, he heard the obvious sound of fist meeting flesh, and a grunt of pain. On the far side of an oak tree, he saw David and Egmanton's soldier rolling on the ground.

God's Blood, Philip thought in shock, his suspicions had been correct. His fear for Anne's safety gave way to the darker, single-minded emotions of a battlefield, where all that mattered was defeating your enemy.

David got in a particularly good kick, and then saw

Philip. "They're just beyond!" he shouted in obvious relief, and then took a fist to the mouth.

David's opponent had seen Philip, too, and now struggled to get away, but David held him fast. Philip sprinted beyond them and into a clearing beside the stream. He saw Anne pressed against a rock, bare legs spread wide, and Egmanton between them holding her down.

Philip launched himself at the enemy, caught him around the waist and knocked him hard to the ground. Somewhere deep in his mind, he knew he need only reveal Egmanton's crime, and that would be enough, but the soldier in Philip, once released and angered, would not be denied. He held the baron down and pummeled his face with his fists.

"How do *you* like being restrained!" Philip shouted.

Egmanton bucked beneath him, but could not throw him off.

At last, Philip heard voices, felt someone take his shoulders, and he allowed himself to be pulled away.

David restrained him. "Enough, Philip. She is safe."

He found himself breathing heavily, listening to the satisfying sounds of the baron groaning. He turned and saw Anne standing alone, away from the rock, hugging herself.

Philip tried to move, yet still David held him fast by the arms. "See to the baron," Philip said. "I'll go to Lady Rosamond."

David's reluctance to release him was obvious, yet at last Philip was free. Anne looked up at him, dry eyes wide, her face set in calm lines. She was trying to be so brave, the perfect Bladeswoman. His need to hold her was so fierce that he ached with it. He could still picture her bare thighs, and Egmanton between them, and it shook him.

He didn't know how to ask, what to say, but at last he murmured, "Are you well?"

She nodded. "You arrived in time."

He closed his eyes momentarily in relief, and then asked, "Did he just . . . lose control and attack you?"

"It was deliberate," she said, glancing beyond Philip.

He turned and saw Egmanton's soldier limping toward his master, just as David helped the baron to stand. Philip remained aware of them, in case the two men attacked David.

"Deliberate?" Philip repeated in shock, glancing down at the blood on his knuckles.

"He thought if there was a chance I was with child, I would be more inclined to marry him." Her voice was bitter. "I thought that only happened to women too powerless to object."

Frowning, he studied her, wondering if she meant more than she was saying. But he did not have time to ask her, because he heard Egmanton's voice behind him and turned around. His face bloody and beginning to swell, the baron marched through the clearing and back into the trees, along with his soldier.

David approached them and nodded to Anne. "My lady? How badly did he hurt you?"

She shook her head. "Not badly."

"Forgive me," the knight said. "I could not get past his soldier in time."

"But you kept him out my way," Philip said.

"I am very grateful to you both," Anne said. "But I fear Lord Egmanton will not take this well."

"He could dispute our account," David said heavily. "And we are amongst his people."

Anne closed her eyes. "I should never have allowed him to lead me away. I thought he would not be so foolish as to try anything with the hunting party so near." She laughed with no amusement. "And to think I thought he was rather naive."

"Do not blame yourself," Philip said. "You are trapped having to behave a certain way."

She looked at him with worried eyes. "Yet you are the one who might suffer."

When Anne emerged from the trees into the meadow where the hunting party gathered, the mood was somber. The steward and bailiffs turned to glare at them, and Egmanton was already mounted on his horse. He rode past them, not looking at Anne, and she had no idea what he might have said to his men.

His injuries looked painful, and she was secretly glad.

The cooks and servants were already putting away their equipment and the food. The Egmanton sisters, pale and frightened, avoided Anne. Had they been told that it was her fault?

Walter and Joseph came to them, leading their horses.

David took his reins. "What was said when the baron returned?"

Walter looked at Philip. "That you had attacked him for no reason."

Anne could not control her gasp. If everyone believed the baron, then it was as if he hadn't tried to force himself on her.

Philip rolled his eyes. "If I had attacked for no reason, I think I would already be under his soldiers' control."

David said, "His soldier prevented me from going to Lady Rosamond."

Walter narrowed his eyes, and glanced at where Egmanton had ridden between the trees.

"Forgive my crudeness," Philip said to Anne, "but when I arrived, he was already on top of her."

Walter's gaze softened. "My lady, how do you feel?"

She smiled faintly. "Well enough. But I feel the need for a hot bath."

"You're shaking," Philip said, putting an arm around her.

Anne stiffened as all three knights frowned.

Philip removed his arm.

For just a moment, she'd been warm, but now she could not control the shivers that wracked her body. What was wrong with her? It was a warm summer day. She hated feeling so weak.

"You are suffering from the shock of the attack,"

Joseph said in a kind voice. "It will fade away soon."

She nodded. The men fussed over her horse, and tried to help her mount as if she were an invalid. But it wasn't until they emerged from the forest, that she pulled up to look at Markham Keep.

"I wish we did not have to return," she said.

Walter nodded. "I promise we will only remain long enough to pack. Newark is not far off, and we can be there before nightfall."

She sighed her relief. "You have my gratitude—you all do."

But when their horses clattered beneath the gatehouse, they were met by a sea of soldiers.

Anne drew in her reins, and her mount danced to a halt. "What is the meaning of this?" she cried. She did not see Lord Egmanton in the courtyard.

A man stepped forward. "I am Sir Martin, captain of the guard. I have orders to take Sir Philip into custody."

"You will not," Anne said firmly. "Sir Philip but rescued me from an unseemly attack."

"I will carry out my orders until I am told otherwise."

When Anne would have said more, Walter rode up to her side and shook his head.

"My lady, we can resolve this peacefully rather than attempt to battle here in the courtyard."

She looked back at Philip with wide eyes, but he smiled at her.

"Do not worry for me, my lady," he said, dismounting. He unbuckled his belt and handed his dagger and sword, still in their scabbards, to Walter.

Two soldiers came to walk at his side.

"Where are you taking him?" she demanded.

"To the dungeon, my lady, where all prisoners await their hearing," said the captain. "I promise he will not be mistreated."

If ever Lady Rosamond's forceful personality was needed, it was now. "If you harm him in any way, I promise that the king will be told, and his might will be wielded in my favor."

Sir Martin bowed to her. "I understand, my lady."

Anne was glad that her trembling had finally fled in the face of her anger. When her knights stood around her after their mounts had been led away, Markham Keep's soldiers finally dispersed, leaving them alone.

"What now, Walter?" she asked.

"We go inside and confront Lord Egmanton with his deception. I assume you can play the part of the aggrieved countess?"

"Gladly," she said with cold determination.

But as they went inside, she could not help but blame herself for this whole dilemma. Philip had warned her that a man could misunderstand her playfulness, could go further with intimacy than she had meant. His imprisonment was her fault.

Chapter 13

When she returned to her bedchamber, Anne was grateful for Margaret's kind treatment of her. There was a hot bath waiting, and she sank into it to banish the last of her shivering. But she did not linger long—she had to win Philip's release. Margaret helped her dress in the most royal gown she'd brought, decorated with enough gold and pearls to shine at court. When Anne finally descended into the great hall, she knew that candlelight caught and reflected in the gown, making her glitter like a rare treasure.

Lady Egmanton was seated on one of the two chairs on the raised dais. Her daughters stood nearby, holding hands, looking confused. But Anne saw several maidservants turn sympathetic gazes on her. Anne had been spared, but perhaps these women had not been so fortunate.

The baron himself was standing before the hearth, talking to his steward. When he turned at Anne's entrance, she saw the bruises that swelled his eyes, the crusted blood in the corner of his mouth. Though he glared at her, Anne ignored him and went right to the true power of the household, his mother.

Instead of taking a place below the dais, Anne stepped onto it before the affronted baroness.

"Your son has wronged me," she said in a cold, powerful voice that rang through the great hall. "He tried to take what I have only given to a man in marriage."

Lady Egmanton's eyes went wide, as if she hadn't imagined Anne would speak so plainly. "Your man attacked a baron," she protested in a high voice.

"Your son deserved more than a black eye for his cruel behavior." Anne plucked at the threads attaching her sleeves to her dress, and since they'd been loosened by Margaret, both came free, sliding off to the floor. Anne lifted her arms so that the baroness could see the bruises mottling her skin above both elbows. "*This* is what was done to me, and if Sir Philip had not intervened, your son had planned to do more."

While Margaret picked up the sleeves, Lady Egmanton looked at her son, who kept his chin raised, although at last worry flickered briefly in his eyes. Anne knew she could take these charges to the highest court in the land—and both Egmantons knew it, too.

But when the old woman turned back to Anne, Anne could have sworn she saw faint relief in those eyes, as if her son had done a good deed by ridding them of Lady Rosamond's favor. Anne felt nauseated by the whole family.

"I wish nothing more to do with you or your offspring," Anne said, turning her back on the baroness.

"You will release my knight at once, and we will leave this keep immediately."

No one said a word as Anne ascended the stairs again. But she met the gaze of Walter, who nodded to her, his expression full of satisfaction.

The dungeon dug out beneath Markham Keep was as damp and cold as the French dungeons Philip had been in—or even the one at Alderley, where he and John had spent a night when they were trying to rescue Lady Elizabeth. At least they had left him a candle. He imagined that the never-ending darkness might drive a prisoner mad after awhile. He had a wooden pallet, a blanket he didn't dare touch, and two buckets. He thought the one had only brackish water in it, but he wasn't about to try it until he was desperate. Though the door was made of solid wood, he did not bother to test it. He had faith in Anne's ability to earn his release. After all, she was Lady Rosamond, wife of an earl, daughter of a duke. And Egmanton was a mere baron.

But it was at least an hour before he heard a door creak open somewhere in the distance. Through the cracks of the door he could see the wavering light of a torch approaching. With the jingling of keys, a lock turned, and the door swung open. But instead of being allowed out, Philip was ordered back by a Markham guard. Walter entered, and the door shut behind him.

Walter looked around. "Comfortable accommodations."

"I'd ask you to have a seat on the pallet, but it might not hold us both." Though Philip was relieved to see the knight, there was now a wall between them because of what the League had withheld. "So I am not to be released?"

"You will be. They are simply delaying it as long as possible." Walter briefly explained Anne confronting the Egmantons.

Philip gritted his teeth. "Their behavior is appalling."

"Before you leave this place, I wish to speak my mind."

Philip regarded him warily, but said nothing.

"You did not handle the situation well."

"You did not see what I saw," Philip said in a low, cold voice. "He was between her bare thighs and she was fighting him. I was worried that he'd already—"

"Believe me, I understand," Walter interrupted, his voice tired. "But it was only necessary to get Lady Rosamond away from him, not beat him. You cannot allow your heart to rule you."

"My heart—"

Walter lowered his voice. "I know you have been alone with Lady Rosamond more than once, that there is an attraction between you."

Clenching his jaw, Philip waited to hear what the captain would say.

"Lady Rosamond will move on with her life someday, perhaps with you, but for now you could have jeopardized our mission with your rash behavior."

"Lady Rosamond's life is at Alderley," Philip said, "not with me." He wanted to tell the knight that Anne had already decided her life was with the League, but it was not his place to make such a revelation.

Walter arched an eyebrow. "I owe her a debt. If she wishes to spend time with you, regardless of how it will end, then I will allow it, as long as you are seen to be acting as her bodyguard. She seems to need your companionship. It cannot be much longer before we are finished." He turned toward the door. "You will be released as soon as we are ready to depart."

When he had gone, Philip propped his arm on his bent knee and closed his eyes. Once he would have believed Walter's words at face value, but now he could no longer trust him. The man's devotion to the League was more important than anything else. Was he just trying to appease Philip? Would he do anything to make sure his mission succeeded?

Walter had said Anne needed Philip, but she obviously didn't think so. The desire between them was proving dangerous. Philip kept trying to resist, and only found himself ever more desperate for her kiss, for her touch. And she seemed to feel the same. But they each had separate plans for their lives. He'd even told her some of his past, so that she would understand.

He remembered his jealousy over Egmanton, how the thought of Anne hurt had been a blow such as he'd never received before. There had been a despairing look in her eyes as she remembered being a woman of little power. What had happened to her? She needed him, yet the last time he had been so desperately needed by a woman, it had changed his life. Was he just going to allow that to happen again, all because he could not stop caring about Anne?

They had too late a start to reach Newark that night, and rather than risk their horses being injured traveling in the dark, the small party ended up making camp in a deserted hunting lodge near the edge of Sherwood Forest. It was nothing but four walls and bare earth, with a thatched roof overhead, but they would be safer from attack than if they slept outside.

While the knights prepared for the night, Anne tried to ignore her sadness as she watched Margaret lay out their bedding near the hearth fire. Joseph had snared several rabbits, and as they ate with their fingers, she found herself watching Philip. She'd never been so relieved as when he'd been released, unharmed. It saddened her that he was no longer as jovial with the Bladesmen. She could understand that she hadn't been told things they'd considered unimportant, for she'd spent her life as a woman and a servant. When Philip had been a soldier, surely he'd been used to taking orders unquestioningly. But once he'd tasted life's freedom as a knight, made choices because of the knowledge he'd been given, it would be difficult to learn that he'd been manipulated.

After pulling the meat off a small bone, she licked her fingers, then found herself meeting Philip's gaze across the fire. For just a moment, he revealed a smoldering intensity as he watched her eat, but it was gone so suddenly, she wondered if she'd imagined it. But no, she knew how little they could resist each other. He seemed almost hasty as he turned to speak to Joseph. But his stare had been real, because it left her feeling as warm and languid inside as if he'd caressed her. Last night, she'd tossed restlessly, barely able to sleep, for wanting what they had not finished.

Philip took the first shift guarding the lodge that night, and Anne lay down, feeling secure. He paced between the two shuttered windows and the door, occasionally peering out to listen.

Again, sleep would not come to her. She could feel Margaret's blankets twitch as she slept, heard several different snores. An owl hooted overhead, and the running of the stream outside seemed so loud in her ears.

At last she sat up and wrapped a blanket tighter about her shoulders against the chill. Philip came over and knelt down nearby.

"Is something wrong, Countess?" he asked softly.

She inched closer to the fire, grateful he'd been keeping it well fed. Awkwardly, she said, "I am sorry that you had to suffer today for the results of my flirtation."

He sat back on his heels, his expression surprised. "Suffer? I spent a couple hours being chilly. I'd hardly call that suffering." He grinned. "And you rescued me."

She found herself playing with the long braid of her hair. "But what if it happens again? I am supposed to be at ease with men. Am I doing something wrong?"

He rubbed his hands on his thighs and looked at the fire. "You are doing nothing wrong except being trusting. If you feel the need to be alone with a man, then do it on your terms, when you can be protected, and not because he suggests it."

He wasn't meeting her gaze, and his lips were pressed thin.

"But you don't like when I have to do that."

His gaze met hers. "Nay. But it is not my place to object."

"And it would not affect my decisions," she said, lifting both hands apologetically. "I am . . . Lady Rosamond. I have a mission."

He smiled. "I know."

She hesitated, then confided, "'Tis coming to me so much easier now. I even think I'm beginning to delude myself, as if I've become her."

"How?"

"'Tis too easy to imagine it really is me these prospective grooms want. I have much to learn to distance myself from the character I portray. I know this is an opportunity to meet different kinds of men, to understand how they think. This knowledge will allow me to serve the League."

"I guess that is one way to use your experiences." He studied her. "So you've learned a lesson about the Lord Egmantons of the world. Back in the forest this afternoon, you made a comment about believing such attacks did not happen to women with power. Were you remembering something else?"

She was tempted to deny any hidden meanings, but she owed him the truth. Linking her hands together, she stared into the fire and said, "Do you remember several days ago when I told you that my parents thought I'd ruined my chances at a good marriage?"

"Aye. They took away your dowry when you wouldn't marry the man they'd chosen. You said you hadn't even told them you were leaving Alderley on this journey."

"'Tis because they no longer consider me their daughter."

He hesitated. "That seems a harsh reaction."

"'Twas not simply that." She took a deep breath and faced him, and the fact that he watched her gravely suddenly gave her courage. "They bade me return home, to meet a man whom they had interested in me. I obeyed them, since they were my parents and my duty was to them. After all, I knew my whole life that I would marry. I had just hoped I would have some say in the matter."

"But they had already chosen this man."

She nodded. "Perhaps I like being Lady Rosamond because of the control I have. I didn't have any when I returned home. They bade me spend time with the miller, and he was old and filthy and had too many children already, but he was going to give my father land to marry me. He tried to force himself on me, just as Lord Egmanton had done. When I fought him off, he confessed his confusion, because he said my parents understood his need to see if I was fertile enough to give him more healthy sons to work for him."

Philip's eyes widened. "Your parents gave him permission to bed you?"

She was surprised how much it still hurt. "After eight years of age, I had spent most of my life with Lady Elizabeth, so I no longer knew them well, but their desperation, their disregard of me, wounded me deeply."

"I know many villagers who did not marry until the woman had proved she could carry a child, but to have it forced on you is a terrible fate."

"I should not have blamed the old miller for what my parents had promised, but I kicked him and ran. When I went home to gather my belongings, my parents told me never to return, that I was no longer their daughter. To my dismay, I was more relieved than sad."

"Because now you could make your own choices," he said shrewdly.

"Aye, I thought so. But after consideration, I realized that with no dowry, I was even more limited."

"Until the League asked for your help."

She smiled with growing enthusiasm. "It opened up a new world for me. I am no one's servant here, and I am helping people. It is my chance to do good in the world, to live an exciting life."

"A dangerous life," he said.

"I know, but you choose that every day, do you not, with your tournaments and mercenary work? And you would deny me my choice?"

He smiled faintly. "I seem to be able to deny you nothing."

Oh, that wasn't true, but she didn't want to force him to change. Like everyone, he was partly ruled by his past. He had mentioned his mother being a seamstress to Lady Kelshall. It had taken her a few hours after the trauma of the day, but at last she had remembered why it had seemed familiar.

"Philip, after you mentioned that your mother worked for Lady Kelshall, I finally remembered where I had heard that name."

He didn't seem surprised at the change in subject. "I already know."

"What do you mean?"

"We're near Kelshall Castle. I had heard that my old mistress had died several years ago, so I questioned Walter. We're going there next."

"I was concerned that you would be upset that your first master was on my husband-hunting list."

"I haven't had time to think about it," he said, wearing an ironic smile. "He is a good man, who deserves to find another wife to cherish. I am just saddened that I have to be a part of misleading him, especially since he only has a daughter, and no heir of his own blood for the earldom."

"He would understand, if he knew the reason," she said softly, tossing her broken twigs into the fire. "Do you want me to request that we avoid Kelshall Castle?"

He shook his head. "Then we'd only have to answer

Walter's questions. Fear not, the past is behind me—as it is for you."

He was watching her again, so intently. Even now, the lure of his body could easily make her forget caution. She murmured a good night and crawled back under her blankets. She was developing a terrible weakness where Philip was concerned.

Through half-closed eyes, she watched him put more wood on the fire. Every moment she spent with him, whether talking or being held in his arms, seemed worth the hurt she would suffer in the future when she left him behind. Soon she would stop playing Lady Rosamond, and take on a new character, never again plain Anne the maidservant. But until then, she and Philip played with fire, she thought, watching him move silhouetted before the flames. Yet she couldn't stop—didn't want to stop.

Chapter 14

Six years had passed since the last time Philip had seen Kelshall Castle, and he'd changed from a boy to a man. The castle itself had changed little, although strangely it seemed smaller to him, especially when they rode through the village on their way in. Sheep roamed the village green, and a flock of geese floated contentedly on the pond. They passed the tavern next door to the brew house, and more than one person stepped outside to watch them go by. No one recognized him, of course, although the brew mistress was still the same old woman whose name he couldn't remember.

As the lane led out of the village and toward the castle, he finally saw the old cottage his parents had shared with him. Though a tree branch had fallen on the thatched roof, no one had bothered to remove it. The door hung slanted, and there were no animals in the wooden enclosure. It was obviously abandoned, which saddened him. It would have been easier to see a family happy there, with children playing in the yard.

He noticed Anne watching him from behind her

veil, and he simply nodded to her and turned to face the castle rising above the line of trees. At last the road cleared the trees and Kelshall Castle rose imposing on its own island, surrounded by a moat. There were five towers in the curtain wall, the central one being the gatehouse. The drawbridge was down, and Joseph was riding over it toward them, as if he'd been waiting for them. He'd gone ahead to prepare the castle for Lady Rosamond's visit, and the fact that he wasn't waiting inside made Philip uneasy.

Walter raised a hand, and the party halted until Joseph rode up to them. "Sir Joseph, you have a report?"

The knight nodded. "Lord Kelshall is in residence, as you can see from the banner flying above the gatehouse. He would be pleased for an introduction to Lady Rosamond. But there are also two other noblemen visiting, both of whom also requested an introduction. They claim not to have met the lady before."

Philip looked at Anne, who wore a doubtful expression. Rather than speaking, she turned to Sir Walter.

The captain said, "Their names?"

"Lord Hungerford and Sir Robert Ludlow, both of Northumberland, traveling to London for the king's summons."

Philip narrowed his eyes as he studied Walter, then spoke in a low voice. "And others are summoned, which is why Lady Rosamond will be able to examine them all in London and prove so valuable to the king?"

Walter nodded, then looked to the women. "Do either of you recognize these names?"

Anne and Margaret exchanged a glance, and then both shook their heads.

"I have heard of Sir Robert," Philip offered. "He has made quite the name for himself as a man of honor, yet a skilled knight."

"And I have heard the same of Lord Hungerford," Walter said. "We have no choice but to go in. I am counting on your good opinion of Lord Kelshall, Philip. Let all be attentive to our lady's safety. Philip, please lead us."

Philip arched a brow, but said nothing. He had admitted to Walter his connection to the castle, and now his judgment was being used to assess Lord Kelshall. Philip could not believe his old master would ever become a traitor to England, regardless of who was on the throne. He rode into the lead, and Joseph moved up to his side.

Philip wondered if Lady Beatrice would be visiting her father. They were of an age, and he had been an illiterate peasant boy until she had taught him how to read, how to dance, how to converse with ladies. Except for his accomplishments on the tiltyard, she bore much of the responsibility for her father choosing him to become a squire.

The horses' hooves beat a rhythm over the drawbridge. Beneath the gatehouse, the sun dimmed, but when they emerged into the inner ward, servants gathered along the path, pointing and waving, and even carrying roses. Philip glanced over his shoulder to see Anne accepting several bouquets. As she blushed prettily, he wondered if she found it difficult to accept accolades not really meant for her. It was understandable why she was beginning to feel like Lady Rosamond.

After they reached the wide staircase that led up to the great hall, David helped Anne to the ground. As Philip dismounted, he saw Kelshall at the top of the stairs. Just seeing his old lord brought an ache of gratitude to his chest. This man had seen the potential in a blacksmith's son who had aspired to become a soldier. He had always considered Kelshall a father and mentor more than his own, and to his surprise, he felt guilt for that.

Kelshall came down the steps at a good pace, seeming younger than Philip had once thought. He was still spry and healthy-looking in his middle forties, although he'd lost the hair atop his head, and what was left was gray.

When he saw Anne, he smiled and bowed to her, and she graciously gave him her hand.

"Lady Rosamond," Kelshall said, "how flattered I am that you decided to visit me on your great journey through England."

She gave her throaty laugh that never failed to remind Philip of his desire for her.

"Lord Kelshall, I have heard much in praise of you, so of course I had to come. But I think you will be even more pleased with my visit, when I tell you that I bring with me a former ward of yours, Sir Philip Clifford."

Kelshall spun about to look at her knights, and when he saw Philip his face broadened in a grin. "Philip!"

Kelshall came forward and hugged him, then clapped his shoulders. "How good it is to see you, lad. It has been . . . four years, has it not?"

"Aye, my lord."

Kelshall said to Anne, "When I was returning from France, Philip decided to remain and test himself against the French knights."

"He is very private about his past, my lord," Anne said.

"He always was a modest young man," Kelshall said with a laugh. "So, now, Philip, you are guarding Lady Rosamond on her great adventure." He took Anne's hand to lead her up the stairs. "You know that Philip saved my life in battle. 'Tis why I knighted him."

She glanced over her shoulder at Philip. "Why, nay, I had not heard that."

Philip spread his hands and shrugged.

In the great hall, more than one servant smiled at Philip, and though he remembered few names, he was glad to be recognized. Dinner would be served just after noon, so they were shown to bedchambers to wash away the grime of travel. When they met again outside Anne's door, she had changed into a lovely blue gown. Not for the first time, Philip wondered at Margaret's packing skills, to load so many gowns on one packhorse. But of course, Lady Rosamond had to look her best to capture a husband.

Would Anne be allowed to keep those gowns, or would they return, along with her identity, to their owner? He enjoyed seeing how confident she looked in them. But of course, she had a confidence that had nothing to do with clothing. And that brought his eager mind to how confident she was without them. It was all he could do to follow in her wake as impassively as the other knights, when he really wanted to devour her with his eyes, to remove each layer a piece at a time.

During the midday meal, Kelshall looked to the next trestle table, where Philip and the Bladesmen were seated. "Philip, over the years I have heard much of your talent as a knight. You will of course do me the honor of joining me on the tiltyard this afternoon."

"Surely you would rather spend time with Lady Rosamond, my lord," Philip said.

Kelshall glanced at Anne. "I am sure you would enjoy watching men battle in your honor."

She smiled. "My lord, I think I normally prefer men becoming hot and bothered over *me*, but this time I will make an exception."

A roar of approving laughter seemed to shake the beams in the ceiling.

After the meal, Kelshall found Philip as the crowd dispersed and put an arm around his shoulder. Quietly, he said, "What think you of Lady Rosamond, Philip?"

"She is a good and kind woman, my lord," Philip said, cautiously.

"I like her humor. And the mark of a good woman is that she does not need to have a man focused on her all the time. Lady Kelshall was such a woman, God rest her."

"I remember her fondly, my lord."

"My Beatrice is also the same, thank God."

Philip nodded. "And how is your daughter?"

"She is well and healthy, and so is her son."

"She had no more children?"

"Her husband is not a young man, but thank heavens she was able to give him an heir. Now, do you need to rest, or are you ready to pretend to challenge me?"

Philip grinned. "I have been preparing many years for this day." As they turned toward the double doors leading outside, he saw that Anne was far closer than he'd thought, and he wondered if she'd overheard—and what she'd concluded.

For the next hour, Anne enjoyed herself watching Philip train amongst the fellow soldiers of his youth. She sat on a bench in the shade, admiring Lord Kelshall's skills, and his ability to keep his men loyal to him.

But she had not missed the reference to Lord Kelshall's daughter, who must have grown up with Philip. Was she the kind of woman who ignored the children of her servants? With a father as generous as Lord Kelshall, it was highly unlikely anyone here had been mistreated.

On the tiltyard, she watched Philip renew friendships with soldiers and knights, and laughed with everyone else when the captain of the guard sent Philip for water to quench his thirst, as if he were still a little boy running errands.

But when the exercises had ended, and Lord Kelshall had gone inside to attend to business with several of his tenants, Philip walked away alone, still wearing his sleeveless leather jerkin, his arms damp with perspiration. Anne followed him at a distance, knowing that David remained behind to watch over her. But she felt safe here, in Philip's home, and found herself praying that Lord Kelshall was not implicated in the treason. He had mentioned that he, too, would be going to London soon at the request of the king.

To her surprise, Philip stopped outside the blacksmith's shop and peered inside. She could see the smoke from the fire billowing up from the chimney, and heard the clang of metal on metal as the blacksmith worked. Philip appeared lost in thought, and her curiosity finally got the better of her.

"Philip?"

"Aye, Countess?"

She looked into the interior of the blacksmith shop, and could feel the heat billowing out toward her. "This place has memories for you?"

A corner of his mouth tilted up. "My father used to work here."

"He was a blacksmith?" she asked in surprise. She had known his mother was a seamstress, but he'd never mentioned his father.

"Aye."

"And you did not choose to go into his trade?"

He looked down. "He wanted me to, but nay, I had my own ideas."

"I am certain he was not disappointed that you became a soldier."

"He never saw that," he said ruefully. "He died when I had but nine years, killed in a robbery attempt."

She gasped. "Oh, Philip, how terrible for you and your mother."

He studied her. "I am going to go see the cottage where I lived until his death, so you can stay with—"

"Would you mind if I accompany you?"

He frowned. "It is best not to be outside the castle walls."

"But the village is right next to the castle! And I'm certain Walter and the others would stay nearby. Unless you do not wish it." She wanted to see him surrounded by his past, to see the kind of boy he was.

He studied her. "And then you'd find some excuse to test your Bladeswoman abilities to follow me."

She smiled, and he looked back at her, and once again, it was as if nothing else existed but the two of them, and the desire that wove them together.

"And when you follow me," he continued softly, huskily, "bad things happen."

"Do you not mean to say when *you* follow *me*?"

He finally turned away, releasing her from his gaze. "Go tell Walter."

While Philip saddled their horses, she found Walter at the soldiers' barracks and explained that she and Philip would be riding back to the village not a half-mile away.

He frowned at her. "I will only agree to this because the village is so close. My men and I will follow you."

"But not too close."

Anne regretted those four words immediately, because Walter arched a brow at her. She quickly turned away and went back to the stables, where Philip waited for her, holding the reins of both horses.

He glanced back at Walter. "Did he forbid us?"

"Nay, they will follow."

"I thought his worry about an attack, even on Kelshall land, would keep you here."

"If you don't want me to accompany you, say it now, Philip."

"When you and I do anything together, we never know what will happen."

When Anne realized that they had looked at each other for too long in a public courtyard, she turned away, but said softly, "And is that not exciting, Philip?" She stepped onto the mounting block, put her foot in the stirrup, and then slid her other leg across the saddle. She smiled at him, deliberately allowing him to see her bare calves before she shook her skirts into place.

He looked up at her, brows lowered over blazing eyes. She tilted her head innocently.

He mounted his own horse, and side by side, they rode out into the countryside. She urged her horse into a gallop, lying low over his neck, satisfied by how much her skill with the animal had increased on this journey. Philip caught up with her, but their mad ride was over too quickly as the village came into view between the trees. Looking over her shoulder, she could see the Bladesmen several hundred yards back, and she was faintly curious why they gave her so much freedom with Philip. She slowed as she spotted the abandoned cottage he had stared at earlier.

He half smiled at her. "A good guess?"

"A good deduction."

She slid off the horse before he could help her, and draped the reins over a scraggly bush. The thatching was gone from much of the roof, and a branch had dented another part. Philip walked to the ruined door, and it came off in his hands. When he set it to the side and went in, she followed him.

The cottage was far smaller than what she was used to, only two rooms, with a loft above. Except for a broken crate in a corner, there was no furniture.

"The cottage could be repaired if someone needed it," she said. "Or perhaps the owner built a larger home."

"My mother couldn't even afford this after my father died. Lady Kelshall found us a room in the castle."

"That was good of her." She wanted to ask what his life had been like, but knew he would only tell her what he wanted to.

He walked to an open window at the rear of the cottage and ducked his head to look out. "My father was disappointed when I did not want to follow his trade."

"Fathers always are," she said lightly.

"I *did* try. But I had so little care with his tools that I burned my calf with the point of a sword he was crafting."

"You must have been young."

He nodded and walked out the front door. She followed him around to the small yard and overgrown garden plot. He stopped at a chicken coop, with its roof caved in.

"I used to hide in here when he was looking for me," he said, his smile containing little amusement. "I wanted to watch the knights. When he died trying to protect us from thieves, I was embarrassed."

Anne said nothing as her throat tightened in sorrow for him.

He looked out across the pastureland behind the yard. "I remember thinking so clearly that a *knight* would have defended himself and killed the thieves."

She walked to him and put a hand on his arm. "Philip, you were only a little boy. Maybe it was easier for you to feel anger rather than sadness. After all, you lost your father and your home."

"Kelshall Castle became my home, and I was happier there, where I could watch the men train any time I wanted." He shrugged. "I have never told anyone this, but I guess you understand what it was like to be different than the people of the castle, to be of a class where you never expected to receive what you really wanted."

Anne nodded slowly, but inside, she was thinking that there was another reason he never talked about being the child of servants—because he'd risen above it, become the man he wanted to be. He'd carved out a future for himself, just like she was trying to do. For a moment, she felt a pang of sadness that their futures weren't entwined. But she couldn't give up her only dream in hopes that perhaps Philip would change his mind about what was driving him. Here, seeing his humble background, made her know for certain that he was driven to succeed. She didn't want to go back to that existence where she depended upon other people for her mere survival. Now she was in charge, she controlled her own life, and it was a heady feeling.

She dropped her hand from his arm. "Is Lord Kelshall's daughter your age? I heard him speak to you about her."

"Aye. She was my friend."

She had suspected as much. "It is unusual for the lord's daughter and a blacksmith's son to be friends. She must be an unusual woman."

"She taught me to read. Lord Kelshall had no sons, so he decided his daughter would be as educated as any boy. And Beatrice decided that I had to be educated, too, after she found me eavesdropping on her lessons. I was her project, so she made me sit beside her in the lady's garden, where she practiced printing her letters on her wax tablet."

So curious she could barely keep it from her voice, Anne murmured, "That was very good of her."

"When we were older, it was dancing. She had decided to turn me into a squire, which I thought was laughable. But eventually it happened, as if by magic. Then she had no reason to hide my tutoring, because it is the duty of a squire to wait on his lord. She taught me how to converse with ladies. She taught me—"

Anne stiffened. No wonder he wanted a nobly born woman for his wife. He couldn't have Lady Beatrice, but she was still what he was looking for. It made so much sense.

He turned to face her, and suddenly he was too close, looming above her.

"I can tell what you're thinking," he said. "Your pretty brain is working hard to figure out my past. Nay, Beatrice was not some experienced young lady, wanting to teach an illiterate servant about the pleasures of bed out of sheer sport. She was a frightened girl of seventeen, offered in marriage to a man old enough to be her grandfather."

Anne took a deep breath in sympathy.

"The king had decreed it, to join two great families. She had been meant for the son, but he had died of the plague, and so the father took his place."

He watched her as if wondering what she was thinking. He reached out and touched a curl that had come loose in her hair and wound down her neck. He moved it between his fingers like a talisman. She trembled.

"She came to me the night before her wedding," he said in a husky voice, "and begged me to give her one good memory to keep with her in a marriage she dreaded."

Pain tightened Anne's chest, as she imagined herself that frightened young girl. She had come so close to having the same thing happen to her.

"I didn't love her as a man should, but she was my friend, and I pitied her. So I took her to my bed. We were young and awkward and eager. And then she married someone else."

Chapter 15

When the words left Philip's mouth, it was as if a spell was broken. He did not see the past, only Anne, staring up at him with sympathetic eyes. He was touching her soft hair. He'd only meant to show her where he came from, to allow her to see how far he'd risen. Instead he'd told her a secret that could cost Beatrice her life.

He cupped her face in both hands and said urgently, "You can never tell a soul what I've just revealed."

"I won't," she whispered. "You have my vow."

A single tear glistened at the corner of her eye, and without thinking, he kissed it. He hadn't meant to make her sad.

She swallowed. "I heard Lord Kelshall say that his daughter had given her husband his only son."

Philip searched her eyes, felt her sympathy as her hands clutched his waist. "He was born nine months from their wedding date. He was the only child she ever had."

"Does he look like you?"

He closed his eyes, and the pain that he always kept buried in another part of his heart now seemed too real. "I was already in France with Kelshall when I heard that she was with child. He was so proud as he told me her missive said that the babe looked just like her, fair hair and all. I think she wrote that so I would know. And perhaps he's not even mine, but when Kelshall said today that she'd never had another . . ."

It had felt even more real. When he'd thought she'd had a half-dozen children, he'd been able to assume that the first child wasn't his.

"Have you ever seen him?" she asked.

He shook his head, and then pressed his forehead to hers. "I don't want to. Maybe I've left a good part of myself in the world, the best deed I could have accomplished. Perhaps I'm the one who made her a mother and gave joy to her days."

He lifted his head to look back at the cottage, and she held his waist tighter, as if she didn't want him to go.

"I was always ashamed that my father was just a man who labored at a menial task, not a soldier, not a knight. And now I am the recipient of my own prejudices—if my son ever knew what I was, he would be ashamed."

"Philip—"

"Nay, you do not have to point out my folly," he said, letting his hands slide down her neck to rest on her shoulders.

"You were so young, too young to understand," she insisted.

"And it took me a long time to mature, to realize that my father might not be a knight, but he was his own man, who stood up to thieves to protect his family, and died for it, because he was only one man against many. I couldn't help him."

Her fingers touched his face, and she rose on tiptoes. It seemed so natural to bend to her, to kiss her gently, to taste the saltiness of her tears on her lips. Beneath that, she tasted of sunshine and sweetness, and he wanted to lose himself in the warm curves of her lips. With each kiss, she opened more fully to him, until he held her tight against him. He pushed her until her back was against the apple tree he'd once spent hours in. Their tongues eagerly mated, and he could feel the pounding of her heart against his.

She was not resisting him, and he let passion sweep away the other emotions he didn't want to feel. He pulled her away from the tree and pushed her back into the tall, overgrown grass. She fell back and reached for him, and he tumbled down on top of her, catching most of his weight on his hands and knees. They came together in a clutch of arms and legs until he lay between her thighs. Their kisses were open-mouthed and frantic, and she wrapped one leg around him, her foot pressing into his ass. She moaned and writhed as his hands roamed her body, his palms filled to overflowing with her breasts. Her nipples were tight against his palms. She suddenly rolled, flattening another patch of grass as she rose above him. When she reached for his breeches, he caught her hands.

"Anne, remember where we are," he whispered, staring up regretfully at the beauty of her passionate face and her wild hair. "I don't want your first time to be like this."

She leaned over him, her hands kneading his chest. He groaned.

"You will be my first time," she said hoarsely.

"You're a virgin, Anne."

"And there will be no husband to save my virginity for."

And she didn't seem sad about it, which only made him hotter, harder. With a groan, he pushed up between her thighs, the length of him cradled in her hot moistness.

"Lady Rosamond?"

The distant call came from the front of the cottage. Philip vaguely recognized Walter's voice. Yet he was so overcome with need, he almost pulled Anne down to hush her until they were gone.

He tried to remember who he'd fought so hard to become. He'd spent much of his life proving himself to other people, first the Kelshall soldiers, then the earl and the League, and then his friend John, Lord Alderley. And now he was trying to be worthy of some wellborn wife who didn't even know yet.

And here was Anne, offering herself for their mutual pleasure. It was hard to remember his honor when she looked at him with dark, hot eyes.

When Walter called again, she rose unsteadily to her feet, smoothing down her skirts. As he stood up, he saw that her hands were trembling as she fingered her hair into place, pinning her headdress. Her mouth was wet; her breasts rose and fell with a rapidity that almost undid him.

"I guess we're going to be escorted to the castle," she said ruefully.

He admired how normal she sounded, when he himself was still burning with emotions, with the past, and with desire.

Anne somehow made it through supper, having to smile mysteriously, and laugh with that throatiness that seemed to make men think differently about her. She could be Lady Rosamond, while at the same time, inside, she was simply Anne, thinking about the secret Philip had carried for the last six years—and the secret passion that burned between them.

Sir Robert Ludlow, blond and earnest, distracted her after supper with a song in her honor; the lords Hungerford and Kelshall took turns leading her in dance. When Sir Robert interceded again, she laughed and allowed him to lead her away. Out of the corner of her eye, she saw Philip talking with a man she didn't recognize, and she hoped he was letting himself be distracted from the memories this place brought out in him.

"Lady Rosamond?"

She gave a start, realizing that Sir Robert had said her name more than once. "Forgive me, sir."

He smiled and patted her hand where it rested in

his. "I asked if I could distract you with a game of Tables."

He was leading her to where the game board was set up. There were long rows with round playing pieces lined up on them, and she looked at it with regret.

"I'm afraid I've never learned how, Sir Robert."

He seemed astonished. "I thought every young noblewoman learned this entertaining game."

Elizabeth had tried to teach her, but Anne had always felt such frivolity not suitable for a maidservant. Her evenings had been for sewing, or preparing Elizabeth's garments for the next day.

But now, she just smiled prettily and shrugged.

"I will play you, Sir Robert." Philip approached her from behind.

It was all Anne could do not to blush with yearning.

"Then Lady Rosamond can learn as she watches," he added.

As the two knights sat on either side of the game board, Lord Kelshall approached and looked down at them all fondly. "My daughter Beatrice taught Philip to play long ago. She was so very patient." He clapped Philip on the back. "Perhaps she is teaching her son, now, eh?"

Anne watched Philip, but all he did was smile and nod, as pleasant as always.

He would never know if the child was truly his. But he had come to peace with it, she told herself. Lady Beatrice had asked a sacrifice of him, and in the name of friendship, he had acquiesced. Anne did not want to think of him in the arms of another woman, but like all men, he could not be innocent at his age.

But Lady Beatrice had taken his innocence even as she'd given her own. And she'd made Philip a traitor to the man he'd worshiped as a father. Anne could not forgive her for that.

When Anne retired to her chamber, she couldn't sleep. It bothered her that they were all just assuming that Lord Kelshall couldn't be involved in the treason, just because he had helped raise Philip. Only last year, a king had lost his throne and his life. What if Lord Kelshall had been King Richard's loyal friend? Would he not feel compelled to seek revenge? She could not ask Philip to look into this; it would hurt him to imagine Lord Kelshall as a suspect. Anne would do it herself.

Outside her door, Joseph was her guard, and she invited him in and explained her worries.

"What do you think we can do about this, Lady Rosamond?" Joseph asked with suspicion.

"You stayed downstairs longer than the rest of us, did you not?"

He only nodded.

"Were you keeping watch on the hall for a reason?"

His gaze slid away. "Not for any reason in particular."

"So where was Kelshall when you came upstairs?"

"Going to his private solar with Hungerford and Ludlow."

"The three of them alone together?" she said, feeling a coldness settle in her stomach.

"There may be three traitors, my lady," Joseph said patiently. "But they know someone overheard them. I cannot imagine they would congregate together and risk implicating themselves."

"How do we know Hungerford and Ludlow aren't some of the men who've been following us?"

"We can't know, but the odds against—"

"I want to go to Kelshall's private solar. Perhaps we can hear what is being said outside the door."

"That is too dangerous," he said stubbornly, folding his arms across his chest.

"If they discover me, I can say I was simply looking for them. Men enjoy that."

She thought his handsome face almost cracked into a smile, but he held onto his discipline.

"My lady, I cannot allow you to do this."

Sweeping past him, she opened the door. "We will be safe, I promise you."

He put his arm around her waist and lifted her right off the floor.

Philip stepped into the doorway and came to an abrupt halt.

Though his face showed no expression, Anne knew him well enough to sense his stiffness, his . . . jealousy? She pushed against Joseph's arm, feeling her ribs creak.

Joseph put her down, cleared his throat, and spoke

softly. "Philip, perhaps you can talk sense into her. She wants to eavesdrop on Kelshall to prove he's not . . ."

When he let his words die off, Philip nodded. Anne stood with her hands on her hips and stared with suspicion as Joseph walked out and shut the door behind him.

"What is this about Kelshall?" Philip asked.

Anne ignored his question. "Joseph just left me here alone with you."

"About Kelshall—"

"And you don't seem surprised he did it. What is going on, Philip?"

He walked to the hearth and rested his hand on the mantel as he stared into the flames. "Walter believes that we should have time alone together."

"You *asked* him for such a boon?" she demanded, fury rising swiftly through her. She caught his shoulder so that she could see his face. Had Philip jeopardized her position with the League?

He shook his head, putting his hand over hers. She pulled away.

"Anne, he is an intelligent man who would see the attraction between us even did he not have the training of a Bladesman. They owe you a debt, and would not deny you something you want."

"And they think I want you."

When he only shrugged, she whirled away from him, close to trembling with her jumbled emotions: anger and humiliation and guilt. Perhaps she herself had alerted the Bladesmen to her desire for Philip. Her personal life should not matter to them; if she wanted to take Philip as a lover—

Heavens, they'd almost given their permission.

She groaned. "This is not good. I have to prove to them that I am dedicated to their cause, not to furthering a romance."

"They know you're dedicated."

His sympathy only fueled her anger. "I am the one who can be closest to Lord Kelshall. I can sneak outside his door and—"

"'Tis already been done," he said softly. "I went myself. I had to discover the truth."

By the calm expression on his face, she knew that he had found nothing suspicious, and she felt relieved for him. But to suspect his own lord had to have been difficult for him.

She turned away, tired of the softness in her whenever she looked at him. She could not control herself around him. Walter might have given his permission, but she worried how the League perceived her. Did they think she needed the comfort of a man more than a mission with them?

Or was she counting too much on a future with them? A bleakness squeezed her chest. Nay, she could not think that way. She had already proven her fortitude. She would make it happen.

"Anne—"

If he touched her, she would melt into him again. "Just go, Philip."

* * *

The next day, they were on the road journeying south again, closer and closer to London, and the end. The tension of always worrying about attack was making her feel exhausted, as if her performance was stretching thin like a second skin worn too long.

The weather did not help. Fog and rain chased them as they rode. Even their horses's heads hung dispiritedly. Anne's cloak drooped soddenly about her head, and she began to feel rain trickling down her scalp. Margaret huddled in her saddle and said little.

In front of her, Joseph glanced behind, and then looked again, frowning. She didn't have the energy to feel frightened. She followed his gaze, but saw nothing out of the ordinary, just her other three knights, taking every precaution, as if she might be in danger at any moment. How did they stay so focused?

Joseph pulled up on his horse and let her pass him. She glanced behind to see him talking to Walter, who finally nodded. Joseph urged his horse into a cantor and rode back the way they'd come, disappearing into the wisps of fog that hid the road.

One minute merged into the next, and Joseph finally returned. But Anne only knew that because she suddenly heard them talking in low voices, as if they were trying to keep quiet. She straightened in her saddle and slowed her horse. Margaret kept going as the knights caught up with Anne.

"Walter, is something amiss?" she asked.

For a moment he was quiet, and she had another of

those eerie feelings where the Bladesmen seemed to be conversing without speaking. Philip watched them, and for once seemed to understand.

At last, Walter said, "My lady, a party is journeying behind us, less than half a league. Joseph saw them through a break in the fog."

"Perhaps they are simply as anxious to reach Stamford as we are," Anne said. But she straightened in her saddle, shaking off her sleepy daze.

"They are traveling quietly for the size of the retinue, and they have not come any closer. Sir Joseph says it is a party of six mounted men, who should be traveling faster than us, loaded down as we are with extra packhorses. It could very well be our watcher, forced to stay too close in this weather. While the fog is still thick, we will conceal ourselves off the road and allow them to pass."

She followed Walter's horse as the road curved down into a weedy ditch, then up the far side. An overgrown hedgerow, which separated the pastureland from the road, blocked their path. They were lucky enough to find a small wooden gate fifty yards farther down, and they went through.

Once they were hidden from the road, they dismounted and waited. Anne held her horse's bridle and petted her nose, trying to keep the animal calm. Soon they could hear the jingle of many horses. The sound of voices faded and appeared, distorted by the mist and the bend in the road.

Her stomach churned, even as she told herself to be calm. A Bladeswoman would face such dangers every day. Philip was standing near her, looking as intent, as impassive as the rest of the knights. He must have often faced the unknown.

Beside her, Margaret was visibly trembling, and Anne put an arm about her shoulder.

The voices became clearer, and they could hear an occasional phrase.

"She's not here."

Anne stiffened.

"Lost . . ."

" . . . Lady Ros . . ."

Before her eyes, her knights as one unfixed their helms strapped to their saddles.

"What are you doing?" she whispered.

Against her ear, Philip said, "If it is you they are after, we cannot let them get ahead of us, where they could ambush us farther down the road."

"So you'll just attack, not knowing—?"

"We'll know for certain if our mission has been compromised."

With his helm under his arm, he mounted his horse, as did the Bladesmen. The squeak of leather seemed unnaturally loud. She found Margaret's hand clutched tightly in her own.

The men rode back through the hedgerow gate. She wished she could be of help. They had volunteered no information about what to do should they not return. Were they so foolishly confident?

"You were so brave to accept this assignment," Anne whispered to Margaret.

"You, too, milady."

Someone barked an order, and both women jumped. Then there were several loud clashes of sword against sword, another shout, and then silence.

"Heavenly God," Margaret murmured.

They could hear voices, but could not make out what was being said. There did not seem to be a battle.

At last the gate opened, and Philip leaned in. "You can come out now," he said in a normal voice.

"Who is it?" Anne demanded.

"Your suitor, Sir Robert Ludlow. He says he wanted to spend another evening with you."

Anne gaped at him. "How do you know he's telling the truth?"

"If he wanted to harm you, he could have done so any time in the last day. But it is better to have him out in the open, where we can see him. Fear not, we will take no chances."

When Anne appeared on the road, leading her horse, Sir Robert bowed low to her.

"My lady, please forgive me for this terrible fright I've caused you."

"Sir Robert, why did you not tell me you were leaving at the same time as we were?" she asked. She did not know what to think of him. Could his pale good looks be hiding a terrible secret?

He looked embarrassed. "Because I did not wish

Hungerford or Kelshall to know that I wanted more time with you."

She withheld a groan. "Then next time, at least mention it to me."

"There will be a next time?" he said so hopefully that he looked like an anxious puppy.

"I will not commit to that." The tiredness in her voice was obvious even to her. "Now can we be on our way, so that we don't have to sleep outside in this terrible weather?"

Yet she felt skittish as their parties merged. It would be so very easy to underestimate him.

Chapter 16

The inn at Stamford did not have a private dining room, so Anne and Sir Robert ate together at a table in the public room. Her knights and his knights, nine of them in all, were seated at several tables they'd pushed together. Wine and ale flowed freely, and their voices rose throughout the evening. Anne kept stealing astonished glances at Walter, who was wearing a silly grin. It was that, more than anything, that convinced her that the Bladesmen were deliberately getting Sir Robert's knights drunk. To incapacitate them for the night? she wondered. Or to see what secrets they told?

She would discover what she could about Sir Robert.

He smiled at her as he dipped his spoon into his chicken stew. "Lady Rosamond, you have undertaken such a long journey."

"'Twill be worth it in the end," she said, picking through the thick broth.

"Ah yes, a new husband. You must have enjoyed your first marriage."

Though she let a wistful expression cross her face, it was difficult to imagine the peace and security marriage might bring. "Aye, the late earl was a wonderful man. I crave that companionship again. And of what use is wealth if you cannot enjoy it with someone?"

He laughed. "I have spent much of my life earning wealth and land, all to make a wife comfortable."

She hesitated. "You must have used your skills in battle well."

"It has been difficult these last few years with three different kings coming into power."

She kept smiling, while inside she felt suddenly alert.

"I kept to myself as much as possible, doing as I was bidden. It is easy when one is only a knight, owing loyalty to another nobleman rather than simply the king himself."

"So you did not have to choose sides?"

"The lord I owed my allegiance to, Lord Hungerford, had to make that decision, and luckily he chose wisely. He weathered well the change in reigns. It is about protecting one's own property, after all."

"Many men are not lucky enough to align with the correct side," she said.

He nodded regretfully, and then changed the subject. "But tell me more about you."

He smiled again, charming and boyish. He seemed to have come through the wars unscathed, the sort of man who would not care who was in power. Why would such a man risk himself to overthrow a king?

"Surely you've heard too much about me," she said, smiling at him.

"Do you play an instrument?" he asked.

She blinked at him in surprise. "Aye, several. But my favorite is the lute." Elizabeth used to have Anne entertain her guests, and it was the lute that kept Anne company when she'd been imprisoned in the tower.

"We would suit well, then, because I love to dance."

At the other table, Philip suddenly lifted his voice in song, and for a man in his cups, he wasn't terrible.

Sir Robert looked askance in amusement. "And I sing, too, perhaps better than your man."

Anne laughed and felt Philip's gaze on her. He had been watching her flirt with one man after another. What would he think if he knew that this time it wasn't so difficult, that Sir Robert wanted to know more about her than the size of her property? Was Sir Robert the sort of man who would want his wife to be amusing and accomplished, yet wouldn't care what her background was?

The drunken knights soon grew too boisterous, and the innkeeper asked Anne and Sir Robert to put them to bed.

Anne stood up. "And I should find my bed, too, for Sir Walter will want to begin the day early."

Sir Robert looked at her captain, who had his arm thrown around Philip and was staggering toward the staircase. "I think Sir Walter will not be so eager to awaken."

She sighed. "You don't know him."

"Are you headed to London?" he asked.

She knew he was hinting that they could travel together. "Nay, sir, we have another nobleman to visit."

His expression fell for a moment before he looked cheerfully resigned. "Another challenger in the battle, then."

"You compare my search to a battle?" she asked, smiling.

"Perhaps not for you, but for those of us in the running, aye, it feels that way. Only this victory matters so much more."

She felt herself blushing. He was the first nobleman who'd reached beneath the Lady Rosamond masquerade and touched Anne herself with his sincerity.

As Anne was preparing for bed, she heard a tap on her barred shutters. She pulled on her dressing gown, knowing it was probably a bird, or the wind. But the tapping continued, far too rhythmically, so at last she went to the window and bent her head to listen.

"I know you're there," said a voice outside.

"Philip, what are you doing out there?" she whispered.

"Trying not to fall to my death. Might I come in?"

She opened the shutters, then stepped back as he dropped to the floor. He straightened and looked about her small chamber, and he seemed so much bigger in this confining environment.

"You do not look very drunk," she said quietly, try-

ing to distract herself from dark memories of fever-
ish embraces. Even when she wanted to be angry with
him, she lusted for him.

"I am a master at hiding my intentions."

She arched a brow. "And your intentions were to see
if the knights were hiding anything?"

"They seem harmless." He smiled. "I did not hide
my intentions so well from you."

"Fear not, your reputation as a master spy is safe. I
just know you well."

His smiled faded. "And I know you well, Countess.
You were trying to get information from Sir Robert."

"I don't know what you mean." She turned away
from him, but there was only one stool upon which to
sit in the small chamber—and the bed. She knew better than to sit there, so she settled on the stool. "And
you should go. You may have gotten *permission* to seduce me, but I don't have to play along with the plot."

He watched her too closely, and then spoke in a soft
voice. "I'm not here because of that. Your wish to join
the League is commendable, but I worry that the longer you are bold Lady Rosamond, the more you believe
that becoming a Bladeswoman is something you yourself control."

She closed her eyes and propped her head in her
hands. Her first thought was to deny everything, but
this was Philip, who was beginning to know her too
well. "Is it so wrong to want to choose my own destiny?" she whispered.

He knelt down in front of her, and she could see the concern in his expression.

"'Tis only wrong if you want something that might reject you."

"I know you're right," she said tiredly. "'Tis all going to my head. I no longer even feel like a serving girl—I don't remember the last time I helped Margaret. I watch her serve me as if it is my due."

He put his hands on her knees. "You are only doing what you're supposed to. Margaret knows that."

"I want to be a member of the League so desperately, Philip," she whispered. "I am determined to make this work."

"I wish I could say something to make this easier for you. I just don't want you to be disappointed."

"Life always has the possibility of disappointing us. That's why we grab a hold of it with both hands and take what we want—or what we can get."

They stared at each other, faint smiles fading, desire rising. It always did between them. What was she to do about it? Just do what the League was allowing her, and take him as her lover?

Inhaling a ragged breath, she looked away. "Sir Robert seemed sincere in his pursuit of Lady Rosamond. His knights did not act suspiciously?"

He stood up. "Nay, they all seem to be exactly what they are."

"Not traitors."

He shrugged. "It doesn't look so, but—"

"But you'll take precautions."

He smiled. "Aye."

"I was rather amused by how Walter behaved this evening."

"I wasn't. I had to practically carry him up the stairs. I think he enjoyed it a bit too much."

She nodded in agreement. The silence between them stretched and finally became uncomfortable.

"I should go," he said.

She didn't want him to, but she was confused enough about everything in her life. She might do something desperate and make everything worse. "Have a good night—and don't fall."

He boosted himself up onto the windowsill. "Bar the shutters when I go."

"I will."

When he was gone, she leaned back against the wall, feeling her confidence fade. Philip's words had struck something within her, but they also made her wonder—did he know so much about her feelings because he, too, was looking for a place to belong?

There was a soft knock on the door, and she wanted to groan. What now?

As she'd been trained, she did not open the door without first asking, "Who is it?"

"Margaret, milady."

Anne opened the door to find Margaret looking up at her, and behind her, David, standing against the wall for his guard duty. She invited the maid in, thanked

David for his service, and closed the door.

Margaret smiled. "I was wonderin' if ye wanted a bath sent for, milady."

Anne sat down on the edge of the bed, and patted the spot beside her. "Sit down, would you please?"

Margaret looked confused, but did as asked.

Anne took her hand. "I know we were both thrust into this strange situation, Margaret, but I feel that I owe you an apology."

The maid's eyes widened. "Whatever for, milady? You have been nothin' but gracious to me."

"Thank you for saying so, but I'm embarrassed because it has been easier and easier for me to treat you like a maid."

Margaret frowned in confusion. "But that's what I am."

"But so am I," Anne said softly. "I don't even remember the last time I asked if you needed my help."

"But, milady, we are playin' roles here," she whispered. "And I was in the wrong at first, when I felt angry about bein' here instead of with milady. 'Tis milady we are both helpin'."

Anne laughed. "There is enough apologizing between the both of us, I guess. So tell me, is the man you met in Doncaster going to be able to see you again?"

Margaret nodded shyly. "Milady, he serves the household of the next lord on yer list."

"Really? You will have to introduce me to him."

"And you, milady, do ye have someone of yer own?"

Anne opened her mouth, and then shook her head. She could hardly call Philip "her own."

"I heard voices in here earlier," Margaret said slyly. "That Sir Philip is always around ye."

Anne waved her hand. "He is a knight, and I am a"—she lowered her voice—"maidservant. He has the chance to rise even further at court."

"But he wants ye, milady, in the way a man wants a woman."

Anne did not think her face could feel any hotter.

"And ye want him?" Margaret continued.

Anne could only nod.

"Then ye should take the chance and have him."

She could think of no protest. She did want him.

"Milady, it might be only a matter of time before another man insists on havin' ye, and ye have no choice in the matter. That's a far cry of a difference."

"Has that happened to you, Margaret?"

The maidservant nodded, her face shadowed by remembered pain. The hard lines at the corners of her mouth faded as her expression cleared. "But now, me man will soon take me away and make me his in the church, before God."

"But why didn't your mistress protect you?"

"I couldn't tell her," Margaret said, twisting her fingers together. "'Twas her brother who wanted me, and 'twould have hurt milady fierce to know that he used me."

Anne sighed. "I am sorry, Margaret."

"Shall I bring Sir Philip to ye now, milady?"

The maid seemed filled with excitement, as if they shared a grand adventure.

Anne laughed. "Nay, but you could send a bath up, as you mentioned. Take word for me to Sir Philip to come to my bedchamber when his shift at my door is finished."

"And ye care not if the next knight sees him comin' in?"

"Nay, he'll know to come secretly as he did before."

Margaret glanced at the window speculatively, and Anne chuckled.

After Margaret had gone, and Anne had soaked in the tub, she was wearing her dressing gown when again someone knocked on the door. Margaret would not have told Philip already. But when she asked who it was, Philip identified himself. Frowning, she opened the door. When she saw David behind him, she gathered the neck of the dressing gown closed with discomfort.

"Philip?"

"Come next door with me now."

"But—"

He caught her hand and pulled her forward. She glanced helplessly at David, who only followed impassively. Philip opened the door and led her inside. The chamber was already crowded with Walter and Joseph—and Sir Robert.

All the men turned to stare at her, and she tried to be dignified as she crossed her arms over her chest. She was wearing nothing under the dressing gown.

"Philip?" Walter said.

"She's involved," Philip answered. "She should hear this."

She looked between them all and focused on Sir Robert, who smiled at her faintly. And then she realized who he must be. She turned a questioning gaze on Walter, afraid to reveal anything aloud.

"Aye," Walter said heavily. "Sir Robert is a Bladesman."

She sank down on one of the beds in surprise. "Then by all means, do not let me interrupt you."

It was Sir Robert's turn to look curiously at Walter, who said, "You may speak before her. She knows all."

She swallowed heavily, feeling privileged and excited, although she tempered herself, knowing that Walter had not meant her to hear this. But of course, she was not of the League—yet.

"As I was saying," Sir Robert said casually, smiling at Anne in a flirting manner, "we received your missive, Sir Walter. You are not the first guardians of a noblewoman to report curious happenings. Although no one else has been attacked."

"Except Lady Staplehill," Philip said dryly. "And that was far beyond an attack."

Sir Robert's smile faded and he nodded. "You are right, Sir Philip. I meant recently. We still have not connected that poor woman's murder to any of this."

"What else has happened?" Anne asked.

"The homes of two noblewomen were invaded mysteriously at night, but nothing was stolen. Another woman felt certain she was being watched, just as you have felt. Her husband ended up killing someone who was following them while they traveled."

"But the noblewoman wasn't harmed?" Walter asked.

Sir Robert shook his head. "But all of these women attended the Durham tournament. There is little else to report. The League believes that you should continue with your mission."

Anne took a deep breath and found herself watching Philip, who looked wary and resigned. But he did not say anything. Perhaps at last he trusted her decisions. She couldn't look at him anymore, so warm were her feelings toward him. He had insisted she be kept informed as much as the members of the League. She wanted to reward Philip right now, but restrained herself from dragging him to her bedchamber.

"My thanks for your information," Walter said, as Sir Robert walked to the door.

Anne smiled at him. "And good luck in your search for a wife—if that was true."

His gaze was appreciative as he looked briefly down her scantily clad body. "'Tis true." Then he glanced at Philip, and touched his hat as he departed.

Anne gritted her teeth. Was their relationship as palpable as a scent in the air?

Walter was watching her, and she stood up.

"My thanks for allowing me to participate," she said, though he well knew he was not the one to thank.

He only inclined his head. Without looking at

Philip, Anne allowed David to lead her back to her bedchamber.

Philip had the shift after David, and he walked the long corridor to keep awake. He could hear loud snoring from the occasional chamber, but behind Anne's door was silence.

A door opened as he passed by, and he turned quickly, only to find Margaret clutching a dressing gown closed at her throat and yawning.

She looked up and down the corridor, then whispered, "Sir Philip, milady asked me to tell ye this message. She wants ye to come to her when yer duty is over."

"She has something more to speak to me about?"

Margaret shrugged. "It is not fer me to know such things. Good night."

Well, at least he had enough to think about to keep him awake. He spent the rest of his shift painfully aroused.

When Joseph relieved him, Philip went into his chamber, but did not close the door all the way. He could hear Walter breathing deeply, evenly. Keeping his ear to the door, he listened as Joseph paced. When the knight turned and walked away, back down the long corridor, Philip stepped outside his door, closed it silently, and ducked around the corner before Joseph could see him. The most difficult part of his journey was over.

After climbing down from the roof, he found Anne's shutters unbarred. He was able to open them, slide inside, and drop to the floor. A single candle burned in its holder on the small table, not two paces away from the bed.

In the gloom he saw the shape of Anne beneath the covers, the mound of her hip as she lay on her side, facing the wall. She was covered all the way up to the crown of her head, as if she were cold. He wondered what she wore to bed, and then immediately berated himself.

He would not wake her up. Whatever she had to say would wait until morning.

Just as he took a step back to the window, she whispered, "Philip?"

He froze. Her voice sounded deep and sleepy, with that huskiness that always made the hair on the back of his neck stand at attention.

Among other things.

Deep inside, an urgent voice told him to ignore her call, to climb back out on his rope, where it was less dangerous hanging three stories above the ground.

Instead he turned his head and looked at her. Although she had not rolled over, she was reaching behind her, lifting the coverlet as if in invitation.

"Anne."

He cursed how hoarse his voice sounded, how much he betrayed. He didn't even know what he'd meant to say. But he was immobile, unable to move to the window. He desperately wanted to slide in behind her, his thighs molding to hers, his chest to her back, his hand pulling up her night rail.

She tugged the coverlet slowly toward the wall, and he watched stupefied as the edge of it slithered up from the floor and flowed over her body.

She was wearing nothing at all. By candlelight, he could see the creamy length of her back, and the mass of her black hair, spread out over the pillow, where her head rested on her arm. His gaze traveled down, over the roundness of her hips, and the tantalizing cleft between. Her legs seemed to go on forever, long smooth lines, delicate ankles and feet.

And then she began to stretch, moving so slowly and sinuously that he gave a soft groan. She lifted her other arm over her head and arched her back. Now he could see the mound of her breast teasing him, daring him.

Oh so slowly, she rolled onto her back, and he stopped breathing. Her perfection had lived in his dreams each night, her breasts so full, tipped the color of dark pink roses. Her belly was smooth and slightly curved inward, leading down to a swirl of black curls where her thighs met.

And all the while he stared at her, his cock straining his breeches, she smiled at him, her eyes narrowed, as if she knew exactly how much power she wielded over him—and how helpless he was to resist.

But she was yet an innocent, and perhaps she didn't know the consequences of where she led him.

He took a step nearer, and stood right over her. "How brave do you feel tonight?" he whispered.

She said nothing, only lifted her arms to him.

"How much are you willing to do?"

She betrayed only a moment's confusion, but the expression faded away. She was far too good at hiding behind a mask. But if he made her do too much, go further than she'd known she could, she might realize that she was only living in the moment.

"I want to see more of you," he told her softly. "Spread your legs."

She hesitated, and he warred inside, part of him praying this torture would be over soon, and the other part praying that she would be his this night.

Then her knee started to move, and his breathing became even more ragged. She put her hand on her knee and slowly lifted it up and out.

She'd called his bluff.

Chapter 17

Anne lay still, barely breathing, baring herself in more ways than one to a man whom she did not know if she could trust. They had been here once before, and she'd been the one to reject him for his honesty. She didn't care about the future anymore. He loomed above her, so broad and powerful and dark. But as the candlelight flickered across the harsh planes of one side of his face, she did not see one hint of rejection or hesitation. His hands were fisted, and he stared at her as if she were a feast for a hungry man.

He'd asked to see more of her, and she complied without thought. She would do anything to keep him here, to feel a part of him.

She'd revealed the most private depths of herself. Then she straightened her leg, pulling it even closer to her body, and she thought he choked.

"Enough," he whispered.

He reached out and took her foot in both his hands, smoothing the bones gently within his warm, callused palms. He slid his hands along her ankle and calf, and then circled her knee with gentle, teasing fingers. Her skin tingled at his touch, and she barely kept herself from squirming, so desperate was she to move her body. He bent her knee back down, and then slid the back of his fingers down her inner thigh, pressing lightly until she parted farther. She could not seem to take a deep enough breath as he stared at what lay so revealed to him.

She almost groaned when he did not touch her. Instead he knelt down at the side of the bed, which brought him so much closer. As he leaned over her, she didn't know what he was going to do. Then he blew softly over her breasts, and her nipples shrunk into hard little points. She whimpered and panted.

"Close your eyes," he said.

She almost balked; it seemed too vulnerable to be blind in the dark when he could see her. But wasn't she already so vulnerable now, naked when he was clothed, open to whatever he wanted to do to her?

He watched her with narrowed eyes, as if he thought she would not follow his command. When she closed her eyes, she thought he might have sighed.

But she couldn't think, could only lie still and tremble, as every part of her skin came alive in anticipation. What would he do to her? Where would he touch her?

She felt his warm breath only a moment before he kissed her lips. With a groan she opened her mouth and let his tongue plunge deeply inside her. She fought it with her own, wanting to taste the inside of him. He touched her in no other way, and she needed to feel him against her. She slid her hands up his arms, and immediately he pulled away.

"No touching. Keep your eyes closed."

She whimpered again, too needy.

Several long seconds passed with nothing except the sound of his ragged breathing. It made her feel as satisfied as if she could see the passion in his eyes.

Suddenly his tongue dipped into her navel, and she gave a start. He laughed softly against her belly, his whiskered cheek lightly scraping her. His fingers suddenly teased the hollow at the top of her inner thigh, and she shuddered.

More seconds passed, building up her tension until she wanted to roll her head back and forth with the anticipation.

Then the warm wetness of his tongue swirled across her nipple and she convulsed, biting her lip so as not to cry out. She had never imagined something could feel so good. How could the pleasure be any deeper, any richer?

When he blew softly across her damp breast, she moaned.

"You taste . . . like heaven," he whispered.

She could feel his breath over her other breast only a moment before he took her nipple deep into his mouth, using his tongue and his lips in a dance that had her writhing beneath him. His fingers found her other breast, and she thought she could not bear the pleasure as each nipple was stroked with tongue or fingers. She wanted to hold his head to her, and instead she clutched the bed sheets with frantic fingers.

He suddenly released her, and it was as if her body was denied sustenance, it ached for him so.

"Oh, Philip, please!"

But still he made her wait, until her skin felt like it hummed.

And then he swirled his fingers through the hair just below her belly, and she gasped, letting her legs sag open gratefully. Aye, this was what she wanted, what her body needed, where every sensation seemed to be centered.

With one finger, he slid lower, parting her, sending the most exquisite pulses of pleasure shooting deep inside her. She felt the moistness of her body and was almost embarrassed, but he gave a groan as if she pleased him. He probed deeper and deeper, to the very core of her, as if he would enter her like this rather than with his penis. And he did, teasing and stroking until she was shuddering helplessly. But still it wasn't enough, it wasn't all she wanted, but she didn't know what to ask or how to say it.

Then his fingers slid higher again and swirled in a circle about the little nub of her flesh. Her body answered with a tense stillness as she concentrated on this new, wonderful sensation. He teased and tormented, plucked and stroked. He set her aflame when his mouth returned to her breasts, and she could no longer remain still, undulating on the bed with each masterful caress.

Just when she thought she could bear it no longer, when each touch was full of painful pleasure, her body seemed to come apart from the inside, shattering into a million pieces of pleasure, suffusing every inch of her skin. She shuddered with it, rocked with it, and still he caressed her, though with ever slower motions.

At last she fell back in exhaustion against the mattress. When she opened her eyes, he was watching her, his head resting below her breasts. She could feel his hand cupping her possessively where she was now so sensitive.

She blinked and looked at him, a slow, secret smile curling her lips. He answered in kind, though his face seemed too tight for his skin.

"You played me like a lute," she whispered.

"Hmm." His voice rumbled against her skin.

She shivered. "Remove your clothes."

As he straightened, his smile faded. "Nay, I should not."

Her mouth fell open and she couldn't seem to find the words. He did not want pleasure from her? Did he think her too innocent? Or did he think she could not handle it?

Before he could speak, she said in a harsh, low voice, "Don't tell me this isn't what I want!"

"You want our coupling now, but will you regret it tomorrow?"

"I've always wanted you!"

He stood up with the slowness of an old man.

He leaned down to caress her breasts in both hands, holding their fullness. Her body arched and sighed with pleasure, needing more. It was her choice to have him, and she would make him realize that. She stood up slowly, and he stepped back, staring at her naked body.

He didn't look like a man who wanted to refuse, and she took power from that. She put her hands on him, touching his flat abdomen to find his belt. As she undid the buckle, she felt the increase in his breathing.

"What do you think you're doing?" he asked hoarsely.

"You know what I'm doing."

Dropping the belt to the floor, she slid her hands down his hips, then up under his tunic, lifting it in her wake.

He grabbed her shoulders as if to push her away, but when he touched bare skin, she could hear his indrawn breath. She felt his thumbs move over her collarbones, and the roughness and heat of the gentle gesture made her tremble. She desperately wanted to press herself against him, but she held back.

"Anne."

He said her name again, harsher this time, with an element of desperation that thrilled her. This was it; he would not be able to resist.

Beneath his shirt, she felt the heat of his skin, his sides so smooth and warm yet hard with muscle. She could not hope to remove his garments by herself, with their height difference, so she concentrated on touching him, running her fingers forward along the waist of his breeches.

She could hear the breath gasping in and out of him. It ceased completely when she dropped her hand lower and cupped along the length of him, so very different from her own body. He hissed in a breath. He felt long and hard, and she wanted to see him, but her sense of touch would have to do.

Suddenly he tried to back away from her, but he hit the edge of the bed and abruptly sat down. Giddy at the opportunity, she moved forward and straddled his lap. She put her arms around his head and held him to her, his face pressed into her neck.

"Take me, Philip," she whispered, stroking her hands through the silkiness of his hair. Holding onto his shoulders, she arched backward, feeling his face slide down her body. It seemed like forever, but at last his cheek was pressed to the upper curve of her breast, his mouth so close to where she wanted it.

"Make love to me, Philip."

She slid along his thighs until their hips were pressed together. It felt so good to clutch him with her thighs, and to feel the long ridge of him that made her groan. But he wasn't touching her with his hands, made no effort to hold her, and in desperation she rubbed herself against him, a long smooth stroke that gave her so much pleasure.

At last she felt his big hands cup her bottom and hold her tight to him, immobile. She whimpered and tried to move, but he didn't allow it. Letting go of his shoulders, she fell back on his thighs, head dangling past his knees. He was trembling as much as she was, and they seemed at an impasse, for he said nothing.

At last, with a groan, he slid his hands from her hips and up over her rib cage to cup her breasts. She gasped and started to move again, and this time he didn't stop her, only caressed and kneaded her, teasing her nipples, pressing himself between her thighs.

She clutched at his back and started pulling on his tunic. As he leaned over her, his open mouth found her breast. His tongue weaved circles about her nipples, distracting her, but still she tugged until the garment began to come between them.

With a muttered curse, he straightened and pulled it off over his head. This time he nipped her breasts with his teeth, yet still she pulled relentlessly on his shirt. That came up over his head, separating his mouth from her body. When he yanked at it, she heard a seam tear and felt a primitive satisfaction.

But now when he leaned over her, the heat of his bare stomach was against hers, and she delighted in tracing the muscles of his shoulders and back with her hands. He felt so very different from her, and she reveled in it.

He could not so easily leave her now, not half undressed. With her arms about him she held him to her, moving against him, whimpering softly when his breeches came between them.

She gasped when he turned and deposited her on

her back in the bed. He dropped his breeches, and suddenly he was above her, his bare knees pushing her thighs wide. She reached for him, felt the rough hair on his thighs. Though she tried to feel higher, he moved away from her, down her body, following with his mouth. She moaned when his lips traveled over her breasts and continued on down. She shivered when he passed her navel, stopped breathing when his shoulders spread her thighs even wider. His warm breath stirred the curls at the center of her.

Uncertainly, she whispered, "Philip—" then had to bite her lip to keep from screaming when his tongue parted her and swirled a long path from the tender nub straight down until he licked inside her. She writhed and moved, unable to stay still until he held her down. He sucked her forcefully, and then gently licked to soothe her. He teased and tormented, never doing one thing long enough. She was awash in circling desire, damp heat, embarrassment and excitement. When his long fingers probed inside her, she felt the resistance and so did he, for he withdrew, leaving her frustrated. He cupped her hips and tilted her even higher to him, working the magic that wound ever tighter between them, drawing them together with invisible bonds. His tongue explored and tasted and caressed, until as she rode higher and higher, she moved less and less, seeking, rising, waiting—

And then he stopped and rose over her, smothering her cry of neglect with his wet mouth. When he came down on top of her she whimpered her satisfaction at the heavy weight of him. With his thighs he pressed her ever wider, then he pulled up on her knees until she felt him probe against her.

"Yes," she whispered, urging him on, thrilled that at last she would have him.

He needed no urging, for he found her entrance and sank in. To her surprise, pain flared and she gasped. He froze, waiting, as if he thought that she would reject him at so crucial a moment.

But she pulled on him until he bent to kiss her. She slid her tongue between his lips in imitation of what he did to her.

And then his hips began to move, and the pain was forgotten in passion that swept her body from toes to head.

Chapter 18

Philip felt the hot cradle of Anne's body as if he were coming home. He had longed to be there, deep inside her, her thighs clutching his hips, her hands on his chest playing with his nipples as he had done to her. He rose up and came down over and over again, with each thrust a little closer to the heaven they both craved.

He did not think about the past or the future, only the here and now, locked in darkness, warmed by the heat of shared nakedness. He could not get enough of the taste of her, bent his back so that he could kiss her over and over again. She tasted of Anne and passion, and he craved it as if she were a long-denied sweet.

He could feel the pleasure rising through her, knew by the frantic way she met his hips and clung to him, her breath hissing in and out of her lungs. He held out until he felt her quake in his arms, felt the ripple of her sheath clutching at him. He smothered a groan into the pillow beside her head and gave himself over to the pleasure that stole him away, shook him until he was shuddering and weak against her. He collapsed at her side in the narrow bed and held her to him.

They said nothing for endless long minutes, as their breathing evened, and perspiration cooled on their skin. Her heart still beat wildly against his, and he caressed her back, sliding his fingers through the long curtain of her hair.

He lifted onto his elbow and simply stared at her voluptuous beauty. The candlelight flickered warmly against her skin, all ivory and shadows. Her long hair, as black as the rest of the chamber, swayed down past her shoulders, curling evocatively beneath one breast.

Then she reached for the candle and lifted it above them. "You are beautiful," she murmured, her dark eyes warm with appreciation.

He lay still, enjoying her admiration.

"I want to remember everything," she said.

"I do not yet have to leave," he answered. "My duty is to watch over you." He tried to take her free hand.

She only lifted the candle higher. "I seem to be watching over you." As the candlelight found his lower leg, she frowned. "That is the burn from the sword tip so long ago?"

He bent his knee so that he could see his calf. "Aye, it is a reminder never to be clumsy."

"You are certainly not clumsy," she breathed, finally setting the candle down.

"And you have so much experience to know?"

She laughed softly. "Nay, as you can now attest to."

"I noticed nothing except willingness and eager passion."

He reached for her, turning to pull her atop him. She sighed as their limbs entwined, the roundness of her breasts against his chest making him shudder with renewed desire.

She gave a little gasp as his cock hardened between them. "Do we have the time?"

"If you're quick."

He spread her thighs and surged up between them, entering into the moist heat of her.

"Like this?" she said breathlessly.

"Aye, my lady, like this."

He taught her to ride him, gladly gave her the secrets to controlling him, and then sank back into the pleasure of watching her undulate above him.

When they were both sated, she lay at his side, then lifted to prop herself on her elbow.

"I wish to thank you for teaching me," she said, her expression earnest.

He trailed a finger over the tip of her breast, watching with satisfaction as it shriveled in response.

And then her words sank in. Teaching her? She could not believe that what they'd just shared was as simple—as emotionless—as that.

"I wanted you to be my first," she continued, further confusing him. "Now I understand why Lady Rosamond wishes to marry again. Why would she want to give up this?"

Her first *lover*? He had known that's what he was,

but the mere thought of another man having her made a blaze of anger burn in his brain.

But she wasn't his.

He had been Lord Kelshall's squire, John's second, the League's hired knight—and now Anne's lover.

Her very temporary lover.

Was that not what he wanted? Did he not wish to be on his own, to make his own future?

Instead he had let an innocent seduce him for her own satisfaction. He could not be angry that it had happened—and told himself to feel relieved that she wanted nothing more permanent from him. His sexual frustration of the last fortnight was over.

Then why was he so disappointed that the League was more important to her than he was?

He rose up onto his knees and stepped over her onto the floor. She lay back on the bed, her arm curled beneath her head, and watched him with a look of sleepy satisfaction.

And he wanted to take her all over again.

Her eyes widened at his erection, but he turned his back and searched for his clothing. When he was dressed, he chanced one last look at her, and found her still beautifully naked, eyes half closed, her smile dreamy.

"Thank you," she whispered again.

He bent over and kissed her forehead. "Good night, my sweet."

She came up on her elbows when he climbed up

onto the windowsill. He didn't look back as he caught the rope and went out into the night.

In the morning, Anne could not even meet Philip's eyes when they broke their fast in the public room. She knew she'd blush or stammer, and the Bladesmen would be suspicious. Through an accident of seating, she ended up beside him on the bench. Their shoulders brushed, and her awareness of him continued to rise until she thought she'd shiver with it.

She had slept peacefully, with no regrets for the lovemaking they'd shared. But now, as she had to keep it a secret, it seemed so much more monumental. What did it mean between them? How would it end? Or had it already? Did one night with her appease his curiosity?

When at last they were finished eating, they filed past the innkeeper, who stood talking to several men in the front parlor. One man in particular caught her eye, but she did not know why. She could only see his back; he was tall and broad, with dark brown hair. Under his arm he carried a flamboyant hat that struck a memory within her.

When he glanced at her, she was so shocked that she didn't look away quickly enough. He was Viscount Bannaster, the man who had wanted to marry Elizabeth. Anne had been trapped in the tower for over a sennight because of him.

Anne pushed at Philip's back to hurry him along,

hoping that Bannaster had not seen her. If only she'd already donned her veil, she thought with regret.

They ascended to the first floor, and when the knights and Margaret dispersed to finish packing, Anne pulled Walter and Philip into her bedchamber.

"Walter," she said in a low voice, "I recognized the man speaking with the innkeeper. Philip, did you?"

Philip shook his head. "I only saw him from the back. Who was he?"

"Viscount Bannaster."

Philip's eyes narrowed as Walter said, "He is the nobleman on the husband list that you wished to avoid."

She nodded. "I know we are near his home, but why would he be here?"

"He saw you?"

"I think so, but he did not seem to recognize me."

"The journey of Lady Rosamond has been the stuff of much gossip," Philip said. "Knowing Bannaster and his longing for a rich wife, he could have decided to search you out."

There was a sudden knock on the door, and the three of them looked at each other.

"If it is him, I will make excuses for you," Walter said. "Step away from the door."

The chamber was small, so Philip and Anne could only go to the corner behind the door. They stood side by side, and Philip turned his body so that he shielded her. She wanted to put her hands on his back, to bury her face there and hide.

Walter opened the door. "May I help you, my lord?"

"Sir, the innkeeper told me that Lady Rosamond Wolsingham is staying here. When I heard she was nearby, I had to meet her."

It was Bannaster's voice—she would never forget it.

"She is, my lord, but we are preparing to depart," Walter said.

"I need to speak with her. In fact, you may tell her that I saw her down below, and I have my concerns."

They could not allow him to discuss this in the corridor, where anyone could overhear.

Anne stepped out from behind Philip. "Show his lordship in, Sir Walter."

Walter kept himself between the door and her, but he gave her a doubtful look.

"Lord Bannaster is the king's cousin," she said.

Walter arched a brow, but he stepped back.

Bannaster strode into the bedchamber and looked around until he saw her. His eyes lit with recognition when he saw Philip at her back. "And you, sir, I recognize as well," he said. "Were you not Lord Russell's man?"

"He is Lord Alderley now," Philip said.

Anne withheld a wince. Bannaster had wanted the earldom that came with marrying Elizabeth, but they hadn't needed to remind him right now, when they were at his mercy.

But Bannaster gave a crooked grin. "Aye, I had not forgotten." He gave Anne an assessing look. "You cannot be Lady Rosamond. Although I do not remember your name, when we last met you were pretending to be Lady Elizabeth. And now you have a new masquerade."

Of course he didn't know her; she was only a maid-servant. She was tired of having to apologize for who she was, as if she wasn't worthy enough as herself.

She folded her hands together to hide their trembling and stepped nearer to him. She had no choice but to convince him of the need for secrecy. He respected the king. Being related, there would be no reason for him to want King Henry out of power—Bannaster could lose everything.

"Lord Bannaster, I am Anne Kendall. Lady Rosamond lived with my mistress for a time and recruited me to help her with an important mission for the king."

Bannaster arched a brow. "Recruited you to play her? Why? And what does this have to do with my royal cousin?"

Anne wished she could ask Walter to explain everything, but the League always preferred to keep their involvement quiet. If he wanted to, he would speak. For now, he seemed content to stand with his arms folded over his chest and watch her.

"Lady Rosamond overheard three noblemen discuss treason against the king."

Bannaster's smile vanished, and he glanced tensely between Philip and Walter.

Philip nodded. "'Tis so. Although she saw these men, she does not know their names, and must identify them in person for the king."

"Ah, so that is the reason Henry has summoned all of

his noblemen to court," Bannaster said thoughtfully.

Anne nodded. "I am to distract attention from Lady Rosamond's secret journey to London."

"By looking for a husband?"

"It is what she had announced as her intentions, before this dangerous situation happened." Anne attempted to mollify him. "You were on her list, my lord, but you knew my identity, so we avoided your castle."

He nodded, slapping his gloves against his thigh. "That was an intelligent decision. Thank you for the information. I, too, will go to London and see what my cousin has to say—and meet the brave Lady Rosamond."

Anne stared at him in surprise. "You believe us so easily, my lord?"

"Why should I not? You always struck me as an intelligent woman . . . Lady Rosamond. It would be far too easy to discover if you were lying."

She could feel the tension and uncertainty in Philip, but he only said, "My lord, will you say anything about meeting us?"

Bannaster frowned and said in a low voice, "I understand why you don't trust me. But the king is my cousin, and I would not endanger him."

"We appreciate that, my lord," she said.

"Then good day, Lady Rosamond."

Anne watched him go, curious about the difference in him. He seemed . . . reasonable.

When Bannaster had gone, Walter looked between Philip and her.

"Did you think I made a mistake telling him?" she asked.

Walter sighed. "From what I could see, you had little choice."

Surprised that he trusted her, she forced herself to relax.

"And he is the king's cousin," Walter added. "What motive would he have for turning against his only access to power?"

"Money? The earldom?" Philip said dryly.

Anne shrugged. "He has money. He always claimed that he wanted to marry Elizabeth to help stabilize Gloucestershire after King Henry came to power. Maybe that was true."

"And what greater power is there than a relationship with the king?" Walter said thoughtfully.

"We saw them together at Alderley," Philip said. "The king seemed fond of him."

Walter nodded and walked to the door. "Meet us in the corridor when you are finished packing, my lady."

"I am sure Margaret has taken care of most of it," she said. "I'll only be a moment."

Walter did not insist Philip leave. Anne looked at Philip with a frown.

Philip sighed. "Remember, he believes that we have an 'attraction.'"

"Philip, I cannot allow this affair between us to color how Walter feels about my performance."

His face impassive, he murmured, "You think I would reveal something that would bring you harm?"

"Not deliberately, nay. But if Walter thinks we believe our relationship is more important than this mission—" She couldn't even finish the words, so ill did they make her. Her entire future was in Walter's hands.

Philip cleared his throat. "Do not forget that Walter feels uneasy for keeping secret the murder of Lady Rosamond's friend."

"I do not believe he ever felt guilty. He believed himself to be in the right." Anne went to the saddle bag on her bed, knowing it was already packed, but fiddling with the buckle while she avoided Philip's gaze. "I hope we did not make a mistake last night."

She watched Philip stiffen, saw how he controlled his expression. She was hurting him, and she didn't want to. She was half afraid she was falling in love with him, hurting herself.

"Tell me what you what from me, Anne," he said.

"This is all new to me," she answered helplessly. "I tell myself that we should not be intimate again, but then a part of me . . . aches at the thought of not touching you again. Can we just . . . see what happens?"

He nodded, but she knew she'd hurt him. She wanted to put her arms around him, kiss the hurt away. She was frightened of how easily she could forget about her plans when faced with Philip's pain.

Chapter 19

Philip stared at Anne. They had shared one blissful night, and she was already putting it behind her, looking to her future, one that did not include him.

But wasn't that what he'd been doing throughout this journey—thinking of the noble wife he would earn . . . *someday*?

The tables were truly turned. When they'd first met, he'd rejected her, and now she was doing the same thing to him. He hadn't known how much it would hurt.

For the first time he thought of what it would be like not to see her every day. His stomach twisted, and he faced the fact that he was growing more deeply involved with her, much as he was trying not to.

And yet all he could think about was that bed, and putting her onto her back and reliving the excitement of being in her arms.

Margaret rode in the front of the retinue with Anne that afternoon as they headed toward Bramfield Hall, home of the second to last nobleman on Lady Rosamond's list. London was less than twenty-five miles away. The North Road now wound through undulating fields growing grain for London bread, and fattening cattle for London beef.

It had been many years since Anne had been to the city, and already the heavier traffic on the road made her remember her last visit with regret. The litter she and Elizabeth had ridden in had become separated from Lord Alderley's party in the busy city streets, leaving the girls frightened for an hour before they'd been reunited with Elizabeth's father.

Anne had a new reason to feel frightened. Large parties of travelers were converging on the city, many with noblemen answering the king's summons. Some of them were bound to be the traitors that Lady Rosamond would identify.

But she could not think of that now. She was wearing her veil to protect her true identity. And she had two noblemen to impress before she entered the city herself.

Bramfield Hall was a sprawling manor house, the country retreat of a lord when the pressures of the city—and the plague—grew to be too much. It was in the shape of a U, and the entrance was down the center of a lovely courtyard past the two wings, each composed of two floors. She realized that she would miss the protection of high castle walls.

Inside, she received the cheerful greeting that she always did from the servants, since David had gone ahead to prepare the way. But this time she found herself watching Margaret. The maidservant was flushed with happiness, and Anne could tell when she'd spotted her suitor in the crowd.

"So he is here," Anne murmured.

Margaret nodded happily. "But I will see him later, milady. I'll take care o' you first."

While Lord Bramfield was with his beloved dogs at the kennels, Anne accepted the offer to refresh herself in her bedchamber before joining him for supper. Walter escorted her to the eastern wing, while the other knights mingled with the manor servants.

When Anne and Margaret were alone, Margaret lay out Anne's gown for the evening, pressing the wrinkles out with a hot iron.

Anne watched her, trying not to smile. "I know how excited you are, Margaret. After I'm dressed, you're free to go find your man. You will introduce me?"

"Gladly, milady," the girl said, grinning. She clapped her hands over her red cheeks. "I must look a fool."

"Nay, just a woman in love. And I envy that."

Margaret squeezed her hand.

After finally excusing the maid, Anne sat down at small table and looked at herself in the hand mirror. Margaret had missed a curl when she'd styled her hair, and just as Anne began to pin it in place, she heard a knock at the door.

Walter was guarding her, so she called for the person to enter. Both Walter and Philip came in, looking grim.

"What is it?" she asked, rising to her feet and coming toward them.

Philip glanced at the impassive captain. "I came to tell Walter that Margaret already knows a man here— quite intimately, it seems."

Puzzled, Anne replied, "Aye, I know about him. He is Lord Bramfield's servant, and he has been courting Margaret for several weeks. He is the man she met with in Doncaster."

"He has been following us?" Walter said brusquely.

"Nay, he has been traveling home . . . I think," Anne said, realizing with dismay that she had never asked for any details.

"And he just happens to live here, with a man on the husband-hunting list?" Philip said.

She closed her eyes. "I never thought about it. How foolish could I be?"

They exchanged dark glances, and she felt even more guilty. Walter could not be thinking much of her intelligence.

Philip said, "I'm liking this situation less and less. We need to find Margaret. I want to know why her suitor just happens to live at our last stop before London."

"She is with her young man even now," Anne said.

"I will find her," Walter said, "and explain our situation to David and Joseph. Philip, you wait here with Lady Rosamond."

Philip nodded. When they were alone, he had little to say, only paced.

A half hour passed by the clock on the mantel. At last, Margaret was led into the chamber, looking almost frightened as she stood between Walter, Philip, and Anne.

"Milady?" Margaret said uncertainly.

Anne tried to smile at her. "Margaret, the men have some questions about your suitor. They are just taking precautions."

Walter began. "It seems strange that we should come to the home of your suitor."

"Oh, 'tis not strange, Sir Walter," she said in confusion. Then she blushed. "I asked Lady Rosamond to put Lord Bramfield on the list. And because he was a man she did not know, she agreed."

Philip's frown grew ominous. "And was that your idea?"

"O' course," she said uncertainly. "We did talk about it, Stephen and me."

With no emotion, Walter said, "Margaret, though I do not blame you, you have made a mistake in not telling us this from the beginning."

"But 'tis my private life." Her lower lip trembled. "'Tis my turn for happiness."

Philip put a hand on her shoulder. "I fear this might not be as you think. You have been manipulated into putting this castle on our list."

She looked between them beseechingly, then at last at Anne. "But I never—"

"I know you would never hurt any of us," Anne said

soothingly. "Maybe we can make this clearer for them. When did you first meet Stephen?"

She bit her lip. "'Twas at the tournament in Durham." Her eyes went wide. "I never saw that that might matter! I would never put Lady Rosamond in danger!"

"We must leave," Philip said.

Walter nodded. "Did Stephen see Lady Rosamond in Durham? And has he seen *our* Lady Rosamond?"

Margaret started to cry. "I know not about Durham, but here, aye, he was in the hall when we arrived."

Anne felt a chill of foreboding. "He might know I'm not—"

"I never told him that!" Margaret cried, then put a hand to her mouth to hush her sobs.

Anne enfolded the maid in a hug. "This might all be for nothing, but we cannot take the chance on Stephen telling Lord Bramfield that I am not Lady Rosamond."

Margaret pushed her away. "He would not do such a thing. He loves me. I cannot leave."

"Margaret . . ." Walter began.

But the maid shook her head. "If I leave with you, he'll know somethin' is wrong."

"When we all leave, he'll know the same thing," Walter said.

"Lady Rosamond can convince him." Philip narrowed his eyes in thought.

Anne stared at him in surprise, grateful that he believed in her.

"You're offended that Bramfield cares more about his dogs than greeting you," Philip slowly said.

"Ah. I can do that." She felt relieved at having a plan. She turned to Margaret. "Are you sure—"

"I have to stay," the maid repeated firmly, wiping her eyes. "I love him. I have to take the chance that he loves me, too. I promise I will say nothin'." Margaret suddenly flung her arms around her. "Take care, milady. Tell me mistress everythin'. Tell her I hope to be happy."

"If not, you know she will always have you back," Anne said. "I understand why you have to take this chance."

Margaret stepped away. "Thank you, milady. Farewell."

As the maid left, Anne glanced at Philip. Margaret was taking a chance on love, but Anne just couldn't. Weren't her dreams more important than the risk that Philip might change his mind about his future?

"Pack quickly," Walter said. "I will inform Joseph and David. I will also hint to the steward that you are not happy. Philip—"

"I'll stay here. I never unpacked."

Walter nodded and left.

"I'll hurry," Anne said, folding the gown she had worn earlier in the day. "I shan't bother to change. The cloak will cover my finery."

Philip nodded almost absently, standing near the door, his head bent as if he were listening.

"You expect soldiers to come for us?" she asked, trying for levity.

"Nay, they would come in secret to hide their deeds. That would be far worse."

Her amusement faded and she redoubled her efforts. In only a few minutes she was ready. Philip escorted her to his own chamber where he picked up the knights' saddle bags.

At the top of the stairs leading down into the great hall, he looked at her. "Are you ready?" he murmured.

She nodded, although her heart pounded so loudly he must be able to hear it. Within the enemy's stronghold, they were few in number compared to what could be mustered against them. Was Margaret's suitor down below, watching them? Could Lord Bramfield be one of the traitors?

Anne took a deep breath and thought about her role. She was wealthy and confident, knew she was desired, knew she would be the center of attention. She felt the transformation come over her, and she relaxed into it. She was Lady Rosamond.

In the hall below, servants were preparing the trestle tables for supper. There was no sign of the nobleman, and Anne was glad.

"Who is the steward of this place?" she demanded in a loud voice.

The chattering voices of the servants died away, and they all looked at each other in confusion. Walter, David, and Joseph came to her and stood at her back, while Philip remained at her side.

A man doffed his cap nervously. "He is in his office, milady. Shall I fetch him for you?"

"At once!"

In only a few minutes, another man came rushing out of a nearby corridor. He fingered his beard nervously, as if it were terribly important for Lord Bramfield's household to make a good impression on the wealthy Lady Rosamond.

"My lady," he said, sweeping into a bow, "how may I help you?"

"I am leaving. Have our horses brought into the courtyard."

"But, my lady," he began, eyes wide with confusion, "you only just arrived."

"I sent word of my imminent arrival, and yet *dogs* were more important to your lord than greeting me."

"That is not true, my lady! He thought you would want to prepare yourself first."

"As if I was not good enough for him when I arrived?"

The steward looked aghast. "Nay, 'tis not what I meant!"

"Send for our horses immediately."

He deflated like a peacock about to be stuffed for a feast. "Of course, my lady."

Would it be so easy? Anne wondered. With her nose held high, she swept from the hall, ignoring the angry glances sent her way. She tried to tell herself that of course Bramfield's servants would be upset that she'd slurred their master. They could not know that he might be a traitor.

But who here did? She had not seen Margaret anywhere. Hopefully she was keeping Stephen away until they'd gone.

Deep inside, Anne found herself praying that all of this was a mistake, and the only thing that would suffer would be Lord Bramfield's pride.

Once they were on the way, they did not stay on the main highway, but rode parallel to it a league away. They were all quiet, and Anne found herself looking about her constantly. But all she saw was cattle amidst the hedged fields, and the occasional farmer.

Walter did not want to sleep outdoors, nor did he want to stay in Ware, so close to Bramfield Hall. They settled on Waltham Abbey, the nearest town to the south, where there would be more witnesses should anything be tried against them. They reached it by nightfall, and although the first inn had no rooms available, the second did.

"We should have tried to hide somewhere less conspicuous," Philip said, as he examined Anne's bedchamber.

The other knights were settling into the chambers on either side of hers. She told herself she was safe; they were skipping the final nobleman on the list to be in London tomorrow.

But a thread of worry and uncertainty never left her, and she sensed it was the same with the Bladesmen. They had not bothered to disguise their relief when they'd entered Waltham.

"Would you have rather we find a barn to hide in?" Anne asked lightly.

"Aye."

She rolled her eyes. When someone knocked on the door, she went toward it, but Philip stepped in front of her, giving her a frown.

"Who is it?" he asked.

"Walter. I have brought supper."

Philip pointed to a corner, and Anne sighed as she obeyed him. He opened the door, and Walter, David, and Joseph all came in, making the room far too crowded. David and Joseph placed trays on the table and began to divvy up the food. Anne sat down on the bed, and Philip sat beside her. None of the other men looked askance, for with only two stools, Joseph, the youngest, had to stand.

To her mortification, she felt Philip's presence at her side far too physically. The straw mattress tilted with his weight, and she had to hold herself upright not to lean into him. She could feel the warmth of his body, knew he was deliberately not looking at her. Did he feel it too? All the worry of discovery, the excitement of the chase, only made her even more aware of the intimacy they had shared. Her body wanted more, and her rational mind did not seem to care how it would look, how it might affect her future. Controlling herself required an effort she hadn't imagined. Would it always be this way? When they had parted, would she forever think of him?

The men shared a pitcher of ale, and although they poured her a tankard, she refused it, concentrating on the lamprey pie.

When they had all finished, Walter stood up. "I will take the first shift outside your door, my lady."

"I won't risk leaving her alone," Philip said. "After all, if I could come through the window, so could someone else."

Anne wanted to protest, to say that it didn't have to be Philip, but Walter spoke quickly.

"Agreed. Good night, my lady."

Clenching her jaw, she watched them all file out after once again deliberately leaving her alone with Philip.

And he paced, wearing a frown.

She made herself calm down. She had done well today getting them out of Bramfield Hall. Walter would remember that.

She finally realized that she was still wearing the fine gown she'd meant to impress Lord Bramfield with. On one of Philip's passes, she presented her back, determined to ignore the feel of his hands on her body.

"Would you help unlace me?" But her voice shook, and she silently cursed her weakness for him.

When she didn't feel his hands on her gown, she looked over her shoulder. He was wearing the strangest look on his face, and he had a hand pressed to his stomach.

"Philip?"

"I find myself suddenly not feeling well," he said.

To her shock, he swayed and braced his hand on the table. She touched his arm and realized that he was trembling.

"Philip, you should lie down."

He closed his eyes. "I think I should find the chamber pot."

He barely lifted the lid in time before he became violently ill. She stood behind him, feeling helpless.

"Something is wrong," she said. "You need help."

"Nay!" He lifted a hand to her. "Don't leave this chamber!"

But that seemed to take the last of his strength, for he collapsed onto his side, groaning. And then he was silent, which was far worse.

She dropped to her knees and put her hand on his forehead. He was damp and hot, but his chest still rose and fell. What if he were dying? she thought wildly. She could not just sit here and do nothing! She would go to Walter, who would surely send for a physician.

She listened at the door carefully, and then opened it, only to find a stranger standing there, smiling at her.

She tried to slam it shut, but he held it open with his hand and stepped inside. He was tall and wiry, with plain brown hair and nondescript clothing, but with eyes that showed secret amusement.

As she took several steps backward, she saw no one behind him in the corridor. Where was Walter?

And then he shut the door. The finality of the sound made her feel sick with fear, but she forced herself to remain calm. She would have only herself to rely on.

"Lady Rosamond?" he said politely, doffing his cap, as if a man were not lying unconscious on the floor. "Or do you wish to tell me your real name?"

She made a sudden run for the door, but he caught her around the waist.

"There is no one to help you, *my lady*," he said, exaggerating the title.

Though she tried to elbow and kick him, he avoided her blows.

"It seems your guard needed to rush desperately for a chamber pot."

"What have you done to my men?" she demanded in her most authoritarian voice.

"I promise you that they will not die."

She was too frightened to hope it could be true. "And I should believe you?"

"Well, of course you should. We had to alter the ale. Since I assumed that you would imbibe as well, and I can't have *you* dead, the poison is not fatal."

Hoping to keep him talking, to delay him, Anne asked, "Were your men the ones who attacked us days ago?"

He gave an exaggerated sigh that ruffled her hair from behind. "Such a terrible mistake. It almost gave the whole situation away. Some people have no patience." He leaned down to speak in her ear. "Enough questions. Be good, and I'll release you if you promise not to run."

She nodded resentfully, and when she was free of him, she backed away.

"Now, if you come along quietly to my master, I promise not to have my men permanently take care of yours in their incapacitated state. After all, you would not be very forthcoming if I had them killed. And leaving several dead bodies would be far too messy—and noticeable."

Though she fought her emotions, her breath caught on a sob. What could she do? He was trying too hard to convince her that he wouldn't have her men killed. Two more men came through the door, and she knew the terrible weakness of futility.

Would Philip and the others be killed, one way or another?

Chapter 20

The pounding in his brain was so unbearable that Philip awoke. He did not want to open his eyes, for fear that light would make it worse. But something deep inside kept urging him on, until he finally rolled over onto his stomach and pressed up onto his hands and knees. His head hung freely, dizzily, and his stomach heaved, but there was nothing left.

And then memory returned, overshadowing his pain as he straightened onto his knees. "Anne?"

There was no answer.

He heard something whoosh through the air behind him, and he threw himself to the side on instinct alone. A man stumbled past him, his sword coming down heavily and sticking point-first into the wooden floor. Philip brought his knee into the man's back, sending him face first onto the bed. Somehow Philip lunged to his feet and grabbed the sword. As his opponent turned around, Philip held the sword before him.

"Where is Lady Rosamond?"

Wide-eyed, the man pulled a dagger from his belt

and rushed at him frantically. Defending himself, Philip parried the dagger away, and accidentally gouged the man's neck. He went very still, hand clasped over the wound, while blood seeped between his fingers. Then he fell back on the floor and died.

Cursing, Philip caught the table to steady himself.

"Oh, God, Anne."

It was a prayer and a question all at once. He staggered into the corridor and opened the next door, only to find the three Bladesmen in varying states of moaning and stirring. The smell made him realize how Anne's chamber must have reeked.

Walter was on the floor closest to the door, as if he'd walked through and fallen. He had been on duty outside Anne's door.

"Walter!"

Walter groaned and came up on his elbows.

"The countess is not here," Philip said.

Walter frowned up at him, as if he couldn't quite remember who Philip was. Then his face settled into its customary impassivity, and he climbed to his feet.

"We were poisoned," Walter said flatly.

Philip glared at him. "You are stating the obvious. And they'd decided to finish what they'd begun, because when I came to, I had to defend myself. I ended up killing the man, though I wanted to question him. But Lady Rosamond is gone."

"Have you searched for her? She could have gone for help."

That seemed to jar a distant memory. "I think I was warning her against it when I passed out. I'll see if the innkeeper has seen her."

They quickly cleaned themselves up, and then spread out through the inn. Only a groom had seen Anne, and she had been in the company of several knights, just as when she'd first arrived.

Philip sat down on the bed as the Bladesmen finished recounting what they'd learned. He felt dizzy and weak, but the effects of the poison seemed to be passing. "It does not seem as if Anne was as ill as we were," he said.

"She ate the same food," Joseph said in a puzzled voice.

"But did not drink the ale," Philip pointed out. "That's what must have been poisoned. And she was still unharmed when they took her." He was grateful for at least that, although he could not let himself think of what was being done to her. He got to his feet because he could no longer sit still. "Do we agree that it was Bramfield?"

"We cannot be certain," Walter said heavily. "But that would be my first conclusion. Why else would Anne be taken unless they had recognized that she wasn't the real Lady Rosamond?"

"Margaret's suitor." Philip practically spat the words. "He's been following us, but he never saw Anne up close until Bramfield Hall."

"Then we must assume that the real Lady Rosamond

is in danger, and perhaps even the king, if Bramfield and his cohorts are desperate. They might step up their plan against the king."

Philip narrowed his eyes in suspicion. "Aye, but Anne is the one in the most danger now."

"That is not true," Walter said. "They want the truth from her; they won't harm her. So we have only one choice."

Philip walked to the door. "We rescue her."

"Nay, we go to London."

Philip could not possibly have heard correctly. He whirled around and found David and Joseph watching him with sympathy, but Walter wore a determined expression.

"What did you say?" Philip asked in a soft voice.

"Our duty is clear. Anne is in the least danger."

"But they have her! Why can't you send one man to London as a messenger?"

"But they want Lady Rosamond. We need to ensure that her information gets to King Henry, and that means as many knights as can be mustered. If not, the entire country could erupt in war between the noblemen backing the king, and all who would follow these traitors. We cannot allow that to happen only a year after the last battle. For all we know, Bramfield could have sent someone ahead to intercept Lady Rosamond in London."

"Walter, I will not—"

"Philip, you will listen to me," Walter said sternly. "If you want to be a member of the League, you have to learn discipline, and to take orders for the greater good. You'll get yourself killed going alone. We cannot risk keeping Bramfield from London, where the real Lady Rosamond has to be the witness against him. And there are two unknown traitors to consider."

"I cannot believe you'd do this to a woman who has risked herself for everything you believe in," Philip said in a harsh voice. "She is someone who wants to join your League, yet you'd leave her behind."

Walter looked pained. "She would understand the urgency of the entire mission. And join the League? Why would she think that?"

"She is good at impersonating women. She hoped you would have her continue."

"Philip, that cannot happen," Walter said, sympathy and frustration in his voice. "Too many people have seen her in the guise of Lady Rosamond. She cannot take on another masquerade and have a good chance of its success. And she has no other skills that would set her apart from other women."

Philip imagined how Anne would feel when she discovered that the future she'd planned for herself was gone. He had to be the one to tell her, to comfort her—after he rescued her.

"I have taken orders my whole life," Philip said, "but not this time. I am not going with you."

"You don't mean this," David said, his voice its usual calm. "You've spent your life wanting to be one of us."

"And I'd already realized that was a mistake before

joining you. You're only confirming it for me. First you withhold information about a murder," Philip said, turning back to Walter, "and now you abandon Anne because she's useless to you."

"We are not abandoning her. By finishing the mission we will be freeing her."

"But it may be too late! And I won't take that risk. She's all alone in the hands of a criminal. I can't leave her to that kind of fear. Oh don't worry—I have no intention of speaking of what I know of your mission. I will simply be a good knight rescuing his mistress."

Ignoring David's entreaty, Philip returned to the chamber he had briefly shared with Anne and stared at her things. But although his stomach clenched in terror at the thought of what she was enduring, he did not have time to think about anything but returning to Bramfield.

When he heard the door open behind him, he whirled, prepared to do battle. But it was only David.

"Surely you are not joining me," Philip said bitterly.

David shook his head, barely glancing at the dead man on the floor. "Although I must follow orders, I understand your dilemma. I wanted to give you something."

He put a coin into Philip's hand. At first Philip thought it was only a pound, and started to demand answers, but then he realized something was different about it.

"Do not spend it," David said quietly. "It is your key to accessing the League in London. Go to the northern most haberdashery on the London Bridge. Present this there, and you can leave a message. We will receive it."

Philip slipped it into the pouch at his waist. "My thanks." He gestured to the body. "Have Walter take care of that."

Behind him he could hear David hesitate.

"We will," the Bladesman murmured. "Good fortune."

Philip was feeling too angry to wish the same in return. He only nodded. When the door closed, his shoulders sagged. He had never done anything like this alone, had always followed in the shadow of someone else.

But now, it was time. He was in the right—and he was all Anne had.

He left plenty of money with the innkeeper to store Anne's garments—and to have the rooms cleaned.

The dungeon at Bramfield Hall was damp and cold, even in the summer. At least Anne thought it was Bramfield; she had been blindfolded once they'd left Waltham Abbey. But the length of their journey seemed right, and where else would a lord risk holding her, where no one would hear her scream? She'd tried that, and nothing had happened. And with only a contingent of four knights, Philip and the Bladesmen could not possibly attack to rescue her. She had not been able to sleep all night; in fact, she had no idea if it were morning yet—or if anyone was alive to come for her.

She could not afford to think like that, or she would lose herself in hopelessness. Now she huddled on a rock ledge that had been dug out of the wall, trying not to think of the dampness soaking into her skirts. At least they had left a torch, though it was high up on a wall where she could not reach it. Chains were attached to those rock walls. Would they use them?

At last she heard more than one pair of heavy footsteps coming down the hall. She got to her feet. A key turned in the lock, the door swung wide, and she was face-to-face with the stranger who'd kidnapped her—and he was still smiling pleasantly. That somehow made it worse.

She glared at him. "Where are my men? What do you intend to do now?"

He ignored her first question. "Talk to you, of course. I have not had the pleasure before now. I was assigned to watch Lady Rosamond, and I must have watched from too far away, because to my amazement, a switch was made."

"Then you must be Stephen, Margaret's *suitor*. There was no switch. I am Lady Rosamond. When the king discovers what you have done to a member of his court—"

"You are not a member of the court," Stephen said with patience. "I saw the real Lady Rosamond in York, and at the tournament in Durham, and you are not she. Now all I need to know from you is where the real Lady Rosamond is."

There was no reason to continue denying the truth.

"I cannot help you. I know nothing about Lady Rosamond's whereabouts. And if you were worried about what she saw in Durham, why did you not deal with it then?"

Stephen shook his head sadly. "'Tis a shame, really, because that would have made things so much easier. But we didn't know who we were looking for. My lord only saw a noblewoman eavesdropping, and only from the back. If he could have discovered her identity, he could have explained that he was discussing what might happen if someone were to go against our king, and what should be done to prevent it."

Anne narrowed her eyes and said nothing. Stephen and his "master" could try to change the facts all they wanted, but it would not matter in the end. "Did you kill Lady Staplehill?"

Stephen put a hand to his chest. "Goodness, no! As I explained to you, I was assigned to Lady Rosamond."

"And others were assigned to different noble ladies," she said slowly, "to see who might have overheard your . . . *misunderstanding*. Perhaps Lady Staplehill is the one you have been searching for, and now her death should be the end of your concern."

"That would be wonderful for Lady Rosamond, of course, but sadly, the death was an accident."

"You mean she was *accidentally* murdered, just like we were *accidentally* attacked on the road."

Stephen shrugged, spreading his hands. "Since I was not there, I cannot say. So again, I ask you to tell me where Lady Rosamond is." He took a step closer.

Anne swallowed and folded her hands together to hide their trembling. "And why do you think they would tell *me*? I was used for only one purpose."

"That was my thought, too, but my lord did not see it that way."

There was a sudden commotion in the corridor, and Stephen frowned as he looked over his shoulder. "Excuse me, mistress. I will return in a moment."

He didn't even bother to close the door all the way behind him, because where would she go? But she braced her hand against the rough wall and sagged her shoulders helplessly as the tremors overtook her body. If she proved useless to them, what was to prevent them from killing her to ensure her silence? She would buy herself time by pretending she knew Lady Rosamond's secret location. It would take awhile for them to travel to London and back to confirm her words. Surely Philip would have rescued her by then. Stephen had assured her that he wasn't dead, and she could only hold on to that desperately.

The door opened, and she stiffened as Stephen came in again.

"Mistress, you are a fortunate woman."

She looked around and said with sarcasm, "Strange how I do not feel fortunate."

"I no longer need the location of Lady Rosamond, because my lord has discovered it."

She opened her mouth, but for a moment she could think of nothing to say. How had Bramfield found out?

"Then there is no need to keep me here," she said, trying not to let her voice tremble in desperation.

Stephen cocked his head. "It grieves me to tell you this, but we cannot allow you to leave just yet. You might prove useful. I promise I'll have food and water sent into you."

"Wait!" she cried, running toward the door.

But he shut it in her face, and she heard the lock tumble home.

What if they forgot about her? She was nothing to them. She would die, never having the chance to tell Philip that she loved him, to see if between them, they could find a compromise for both of their futures.

But nay, she would not die.

If she wanted a future, she had to make it happen. Beginning with the wall behind her, she searched for something that might help her, a large stone she could hit someone with, or perhaps a loose rock she could pry open into another chamber. She worked for well over an hour, ripping her delicate skirt and tearing several fingernails, but the chamber was bare.

At last she heard footsteps again, and she moved to the side of the door. Maybe the person would step far enough in that she could duck behind them and out the door. With her back pressed to the wall, she took deep breaths, trying to calm her breathing. As the lock turned, she tensed, but the door only opened a crack.

"Milady?" came a whisper that Anne would know anywhere.

"Margaret?" she said in disbelief.

The door opened wider, and Margaret entered swiftly. But a man followed behind, and Anne reared back until she saw that it was Philip. She gaped at him, he grinned back, and she knew in that moment how terrified she'd been that she would never see him again.

She threw her arms around him. He felt warm and safe and strong.

But by the loud sniffing, Margaret was the one openly crying. Anne turned and enfolded her in a tight hug.

"Thank you so much, Margaret!"

"How can ye thank me, milady?" she whispered despondently. "I brought ye here, into the house o' the enemy."

"You didn't know," Anne insisted, stepping back and holding tightly to Margaret's shoulders. "And you've rescued me! If you felt you had anything to make up for, you've already done it."

"We must go," Philip said, looking back into the corridor. "I fought the guard at the top of the stairs, but he isn't dead."

"And a kitchen maid knows we're here," Margaret added. "She was to bring you a food tray, but she was so frightened of the 'ghosts' in the dungeon, that she accepted me offer to do it for her."

"How did you get back into the castle, Philip?" Anne asked. "Surely they were on guard against a rescue."

"I used John's trick and snuck aboard a cart full of hay. I'm still itching. I was able to find Margaret in the kitchens. Now we must hurry!" He handed her a bundle. "She found you a maidservant's gown, so that you won't attract attention. Put it on."

Margaret helped her unlace the ruined gown and replace it with a shabby gray one of homespun. Philip guarded the corridor. Just as Anne was about to follow him, Margaret caught her arm from behind.

"Milady, I won't be goin' with ye."

"Margaret! You cannot stay in this dangerous household."

"But if I disappear, Stephen'll know ye're gone, and that I helped ye. I'll get away when 'tis safe."

Anne squeezed the maid's hands. "We'll come back for you, I promise."

"Just go, milady." Margaret thrust a wrapped bundle into her hands. "Here are cloaks for ye both. Go with the servants heading into Ware for their daily shopping. God grant ye luck!"

Chapter 21

Philip's heart only slowed down when he led Anne into the woods near Bramfield Hall, where he'd hidden their horses. He still could not believe how weak in the knees he'd gotten when he saw that she was alive and unharmed and still so brave. He never again wanted to see her in danger.

Soon she wouldn't be, for the League would not be using her services again. How would he break the news to her?

"We'll go into Ware and find an inn," Philip said as he tightened the horses' girths. "You stay there, and I shall return for you as soon as I can."

"You will not leave me behind, Philip Clifford."

He frowned at her. "You've told me they know where Lady Rosamond is. Only the League knew that, which means the Bladesmen have a traitor in their midst."

"A traitor in the League?" she whispered with horror.

"Aye," he said grimly. "And it cannot be one of the Bladesmen already involved, for they have known the truth of Lady Rosamond's identity for weeks. Nay, it is someone Bramfield was able to contact. We have to find Lady Rosamond before they do."

"In all of London?"

"David left me a way to reach him."

"And where *are* the Bladesmen? I was surprised when you came to Bramfield Hall alone."

He hesitated. How would she feel to know that they considered her expendable?

"They went on to London to protect Lady Rosamond." He put a hand on her shoulder. "They wanted me to go, too, but I refused."

Her eyes widened. "You . . . broke with the League?"

"They claimed you were in no danger, so their first allegiance had to be to Lady Rosamond and the king. I could not abandon you."

She smiled at him softly and reached up to touch his face. "Thank you. I promise that when we see Walter again, I'll speak to him for you."

"Anne, there is something you need to know."

Her smile faltered. "Has someone been killed?"

"Nay, 'tis something Walter told me. Too many people have seen you as Lady Rosamond, so the League cannot invite you to join."

She stared at him in confusion, until at last her face flushed. "Is it because I did not tell him about Margaret's suitor? It was a terrible mistake but—"

"Nay, never think one mistake would matter! He told me that they think you have done brave, skilled work, but—"

"Speak of my foolishness no more, Philip. We don't have time."

Searching her eyes, seeing no emotion there, he could only nod. "You must go to Ware and await my return."

"So you too believe I'm incapable of helping?"

He stiffened and said in a low voice, "How can you accuse me of that?"

She briefly closed her eyes. "You are right. Forgive me. If you leave me behind, how will you know that they won't capture me again? Then they'll be able to use me against *you*."

If only that didn't make sense.

"This is my decision, Philip, and I want to be with you."

He wished that she would try to persuade him with kisses, anything to show him that she would get over the League's rejection. But she just waited for his reaction.

"Very well, you can travel with me, but you must promise to obey me in all things."

"I will."

Anne and Philip entered London through massive gates in the ancient stone wall. Anne had never ridden on a horse through the city, and now she knew why. The streets were so crowded that several times people had to press against walls to let her pass. Twice, Philip ducked beneath a merchant's sign that hung too low over the street. Stone buildings often had timber upper stories that leaned over the street. The stench of open sewers mingled with the smells of the slaughterhouse, and above it all smoke from cooking fires.

Anne behaved as she was supposed to, perhaps even fooled Philip into thinking that she'd recovered. But inside, all she could think was that her future with the League was gone. She reminded herself that she was luckier than most women; her dear friend Elizabeth would take her back as a lady's maid. She would never know hunger or cold.

But she would never have her own home, for the payment given her by the League would make a poor dowry.

Despair gnawed at the edges of her mind, but she refused to give in to it. She was used to accepting reality. She would be a part of Elizabeth's family, help her raise her children, and try to put away any tiny feelings of envy. She would get over this desolation. And Lady Rosamond was still in such terrible danger.

London Bridge had huge stone gates at either end and another in the middle. Passing beneath the gate, Anne kept her gaze averted from the rotting heads of traitors mounted on pikes. Buildings of three and four stories lined the bridge all the way across, and when she rode between them, she felt like she was on another street rather than crossing the river. They did not have far to ride before they found the first haberdashery. The front window shutters folded down during the day, so that shoppers could see the displayed wares.

After paying a boy to watch their horses, they went

inside. Anne pretended to admire the hats that graced several small cramped shelves, as she'd done once before for Walter, when all she really wanted to do was stare around her nervously. What if the traitor within the League oversaw this haberdasher? But they had no other way to reach Walter and the others.

A man came out from a room in the back and smiled at them. "Good day, sir. What might I do for you?"

Philip put the League coin and another for payment on the man's desk. "I would like to leave a message."

The man stared at the coins silently for a moment, and then studied them with narrowed eyes. "Very well, sir."

So far, so good, Anne thought, sighing with relief.

"Do you have a paper and pen?" Philip asked.

The man handed over a scrap of parchment, a quill, and an inkpot. As Philip wrote, Anne said nothing, listening to the scratch of the pen and the sounds of peddlers shouting in the street. The city was so big, that even if they knew where Lady Rosamond was, it might take awhile to reach her in the traffic. Anne could only hope that they were not too late. God forbid Lady Rosamond end up like Lady Staplehill.

At last Philip rolled the parchment and tied it with a strip of leather. To Anne's surprise, the merchant brought out a pot of heated wax and gestured for Philip to seal his missive.

"My thanks," Philip said, taking back the League coin.

He took Anne's arm and led her out of the shop. After retrieving the reins of their horses from the bowing, soot-covered boy, Philip tossed him another coin before helping Anne to mount.

"So where did you tell them we could be reached?" she asked, as she guided her horse slowly through the crowds back the way they'd come.

"An inn near the docks by the Tower. I've stayed there before. 'Tis mostly frequented by sailors and the like."

As they traveled east along the Thames, Anne could see great cranes lifting cargo from sailing ships. The smells of fish and tar mingled—yet, still, the occasional purity of a white swan swimming peacefully on the river spoke of beauty. When they arrived at the inn, Philip requested a chamber on the northern side of the inn, facing away from the river and its stench.

Their chamber was small; besides a bed, there was only a small table and two stools where they ate a hasty supper in the growing darkness. She watched him above the single candle that lit the table between them, and knew that he watched her.

"How long do you think it will be before we hear something?" she asked, as he set the tray out in the corridor.

After he closed the door, he turned and just looked at her. The tension between them was suddenly palpable, as if the air in the room were too heavy to breathe.

Philip didn't come closer, and his voice was husky

as he said, "I would imagine morning would be the earliest. People aren't encouraged to be on the streets late at night."

"Oh." She watched him, feeling her bones melt at the thought of the passionate hours they'd spent together in a bed. She wanted him desperately, needed him to help her forget what lay in store for her. But surely their situation was too dangerous to allow themselves to be distracted. "How are you feeling? Although Stephen told me you would not die, I feared that he was lying, or that he'd sent someone back to kill you."

"You saw the worst of it," he said.

She nodded, but could think of nothing else to say. She watched him with longing, feeling so overheated that she wanted to strip the clothes from herself. That would be subtle.

When a knock sounded at the door, they both gave a start.

"It cannot be the League already," she said.

He shook his head and turned to the door. "Who is it?"

"The valet, sir, with your bathing tub."

She stared at him.

Philip arched a brow at her and smiled as he swung open the door. Several young pages carried in the tub, and others followed with buckets of hot water. Within ten minutes, they were alone.

Anne dipped her fingers in the water and sighed. "'Twas a thoughtful deed, Philip—unless you're saying that my scent could use improving."

He grinned. "After your ordeal in the dungeon, I thought you would appreciate a luxury."

She gave in to the inevitable. "Oh, I do. Could you unlace me?"

She saw his eyes darken, but all he did was nod. She presented her back. As the gown separated, she pulled it away, and suddenly he was helping it over her head. She loosened the laces of her smock, and pulled that off as well. Behind her, she could hear him breathing deeply.

She took a breath and turned to face him. While his gaze moved down her body, lingering at her breasts, she lifted her arms and began to pull the pins from her hair. One by one her long curls fell down.

Still, he said nothing, only watched. She moved around him to the bathing tub, making sure linen cloths and soft soap were placed where she could reach them. Then she lifted her leg and stepped in. She sank down with a sigh, even though the water only reached her waist.

Philip pulled up a stool to watch, as if she were an actor in a company of players. She didn't mind, because being on display for him made her feel beautiful.

"Now if you were Lady Rosamond," he said in a low voice, "you would have the luxury of a larger tub and more water."

"This will certainly do."

After wetting a cloth, she applied soap and began to rub it leisurely on her arms. She watched him watch her, as she next washed her neck and then down to her breasts. Touching herself was almost as pleasurable as when he touched her. She lifted each leg out of the water to wash it, and then splashed him with her toes. His smile was almost a grimace.

When she washed between her legs, she almost lingered, but felt too self-conscious yet for that. At last she leaned back to wet her hair, then put soap onto her hands.

He suddenly rose to his feet. She was stunned when he took her hands between his and rubbed the soap from them, then massaged slow, gentle circles in her hair.

She closed her eyes and let her cares drift away in pleasure. "This is simply wonderful."

"I do have my uses."

Her body became limp with relaxation, and her head felt like it would tip backward under his ministrations. He cradled her, caressed her, all under the guise of washing her hair, and she could not have been more touched and pleased. She loved this man for how gently he treated her.

"Time to stand up," he said in a hoarse voice.

She almost couldn't, so heavy were her limbs. When she was upright, Philip poured a bucket of hot water over her head, so that the soap sluiced away, leaving her clean. When she reached for the linen cloth, he pushed her hands away and unfolded it himself. He wrapped her in it, patting her skin. She arched like a cat under his touch, but at last she was dry, and there was nothing left for him to do.

He lifted her into his arms and put her into bed. Sleepily, she reached for him, but he backed away.

"You are not the only one who would like to bathe."

"In the water I already used?"

"You were not that dirty."

"Will it not be cold soon?"

"Good."

She didn't understand his response, but she forgot as she came up on her elbows to watch him undress. To her embarrassment, she suddenly yawned.

He smiled. "You are already bored by my naked-ness?"

"Oh, nay, Philip!" she said. "I did not sleep last night, and now that I'm warm"—she huddled within the covers gratefully—"I cannot seem to keep my eyes open."

"Then sleep," he murmured, leaning over to tuck the coverlet beneath her chin.

She would *not* sleep, not when she had him to herself. She watched him from beneath lowered lids. When his clothing was gone, she enjoyed the way the candlelight played on his skin, creating hollows of shadow in the curves of his muscle.

Philip washed quickly, feeling vulnerable without his garments and weapon at hand. He glanced at Anne, and she continued to blink drowsily, her lips curved in a gentle smile.

She was so tempting. He kept thinking of a dozen reasons why he could take her tonight, but in the end, he had a deep need to keep her safe. And that meant he had to remain on guard. He didn't think they'd been followed from Bramfield Hall, but he could not be certain. And if there were a traitor within the League, the message he sent could be intercepted and used against him.

After he was done washing, he dressed again and went to stand over Anne. She reached for him, and after making sure his sword was near at hand, he lay down on top of the coverlet at her side. She rolled against him, caressing him with her hands, lifting her mouth for his kiss.

Though it was the hardest thing he'd ever done, he kissed her forehead. "Sleep," he murmured.

Her face scrunched up in a sweet frown, but the expression relaxed as almost instantly she fell asleep. He smoothed back the hair from her face, and contemplated the softness in his heart for her.

Was this love? This ache when he worried that she was harmed, this tenderness he felt when she slept in his arms? It was not about lust or passion, it was all about . . . Anne.

More and more it seemed that his dreams of a noble life and higher status at court seemed shallow. Had it only seemed important to him because of what his mother wanted? Wouldn't his mother want his happiness above all else? Perhaps he had been foolishly equating Anne with his past, because he had come from the same background. It was time to start finding out what would make *him* happy.

But for now, keeping her safe was all he should think

of. He couldn't sleep, worried that someone might try to break in.

Several hours later, she stirred in his arms and opened her eyes. She stared at him in confusion for a moment, and then lifted her hand to touch his face.

"You have not slept," she whispered.

He shrugged.

"Philip, you need your rest. We'll hear if someone comes. You need to be strong enough to face them."

He put his head down on his arm and just looked into her face, there beside him on the pillow. "I would not be able to forgive myself if something happened to you."

"It won't. Now sleep."

She put her arm around him, and he drifted off.

Before dawn had lightened the sky, Anne felt herself being shaken awake. She opened her eyes to see Philip leaning over her, his weight a heavy warmth that pulled her to him.

"Good morning," she murmured, smiling.

He smiled back. "A good morning to you."

He leaned down and kissed her, but it was all too brief.

"Up with you," he said, patting her rump when she tried to squirm deeper into the bed. "We could have visitors."

She had no choice but to don the same simple gown that Margaret had given her. That made her think of her friend with a pang of worry.

"My escape must surely have been discovered by now," she said as Philip laced up her gown. "Do you think Margaret is all right?"

"Why would they harm her? I think they would be more concerned about coming to London and finding Lady Rosamond. After all, Bramfield must appear before the king with the other nobles. He cannot refuse without looking guilty."

"What if this traitor within the League reaches her before we do?"

"She is surely well guarded. All we can do is hope. Obviously these men have not wished to kill women if they didn't have to. After all, Bramfield assigned a man to watch each lady. If he was inclined, he could have had them all killed, by many different means that would not draw suspicion on himself. Even our Bladesmen believed that Lady Staplehill's death wasn't suspicious."

"Will you tell our Bladesmen what we suspect about a corrupt member of the League?"

Philip hesitated. "I do not think we should risk it if we don't need to. How do we know if they have received corrupted orders? We'll bide our time and make a decision."

"At the last moment?" she said, smiling faintly.

"If we have no other choice."

A knock on the door startled Anne, but Philip looked calm, and even relieved. The sky had only just begun to lighten, so he lifted a candleholder. He motioned for her to move toward the corner of the room. As she did so, he drew his sword.

"Who is it?" Philip said at the door.

"David."

Philip and Anne exchanged a glance, and then he opened the door a crack, holding the sword where it could be seen.

"Are you alone?" Philip asked.

"Aye. I received your message."

"And told no one, as I requested?"

"No one."

Philip stepped back to allow him entrance, then checked the corridor before closing the door.

Anne saw the relief on David's face when he saw her.

"My lady," he said, "Philip's missive told of your rescue. Glad I am that he was able to accomplish it."

"With no help from you," Philip said coldly.

David, so tall and usually so impassive, bowed his head as he said, "Aye, 'tis true. My lady, there are things I cannot say, but it grieved us all to have to leave you."

Things he couldn't say, Anne thought, exchanging a glance with Philip.

"I know it did, David," she said, "but please, I am not your lady. I am only Anne once again. Is Lady Rosamond still safe?"

"Aye, she is, and in our safekeeping."

Anne's relief weakened her.

"Has she gone to the king yet?" Philip asked.

"We were going to yesterday, but then she refused, and she would not say why. And we have no time left, for tonight the noblemen are gathering at Westminster Palace."

Could someone have coerced Lady Rosamond already? she thought worriedly.

"Perhaps she is frightened," Anne said.

"How could that be? She traveled all the way here in secret, never once losing her courage, or so I am told. It is almost finished—and yet she holds back." David shook his head. "It is something else."

"Could I speak with her?" Anne asked, hoping this was what Philip wanted her to do. "She knows me from our years at Alderley."

"I hesitate to ask your assistance yet again, mistress," David said.

"You may ask it. Until Lord Bramfield and his fellow traitors are caught, no one in the entire realm is safe."

Chapter 22

At sunrise, Anne and the two men rode through London, taking many different streets to ensure that they weren't being followed. Peddlers shouted their wares for the housewife: milk from the countryside, wood to heat one's house, and oysters harvested from the ocean.

The house that David escorted them to looked like any other home of a well-to-do merchant off the Strand, made of half-timber and whitewashed plaster, and standing three stories tall. Anne was led within the front gates to a small flowering courtyard. Two men stood guard outside the door, and after David introduced them, they were allowed inside. Another two guards waited in the front hall. How could they even begin to trust all these Bladesmen?

The man in charge, with a heavy beard that partially hid an old scar, eyed David coldly. "I do not care how these people have helped us—I want the man's sword."

"I am here to protect what you guard within," Philip said impassively. "You want to deny me that ability?"

"He has spent weeks with us," David said. "He can pass on my say. You may ask Sir Walter."

"He is not here."

"Then ask my lady," Anne said. "I served her several years ago at Castle Alderley. She will remember the lady's maid, Anne."

Though the knight clearly did not wish to consult anyone else, at last he withdrew deeper into the house. Anne found herself feeling chilled, wondering if Bramfield had already tried to breach the security here. Or would they be lucky, and the corrupt Bladesman only knew that Lady Rosamond was in a secure home in London, but not exactly where—yet. She couldn't imagine it would take him long.

But for now, Lady Rosamond was still here, and she was safe. Anne had not realized how worried and ill she felt, until the feelings had lessened.

At last they were shone up a flight of stairs to the first floor, where chambers were laid out front to back along the narrow house. Lady Rosamond and a maid were seated together in the first withdrawing chamber, their heads bent over embroidery.

When Lady Rosamond looked up, her hesitant expression changed into a relieved smile, and she tossed her embroidery onto a nearby table as she rose. She was as tall as Anne, and her black hair hung freely down her back, as if she could not be bothered to see to it.

Taking Anne's hands, she said, "Glad I am to see you here, and safe, Anne. Your journey as me must have been a success."

Though her words seemed innocuous enough, her expression seemed guarded, and she glanced several times at Philip and David.

"It was, until the end, my lady," Anne said after curtsying.

"I was not told there was trouble," she said quickly.

But . . . something about her manner seemed off. She might only be nervous about her coming meeting with the king, but even that she was putting off.

"My lady," Anne said, "do not trouble yourself on my account. I am fine now, but you do not seem well. Might we speak alone together?"

Lady Rosamond turned her head toward Anne, and the expression she betrayed could only be seen by Anne. There was urgency and relief and—great fear.

"Aye, come into my bedchamber, Anne. We will be but a minute, sir knights."

Anne followed Lady Rosamond, and when the door closed, she was shocked when the lady gripped her upper arms tightly.

"I received a note just yesterday slipped beneath my bowl of pottage, saying that you were being held, and that they would kill you if I went to the king."

Anne wanted to wince from the lady's strong hold,

but she understood the urgency. "You did not show it to anyone?"

"Nay, how could I? They would have insisted I go immediately to the king, risking your life. What is going on?"

"My lady, I *was* being held by Lord Bramfield, but I was rescued. We came here as quickly as we could, because Lord Bramfield had discovered where you were in London."

"But how could he?" Lady Rosamond whispered, pacing in a tight circle near Anne. "The Bladesmen have guarded my secret with their very lives."

"And that is our fear, my lady—that a Bladesman has been corrupted by Lord Bramfield and his traitorous friends. He doesn't seem to have known about you until recently, or I fear the danger to you would have been severe. We do not know whom we can trust within the organization." Anne hesitated. "I know this is dangerous, but do you still wish to go to the king?"

"Now more than ever," Lady Rosamond said firmly. "The gathering is tonight. We cannot allow men like this to threaten us all, including King Henry. But the League cannot escort me."

"Nay, that is a certainty. Would you allow Sir Philip and me to do so?"

"This knight is trustworthy?"

"Oh, aye, my lady, he has protected me and your secret for almost a fortnight. And before that, he was second to Lord Alderley, Lady Elizabeth's new husband."

"Then we will go," she said with relieved determination. "Only how will we explain that I'm leaving the League's protection?"

"I think there is no explanation they will accept. We might have to leave as quietly as possible."

Lady Rosamond's mouth quirked up in one corner. "Have you seen the guards?"

"Aye, I have, but there *is* one thing that you and I know how to do."

Philip stopped pacing when the door to the bedchamber opened. When only Anne peered out, Lady Rosamond's maidservant went back to her needlework.

"Philip, where is David?" Anne asked.

"He needed to speak with someone down below."

She motioned to him. "Lady Rosamond would like to speak to you. And to you, Eleanor."

Philip waited for the maid to precede him. When he was through the door, Lady Rosamond shut it firmly behind him, then leaned back against it and watched him speculatively. There were not many noblewomen who would invite a man into her bedchamber, but he had always known that Lady Rosamond was different—and desperate.

Philip glanced in confusion to Anne, who said, "Lady Rosamond has already been threatened by Lord Bramfield."

After he heard the whole story, he said, "Anne, I do not think that a masquerade is the answer."

"And do you plan to fight ten men in a reckless escape?" she shot back.

"I regret that I must use Anne again, Sir Philip," Lady Rosamond said, "but this mission is even more imperative now. Can you get me to the king?"

"Aye, I can, my lady, I vow that with my life."

"It shan't come to that," the countess insisted. "But we must hurry before your friend returns."

It did not take long for an exchange of garments. Philip waited in Lady Rosamond's antechamber, sword drawn, listening at the door to the staircase.

"We are ready."

He turned around to see Anne dressed the same as when she'd arrived. But this time, Lady Rosamond had exchanged gowns with her maid. She wore her hair hidden beneath a wimple, whose long folds encircled her neck. Eleanor, the maidservant, was now dressed as Lady Rosamond.

They heard footsteps coming up the stairs. The women all looked stricken, and Eleanor bowed her head and began to murmur prayers.

He motioned them all back behind the door. Anne had to pull Eleanor with her.

When the door opened, they heard, "Lady Rosamond?" in David's puzzled voice.

Philip shut the door, and as David turned around, Philip grabbed him by the throat and held him to the wall, sword evident. David was just tall enough that Philip felt off balance having to reach up.

David looked stunned, then bewildered, and at last, full of dawning despair. "You have betrayed us!" he said hoarsely. "And I led you here."

"Nay, I have not." Philip did not lower his sword. "But Lady Rosamond received a missive yesterday morning, threatening to kill Anne if she went to the king."

"That is impossible!"

Philip pressed him a little harder to the wall. "Keep your voice down. 'Tis the truth. Why do you think she hesitated to complete the mission? We have no way of knowing who among the League has been corrupted."

"You knew this before you came, did you not?" David demanded.

Philip nodded. "When Anne was held prisoner, they did not torture her because they had already discovered where Lady Rosamond was. Who else would know this but a Bladesman?"

"You know it is not I, or our fellow knights," David said, struggling.

Philip didn't release him. "I know. Or you would have had her killed much sooner. But David, how can we trust the men you answer to? How can *you* trust them?"

Philip could almost see the thoughts darting frantically through David's mind.

"Then what do you plan?" David finally asked.

"If I release you, will you stand still and listen?"

David nodded, and when Philip stepped back, the Bladesman rubbed his throat.

"We are taking Lady Rosamond out of here in secret," Philip said. He wanted to sheathe his sword, but he didn't yet dare, not with David looking so furious and frustrated.

"That is impossible. Where would she be safer?"

"Anywhere is better than here," Lady Rosamond said, eyeing David coldly. "I can no longer trust any of you. But my mission is yet clear. The nobles have gathered. I must be there with the king."

"He is at Westminster Palace," David said. "If you don't have us to take you there—"

"I shall guide her," Philip said. "We will go immediately."

"Why do you tell me this?" David demanded, finally showing bewilderment.

"Because I trust you, and I hope I am not in error."

David's jaw tightened. "You aren't, but I cannot offer much help against all these men."

"We don't plan to fight," Anne said. "You'll see—it will work."

"And I don't want you to go against your fellow Bladesmen," Philip said, sheathing his sword. "I am not one of you; I can risk it."

David rubbed a hand down his face. "What do you want me to do?"

"Walk down the stairs with me as if nothing is wrong. Anne and Lady Rosamond will walk behind."

Anne glanced at Eleanor. "You can remain in the bedchamber, lying down as if you're unwell."

Eleanor gave Lady Rosamond a frightened look. "I will, my lady. Godspeed." She went back through the far door and closed it behind her.

As Philip walked to the opposite door, he glanced at David. "You are ready?"

"I know not, but I want this to be over."

They went out onto the landing and started down the single flight of stairs.

David casually said, "My thanks for your help with Lady Rosamond."

Philip glanced at him, bemused. "She just needed to be convinced."

Behind them, he heard the two women discussing the ingredients to the mulled wine they were going to use to settle Lady Rosamond's stomach. In the front hall, two soldiers stood on guard, looking out the windows. They were more concerned about people trying to get in, rather than getting out, which would work to Philip's advantage.

David pointed to the rear. "The kitchens are beyond. I'll take you there, Anne."

"I know where the kitchens are, milord," Lady Rosamond said, her voice coarsened and huskier.

"You there," called one of the soldiers. "Anne, is it?"

It took every bit of Philip's concentration to watch impassively. He wanted to rest his hand on his sword hilt, but even that might prove too threatening. The second Bladesman glanced over his shoulder, and then went back to watching out the window.

Anne came forward. "Aye, sir, what might I do for you?"

"The wine you were discussing sounds tempting. Care to bring me a taste?"

"Aye, that I will, sir," Anne said, grinning as she looked over at shy Lady Rosamond. "We'll have several sent out to you. Be patient, because we'll have to heat a large amount to satisfy you all."

He nodded, looking once more at David and Philip before turning back to the window.

"I need to use the privy," Philip said. "I'll return in a moment."

David nodded, folded his arms across his chest, and ducked his head for a glance out the same window the other Bladesmen stared through.

Philip wasted no time following the women into the back of the house. As Lady Rosamond had already explained, the kitchens were a separate building in a rear courtyard. London had had far too many fires for kitchens to remain within the houses, which worked in Philip's favor. The women went into the kitchen, and he to the privy. He was able to watch as the soldier taking a turn about the rear courtyard strolled to the front, out of sight. Philip darted out, met up with Anne and Lady Rosamond, who had also been keeping watch, and circled around to the back of the kitchen, keeping it between them and the house. A willow tree grew in the corner, leaning over them. It would hide them well.

"The walls look so high," Anne said.

"I'm certain the gate is locked," Philip said. "I'll boost you both over. Hurry!"

Anne had no problem stepping onto his bent knee, and then perching on his shoulder. Philip put his hand beneath her ass to push her up.

"I'm at the top!" she whispered.

He steadied her, watching as she leaned over the wall on her stomach, then boosted herself to a sitting position, straddling the wall.

She reached down. "Lady Rosamond?"

The countess was not quite as nimble, and she flinched when Philip had to palm her, but with Anne's help, she pulled herself up.

"'Tis a long way down." Lady Rosamond leaned over the far side.

"I'll help lower you," Philip said. "Slide back toward the tree to give me room."

It took a running jump, but Philip had a grip on the edge of the wall by the second try. Gritting his teeth, he slowly pulled himself up until at last he too was straddling the wall. A deserted alley ran between the high walls of several courtyards. It seemed that Bramfield's men were not so vigilant—or did they trust that they had threatened Lady Rosamond well enough?

"Give me your hands," he said to the countess, who was closest to him.

He lowered her down until she could easily jump, then did the same to Anne, who grinned at him. He jumped down beside them and adjusted his sword.

Anne said, "We did it!"

"We are not done yet," he warned her. "We'll have to find horses to rent, because we cannot risk retrieving our own in the front courtyard."

"What about the Thames?" Lady Rosamond asked as they began to move cautiously up the alley. "We could hire a wherry to take us upriver."

As Philip led the way, he cautiously checked the closed doors of each courtyard they passed. Only two houses down, a man jumped over a half wall, his sword already swinging down. Philip stumbled backward and knew he knocked the two women over. Was the man only protecting his own property? Then beneath the man's cloak, he glimpsed the blue and black livery of Lord Bramfield's servants. Philip unsheathed his own sword and thrust it forward. The other man parried it aside, yet he was too concerned with getting to the women. When he took his concentration off Philip to look toward them, Philip was able to swing at the man, and when their swords clashed and held, Philip swiftly drew his dagger and buried it in his side. The man went down, gasping.

Philip turned and found the women together only a few yards away. They heard a sudden shout from behind the walls of the League's house.

Anne pulled Lady Rosamond forward. "Is he dead?"

Philip knelt down with his back to the women and

quickly slit the enemy's throat. "Aye, he is. He will not tell Bramfield that we escaped the League."

He took both of their arms and began to move them down the alley.

"Bramfield's man?" Lady Rosamond asked in a low voice.

Philip nodded. "The Thames is our best escape. We head west out of this alley, then south to the river. Move!"

Chapter 23

It was several miles of rowing for the boatman to bring them to Westminster, and though Anne told herself to rest, she could not sleep. She found herself watching Philip, unable to imagine going back to a life without him. But what to do about it? After he helped her and Lady Rosamond out of the wherry, they had to tiptoe through mud and debris before climbing up a ladder to reach the street level. Philip went first, then Lady Rosamond, and Anne brought up the rear. She was glad the ladder was set back from the Thames, because otherwise the waterman would have had a good view up her skirt.

The towering yellow stone walls of Westminster Palace glistened in the sun. They had made the decision to leave the river north of the palace and its yard, near a cluster of smaller buildings crowding the road. They didn't want to show themselves to soldiers just yet. How were they ever going to enter such a place secretly?

It was past midday, and there were many people hurrying to and fro. Surely the noblemen had already begun to arrive for the evening's festivities. Anne wished that they would have been able to discuss their plans on the boat ride, but the presence of the boatman made talking impossible. Now she glanced at Lady Rosamond, who, though pale, still seemed determined.

Lady Rosamond quietly said, "The king will be meeting with his noblemen tonight in Westminster Hall itself, for it is the only chamber large enough."

"We have to get inside," Philip said, doubt in his voice. "If we try to enter through the palace yard, the soldiers will question our identities."

"And there could be guests arriving who will know us," said Anne.

"There is a private entrance," Lady Rosamond insisted. "My dear husband, a distant relation of the king, confided the words necessary to gain entrance. We were in London once and—oh, never mind, 'tis a long story. Sometimes a king needs a way to leave his palace without an entourage of soldiers marking his every move."

"It sounds dangerous," Anne said.

"But necessary." Lady Rosamond smiled. "Sometimes one wishes not to be noticed."

"I'm hoping for that just now," Philip said dryly.

Lady Rosamond glanced at the sun. "We should do this after supper, when most people will have gone home for the night."

"Can we afford to wait that long?" he asked. "Is not the king expecting you?"

"Yesterday," she said ruefully. "But he will understand. Might there be a tavern nearby where we can eat?"

"I'll feel safer when we are not so exposed to whomever wants to see us," Philip added. "This way."

He led them to a tavern tucked away from King Street. They ate in the darkest corner they could find, talking little, just waiting, until Anne's nerves felt like thread about to snap. She had come so far—why did this last part of the mission suddenly seem so insurmountable?

And there was Philip, calm and steady and courageous. He got up to play dice against the wall with a group of men, aiding their disguise. He'd gotten them away from the League, killed Bramfield's man, and now was about to lead them into the king's palace. Did nothing bother him? His confidence was part of what she loved about him, probably because she herself had once lacked it in a fundamental way. It had taken her this journey to learn to believe in herself, to believe in her worth as a person, beyond her service as a maidservant, beyond the masquerade as Lady Rosamond, or what the League believed of her. She was worthy of her own dreams of happiness.

Could she share them with Philip? The League rejecting her had forced her to reevaluate herself and what she wanted. How had she thought being a Bladeswoman could be more important than finding someone to share a life with? She had fixated on the League because she had no other hopes.

But what about Philip? He cared for her, she knew, but could he love her? Only love would make him abandon the plans he'd anticipated to bring his family recognition. He wanted a marriage, and she didn't even have much of a dowry to offer. She would have to come up with a way to convince him that love mattered more than status.

After twilight had darkened the world, they left the tavern following Lady Rosamond. But instead of turning up the road to Westminster Palace, she went back toward the river where storage buildings sat in a squat cluster. When they were certain the last people on the road had turned away, they ducked within an alley. Anne heard Lady Rosamond counting to herself as they passed several buildings. Clouds hid the rising moon, and she began to wonder how much longer this would take. With no torch, they would soon be stumbling in darkness. And this "private entrance" was far away from the palace itself.

Lady Rosamond came to a stop. "This is it," she said softly, staring at a door.

There were no windows to peer through.

"What will we be facing?" Philip asked.

"Soldiers. There should be several stationed inside. Allow me to speak."

She knocked on the door, and there was an echoing sound of desertion inside. She knocked again, this time only once.

The door opened immediately, and two men stood there. Though they displayed no weapons, by their stance they were used to swords in their hands. When the soldiers saw only one man and two women, their stiffness faded.

"Who are you?" asked the shorter, squatter soldier, his eyes dark with suspicion.

"Lady Rosamond Wolsingham."

His face scrunched up even more, while the taller man said, "The earl's widow?"

"I am traveling secretly, and I need to enter Westminster Palace. The king is expecting me. I suggest you allow me in, or we can discuss it here in the open."

Anne could hear the refined tone of command in every word Lady Rosamond spoke. The soldiers could, too, because they stepped back and allowed the three to enter. The building was only one large room, lit with lanterns. At the far end, four more soldiers stood in front of a table with stools surrounding it.

"My lady," the squat soldier said, emphasizing her title with sarcasm, "I am Sir Humphrey. If you know about this entrance, then you know what it takes to use it."

Anne glanced wide-eyed at Philip, who stood tense, as if still expecting to do battle.

Lady Rosamond smiled. "I will grant you the words of entrance."

Were they going to be privately escorted? Anne wondered. Or ride in a covered cart or litter?

Sir Humphrey folded his arms across his chest, his smile challenging, as if he didn't believe she knew the words. "Come to me, my lady, and speak them softly."

She stepped toward him, and he bent his head. Whatever she whispered caused his expression to change from skeptical to surprised.

"We must hurry," Lady Rosamond said with urgency.

He nodded. "Aye, my lady, follow me."

Anne felt Philip's hand above her elbow, and as they walked behind Lady Rosamond, she told herself that he cared about her. She had a stray worry that perhaps that was all he would ever feel. How could she convince him that she had not merely settled for marriage with him?

Sir Humphrey guided them to a stack of broken crates, and then moved several aside to reveal a trap door in the wooden floor.

An underground tunnel, Anne thought with excitement. But when she saw the earthen darkness gaping up at them, and a circular stairway disappearing straight down, she began to have second thoughts. But Sir Humphrey lit a torch from one of the lanterns and began the descent. The taller soldier took up another torch, falling back to the end of the line.

The stairway smelled of earth and must, and it grew cooler and damper the deeper they descended. Many minutes later, they reached the bottom. She could see a narrow, arched stone tunnel disappearing into the distance. Silently they walked along it for several hundred yards. They were walking beneath the palace yard, or beside the deep foundations of Westminster Hall or the abbey itself.

At last they reached another staircase, and this time the climb up seemed worse. Anne's thighs hurt by the time they reached the room above, with its curved vaulted ceiling of an undercroft used for storage. There were even more soldiers here, and Sir Humphrey took his leave of them. A silent soldier escorted them through long corridors that twisted and turned so much that Anne lost all sense of where they were.

At last they reached a grand door, and a man dressed in a plain, but finely made doublet was waiting for them. The soldier leading them bowed and departed.

"Lady Rosamond?" the man said to Anne.

As Anne shook her head, Lady Rosamond stepped forward. "I am she. And who are you?"

"I am Sir Edward Colet, the Lord Steward of Westminster Palace. His Majesty has been waiting for you."

"Somewhat impatiently, I imagine," she answered.

Sir Edward arched a brow. "You are the reason for the festivities tonight. Allow me to show you into the Painted Chamber, the king's private quarters."

Anne exchanged a surprised glance with Philip. They would all see the king? Would he remember them? He had attended Elizabeth and John's wedding at Castle Alderley, where he had met Philip.

Sir Edward opened both doors, and Anne walked into an opulence she had never seen before. Every wall was covered with murals painted in crimsons and greens and blues. She recognized scenes from the Bible, and what must be ancient kings of England in battle. All the crowns and armor were gilded with gold that shone in the hundreds of candles hanging from the ceiling and mounted on stands. The far end of the chamber was curtained off, but nearer at hand were groupings of cushioned chairs and small tables. But standing about one massive table, looking at papers scattered across it, was a group of men surrounding King Henry, surely his Privy Council and courtiers and clergymen.

King Henry, tall, and blond, with handsome looks, but blackened teeth, focused his gaze on Lady Rosamond, who stood at Sir Edward's side. Anne and Philip waited just behind.

"Your Majesty," said Sir Edward, "the Countess of Wolsingham, Lady Rosamond."

Lady Rosamond sank into a deep curtsy, then rose, head held high, regardless of her plain and rumpled clothing.

"Lady Rosamond, you were expected yesterday," King Henry said coldly.

With a wave of his hand, he dismissed many of the men, until only a few were left about him.

And then Anne realized that his cousin, Viscount Bannaster was there. He nodded his head to her, and she reluctantly returned the gesture. Why was he here?

"Forgive the delay in my arrival, Your Majesty," said Lady Rosamond, "but our masquerade was discovered, and there was a threat against my companion, Mistress Anne, that I could not ignore."

"Masquerade?" said the king impatiently.

Perhaps he had not cared to know the details of what they'd had to do to come before him this day.

"Who are these people," the king continued, "and how did they assist you?"

Lady Rosamond presented both of them, and Anne thought the king recognized Philip. Next, the lady explained the purpose of Anne's ruse, her capture by Lord Bramfield, and the threatening note delivered to Lady Rosamond in the home where the League had hidden her.

King Henry watched her without expression as she spoke, and when she was finished, he said only, "Bramfield?"

She nodded solemnly. "Aye, Your Majesty. I do not yet know the identities of the other two men who spoke of treason against you. I know you are hosting a gathering of noblemen this night."

"And now instead of a celebration, it will expose traitors," he added heavily. "But not to the public. Their identities will remain a secret this night. Do you understand?"

"Aye, Your Majesty," Lady Rosamond said in a solemn voice. "I do not know their names, but I will never forget what they look like. How do you wish me to identify them for you?"

"Since this is a celebration, I have hired women to entertain."

He looked uneasy about that, as if his morals disapproved.

Anne's nervousness darkened into dread. Entertain? What did he expect Lady Rosamond to do?

But the lady herself did not even flinch. "Might you explain my duties, Your Majesty?"

"The women are to be costumed and masked. Although you will not be present at the end of the evening when their services might be requested, you will pass as one well enough while you move through the crowd and search out the traitors. My cousin, Lord Bannaster, will walk with you, as if you are reserved for someone specific, and you may identify the traitors to him."

"Of course, Your Majesty." Lady Rosamond bowed her acceptance.

Anne was aghast. A countess of England had to impersonate a . . . harlot? There might be a hundred men there, all of whom would be looking at her with base thoughts. And she was to be alone with them?

And of all the king's closest councillors, he had chosen Lord Bannaster. Why?

Anne stepped up beside Lady Rosamond. "Your Majesty, may I speak?"

She knew Philip stiffened, but he did not try to stop her. The king simply looked irritated. And she did not blame him, with the threats coalescing all around him.

King Henry said, "Aye, girl, what would you say?"

"I wish to accompany Lady Rosamond, to lessen the risk to her person."

Lady Rosamond's eyes widened, Anne thought she

heard Philip curse softly, but the king only exchanged an amused look with several of his councillors.

"And how will you protect your lady beyond what Lord Bannaster's presence will do?" the king asked.

Anne realized she might have offended the viscount, and she sent him an apologetic look. Instead of being angry, he looked amused, which puzzled her. She once thought him a man who did not allow others to alter his own plans, but now he seemed . . . different.

"Surely if there were two of us," she said quickly, "would not the gentlemen be less inclined to . . . proposition Lady Rosamond?"

King Henry looked as if he was trying not to laugh. "If you knew these men, you would know that was not the truth. But you are a brave girl to volunteer."

"Then allow me to be at her side, Your Majesty. I have risked my life for this culmination. Let me see it through."

Philip thought for certain that everyone in the chamber could hear his pounding heart. He could not believe Anne would continue to risk herself this way. He had never known anyone as brave—yet vulnerable—as she was.

The king studied her for a moment, and then nodded. "I believe the Lord Chamberlain can find another costume for you."

Anne curtsied. "My thanks, Your Majesty."

Philip stepped forward. "And might I offer my protection for the ladies, Your Majesty?"

The king's gaze sharpened. "Sir Philip, is it? Were you not Lord Alderley's man?"

"I was, but I left to seek my own fortunes."

"I have my own guard to protect the women this night."

"And I wish to be among them. I have guarded Mistress Anne, and now Lady Rosamond, and it is a duty that it grieves me to abandon."

The king shrugged. "As you wish. Sir Edward," he said to his steward, "find him livery." He looked again at Lady Rosamond. "The Lord Steward will further instruct you. We will meet again this evening at the end of the festivities. Know that you have England's gratitude."

Philip followed the women and Sir Edward out of the Painted Chamber, through several tall corridors lit with hundreds of candles. There were paintings and sculptures everywhere, but he did not care for the wealth of Westminster Palace. His sole focus was on one woman.

At last, Sir Edward opened a door to a bedchamber. "Lady Rosamond and Mistress Anne, attendants will wait on you to help you bathe and change. Be quick, for when the feast is over, I will send for you. Sir Philip, you may have the chamber next door, where a page will see to your bath and livery."

As Lady Rosamond stepped into the bedchamber, Philip said, "Sir Edward, I need to speak with you. It concerns Lord Bannaster." He took Anne's hand, when she would have left.

Sir Edward frowned as he waited.

"I will be honest in my question to you," Philip said. "Can Lord Bannaster be trusted?"

Sir Edward wore a ghost of a smile. "You know little of him, I understand, except his foolish mistakes when he tried to win the hand of Lady Elizabeth. His brother was the viscount until his death, and this Lord Bannaster was raised to be a priest."

Philip and Anne exchanged a surprised look.

"He only came in to the viscountcy recently, and still has much to learn. He will aid you well this night."

After Sir Edward had gone, Philip glanced at Anne. "A priest?"

She shrugged. "Then I guess we will have to trust him."

When she tried to release Philip's hand, he pulled her closer.

"I need to speak with you," he said in a low voice. "Come with me."

Anne nodded.

Several maidservants were already approaching from down the corridor, trailed by pages carrying a bathing tub and buckets of water. The servants went into Lady Rosamond's chamber, and Philip pulled Anne into his.

"What is it?" she asked as he shut the door.

He held her by the upper arms. "What were you thinking, to volunteer yourself once again? 'Tis not your fight—you've done your part."

"You heard my reasoning," she said calmly. "Would you do any less?"

"But I can defend myself with a sword!"

"And I will have you and the king's men to defend me."

She put her hands on his face, her skin overly warm because he felt so cold.

"Philip, I am no longer the simple maid who followed every order without question."

"You were never that."

Gently, she said, "I think, at first, to you I was. I was a servant, as you had once been, as the family you came from. Maybe I even reminded you of that."

"Anne—" But he stopped himself. Had he not worried about this? "I care nothing of that anymore."

"I am truly glad, Philip," she whispered.

When she put her hands on his chest and rose onto her toes, he kissed her with all the feeling he had not been able to express yet.

"We have much to talk about," he said in a husky voice.

"And after tonight, we will do so." She stepped away from him, her expression one of regret. "I must go."

He stared at the door after she'd gone, realizing what a fool he'd been. Anne had been the only woman to make him happy, and he'd been too slow to realize that he loved her. Now she was risking herself yet again.

But would she ever be safe if her part in this tragedy

was known? Lady Rosamond had her nobility and title to protect her—Anne had nothing.

And Philip wanted her protected. He paced his chambers, thinking about how this could all turn out. Could he convince her to marry him? Would his name keep her safe?

And how to convince proud Anne that her safety was not the only reason he wanted to marry her? *He* would be the only man in her life, in her bed.

Chapter 24

Anne knew that she looked different by the way Philip's eyes widened when he came into the women's assigned chamber. She and Lady Rosamond, though not yet masked, were dressed in red and gold gowns, respectively, that bared their arms and the upper slopes of their bosoms. Though it was summer, she felt chilled wearing so little.

Lady Rosamond smiled with a touch of sarcasm. "Sir Philip, do you approve our attire?"

"The noblemen certainly will," he said, his eyes narrowed in obvious anger.

Anne tilted her head, intrigued. "But not you?"

"There is only one place I wish to see you looking like that."

She gasped, feeling embarrassed and overly hot all at the same time, but Lady Rosamond only laughed.

"Sir Philip, I will look forward to hearing about your next adventure with Mistress Anne. But for now we must affix our masks and finish our duty to the king."

"Do you believe there can ever be an end to this?" Philip asked her.

The smiled faded from her face, and Anne looked stricken.

But Lady Rosamond was still strong, for she only said, "We do what we must."

They tied on masks that covered the upper half of their faces, leaving their painted red lips bare.

"The king chose this last masquerade well," Lady Rosamond said dryly. "Have we not worn masks throughout our adventure?"

"But never so pretty," Anne said, thinking of the sparkling beads sewn on the masks.

"So when you were portraying me, you weren't pretty?" Lady Rosamond asked, one eyebrow lifted. When Anne stuttered a response, she only laughed before glancing at the door. "Oh, where is that man? I wish this to be over."

Another hour passed before Lord Bannaster arrived. He looked handsome in his green doublet and hose, and Anne found herself trying to picture him as a priest. With Philip bringing up the rear, the women followed the viscount through the palace. Anne could hear the slow swell of music growing louder and louder. Her stomach seemed to twist on itself, and she was breathing far too quickly.

When they reached double doors twice Philip's height, two soldiers stood guard. Together they opened the doors, and a calm came over Anne. She was a woman of loose morals, at ease with men, confident in her power to overwhelm them with her beauty. They would not see her face, so she allowed herself to sway as she walked, emphasizing the curves she knew men admired.

She and Lady Rosamond each took one of Lord Bannaster's arms, and he began to slowly escort them in. Heat and noise billowed out at them. Anne found herself astonished at the height of Westminster Hall, without a pillar in sight to support the roof. Easily a hundred noblemen moved amongst each other, talking and gesturing and laughing. An orchestra played somewhere within.

They weren't the first women to arrive. Others, masked and certainly in more provocative clothing, walked between the men, displaying themselves and entertaining with their smiles and their laughter.

Did the noble wives know what was going on tonight? Anne found herself wondering.

But a woman such as she would not care. Tonight was about the payment received, and the pleasure given, so that she would be hired to return again. A smile came easier to her then. She walked slowly at Lord Bannaster's side as at first he displayed them before King Henry, seated on his throne on a raised dais. The king nodded, but his gaze did not linger. He was a newly married man, and she had heard that his wife was with child.

And then Lady Rosamond's work began. Lord

Bannaster moved through the crowd, smiling at each woman on his arm. Anne gave him a languid smile back, impressed with his acting skills. Lady Rosamond giggled, reaching out to touch the arm of the occasional nobleman.

Did she recognize one of the traitors yet? Anne wondered. Who here would betray his king? She herself saw a few faces she knew: Baron Milforth, who'd kissed her; and his son who was worried that his father would marry the wrong woman.

"My girl, did you hear what I said?"

Startled, Anne smiled up at a man and realized she faced Lord Egmanton, without the oversight of his mother. She felt a flash of fear, remembering how he had forced her legs apart.

But he didn't know her now, hidden behind her mask, and she would never have to submit to him.

"My lord, I was admiring the way everyone simply glitters with jewels here," Anne said, her voice low and husky.

Lord Bannaster was bending his ear to Lady Rosamond, who was pointing and smiling and whispering to him, as if picking out her choice of protector for the evening.

When really she was identifying a traitor. Though Anne caught a glimpse of the man she pointed to, she reluctantly made herself focus on Egmanton.

"Are you available for the evening?" he asked, reaching for her.

Finding it difficult to smile, she playfully batted at his hand. "I am with Lord Bannaster for now, you impertinent man."

She glanced again at the man Lady Rosamond had pointed to, and he seemed so . . . normal. Pleasant to look at, rather short in height.

Egmanton had not given up. "What will it take to make you leave Lord Bannaster? After all, the man was almost a priest. What does he know of women?"

Lord Bannaster suddenly gave the young baron his full attention. "Egmanton, is that you? You are difficult to recognize without your mother leading you about."

Several men nearby snickered, and Egmanton flushed red.

"Perhaps you shouldn't be seen here," Lord Bannaster continued.

Anne looked at Lord Bannaster with interest, while Egmanton's chest puffed like a rooster.

"I do not take direction from you," the baron said.

"Then perhaps you will from the king. It has come to his attention that you abused a noblewoman recently."

Anne held her breath in surprise, but she did not think Egmanton would back down.

"You cannot believe a woman's lies."

Bannaster smiled coolly. "She is not the one who complained to His Majesty. I do believe you will be hearing from my royal cousin soon."

Egmanton gaped at them, his mouth moving but no words emerging.

Lady Rosamond and Lord Bannaster began to move away, and Anne allowed her hand to loosen in the viscount's arm, as if considering remaining with Egmanton. At last, she shook her head, trilled a laugh, and waved good-bye. She glanced at Lord Bannaster with grateful satisfaction. Maybe there was more to him than the man she'd met at Castle Alderley.

As they moved through the men, and the occasional cluster of women, everyone parted before them, looking, lingering. Anne was finding it easier to breathe. This was not so difficult. Then she spied Sir Robert, the young Bladesman who'd followed her from Lord Kelshall's. How much did he know about their escape from the League's house? Surely he was only here to ensure the completion of their mission.

And then she saw Lord Alderley, her dear friend Elizabeth's husband. He was making his way purposefully through the crowd, smiling politely at the women who tried to snare his attention, but continuing to move past. Anne was not worried about him straying from Elizabeth.

She realized that he had a goal in mind. She glanced over her shoulder and saw that Philip was standing against a wall nearby, stiff with attention. Lord Alderley had seen him. Would that matter? Lord Alderley, a member of the League, had been the one to suggest her when the Bladesmen had needed a woman's help.

Before she could see if they spoke, Lord Bannaster pulled her deeper into the crowd. There was only one man left to find. Their mission was almost over.

Then a man took her free hand and tugged; she was so surprised that she let go of Lord Bannaster.

"Dance with me, mistress," the man said.

He spoke so close to her ear that she felt his warm, wine-soaked breath tickling her. Before she could protest, he had her in his arms, and was pulling her even farther away from Lord Bannaster. She glanced back and saw the viscount watch her with concern, and Lady Rosamond saying something to him, but at last they turned away. The mission was more important.

And she was alone in a sea of men.

Her dance partner was enthusiastic; he picked her up and turned her about, moving not quite in time with the music. Anne smiled at him as she stumbled along in his wake, but she was panicking at losing track of Lord Bannaster.

And then she remembered Philip. Nothing truly bad would happen to her under his watchful eye.

But if Philip interfered with a nobleman's pleasure, what would happen to him?

She could not allow him to think she was in trouble. When the dance ended, she curtsied dramatically, giving her dance partner an eyeful of her cleavage.

"A good evening, my lord," she said, moving away swiftly.

"But wait! Have you chosen someone yet?"

She only waggled her fingers at him and continued on. The hall was vast and crowded, but surely she would be able to find Lord Bannaster. But other men were taller. She walked as swiftly as possible, craning her neck past one man's wide shoulders, darting beneath the outstretched arm of another as he spoke.

A woman suddenly took her hand and pulled her close. Anne was overwhelmed by the strong scent of jasmine, but it could not quite mask the body odor beneath.

"Dearie, you move too swiftly. How can you be caught?"

"I don't need to be caught," Anne said, trying to remove her hand from the strong grip. "I am spoken for this night."

"Ah, lucky you," said the woman, releasing her at last.

Anne was not successful finding Lord Bannaster on her own. She turned about, hoping to ask for Philip's assistance.

"My dear, there you are!"

Anne could have sagged with relief at the sound of Lady Rosamond's voice. She and Lord Bannaster came upon her, and Anne gladly took the viscount's other arm.

"I need a lady's privacy," Lady Rosamond continued. "Might you accompany me?"

"Of course," Anne said, knowing that she must have already pointed out the last traitor. "But tell me we will hasten back. I am so enjoying myself!"

The corridor was blessedly cool, and the sounds of merriment and music gradually faded behind them. Lord Bannaster picked up his pace until the women were almost running to keep up with him, but he must have felt the pressing need to return to the king.

To her surprise, he led them back to the Painted Chamber. When he opened the door, Anne glanced over her shoulder and saw that Philip was close behind. He gave her a grim smile and she returned it with relief.

"Wait here," Lord Bannaster said. "I must make sure the king saw us leave."

And then he was gone. They stood rather helplessly in the middle of such elegant finery, beneath the watchful eyes of two soldiers who remained on guard beside the door. When the king did not immediately return, Lady Rosamond sighed and found a cushioned chair to flounce down upon.

"Oh, these shoes do not fit me," she murmured, leaning her head back and closing her eyes.

Anne perched on the chair next to her, and Philip took a seat across from them. And then they waited. Surely over an hour passed. Philip rested his head in his hands, and Anne leaned back to doze beside a sleeping Lady Rosamond. They had yet to remove their masks, in case someone unexpected arrived with the king.

When the door opened, Anne shot to her feet at the same time as Philip. Lady Rosamond followed slowly, yawning into her hand.

King Henry strode in, his fur-lined cloak streaming behind him. Several of his councillors, as well as Lord Bannaster, came with him.

The king stopped and faced them, his expression set in firm, impassive lines. For some reason the nerves that had settled down within Anne's stomach now flared back to life. Philip glanced at her, looking grim.

The king lifted his chin. "The celebration is almost over. Lord Bannaster has given me the identities of the three traitors."

Anne waited, but he did not say their names. Perhaps it wasn't their place to know.

Philip asked, "Who are they?"

The king looked away, suddenly tired. He motioned toward a table, and someone hurried to fetch him a goblet of wine.

"You do not need to know their identities," he finally said. "Only know that you have the gratitude of England."

"What will you do?" Philip demanded. "I speak freely, Your Majesty, but we have earned such a right, have we not?"

Anne held her breath. Perhaps in the world of kings and noblemen and high intrigue, they were owed nothing, and Philip's presumption might only earn him the king's anger. Had not Philip once cared for the king's good opinion? It did not seem so now.

But the king took a deep breath before sighing. "You must understand that it is a time of deep unease in the kingdom. I was crowned less than a year ago, and there are those, uncertain in their support of me, who might see this rebellion as a cause to side with."

Anne did not understand. What was he saying?

"Bramfield and his cohorts know that if I actively

move against them, it could incite another civil war. It is why they so freely came to an event they must have known had been deliberately called for them."

"You will just . . . keep quiet about this information?" Lady Rosamond asked in disbelief.

"Only for now," King Henry said. "I will begin the investigation quietly, and when I have more proof to hold up to Parliament, I will move against these traitors."

"Until then, they are free," Philip said sardonically.

"They know they have been identified." Lord Bannaster showed the anger that his royal cousin did not. "They will not be so foolish again."

"And I have already declared that none of the noblemen can retain an army any longer," the king said. "That will now be the government's domain. Lady Rosamond, you have made possible the futility of the traitors, and risked your life—and the lives of Mistress Anne and Sir Philip. The Crown will not forget."

Anne told herself that this could have beneficial results. Perhaps Philip would win the acclaim he'd long wanted, the status at court that a noble marriage would have brought him. But when she looked at him, he was frowning, his gaze far away.

Suddenly, he said, "Your Majesty, might I ask a favor this night?"

There were restless murmurs among the king's councillors, but the king himself nodded. "Aye, Sir Philip. What is your request?"

"That the ladies be allowed to remain here tonight, safe within the palace."

Sir Edward, the Lord Steward, scoffed, "Think you that we would throw you out onto the streets at midnight?"

"Philip—" Anne began.

Philip shook his head. "I must leave. I have an errand to attend to, but I cannot rest if the women are not protected. And I'll need to borrow a horse."

Lady Rosamond studied him thoughtfully but said nothing. Anne wanted to demand answers, but Philip had carefully chosen to speak before an audience. Had he wanted to forestall her curiosity?

"Go, Sir Philip," King Henry said. "My stables will be open to you."

"I hope to return by supper tomorrow, but until I do, please do not allow the women to leave."

"Philip!" Anne finally said in exasperation.

He gave her a last look. "Stay here, Anne. Wait for me."

Anne was never so terrified as she tried to imagine what Philip had planned. But if there was one thing she'd learned in her quest to become a Bladeswoman, it was that she did not take waiting well.

Was Philip planning to take on the traitors himself?

She could not leave him to go alone, not when she knew that there was someone still at the palace who could help. When she and Lady Rosamond were finally alone in their bedchamber, Anne quickly changed back into the plain garments of a maid, covering her hair beneath a linen cap.

"What are you doing?" Lady Rosamond asked with suspicion.

"I have to go. Philip needs help."

"What do you think you can do alone?" Lady Rosamond demanded.

"I will not be alone, I promise you."

Before the countess could try to persuade her, Anne left the chamber and ran back through the corridors. She had a good head for direction, and she well remembered the way to Westminster Hall. Luckily, the soldiers on guard outside the door thought nothing of letting a maid in. Half of the guests had already gone, which made spotting Lord Alderley, Philip's friend, even easier.

She approached him and waited subserviently as he spoke to another man. When at last he glanced at her over the man's shoulder, she beseeched him with wide eyes.

Lord Alderley excused himself and came to her. Looking around to make sure no one could overhear them, he murmured, "Anne, what is wrong? Where is Philip?"

"Gone, my lord," she whispered, "and I fear for him. The king knows the traitors, but cannot act immediately."

Lord Alderley closed his eyes, his face a grimace. "You think Philip went after them."

"He went alone! It is hard to believe that he would

be so foolhardy, but I know not. We need to involve the League."

"Anne, you know I have only been invited to join, but not yet trained," he said with obvious regret. "I don't know how to contact them."

"I do. Another Bladesman was here this night. I will introduce you if I can find him."

With the hall emptying, and servants beginning to clean, it was easier to search for Sir Robert. In fact, he seemed to be watching her, for he was alone, and when their gazes met, he inclined his head.

Then suddenly she remembered—there was a traitor within the League. Could Sir Robert be he?

But surely, if he was, he could have killed her before now. And she just couldn't believe it of him. Her instincts about people had always been strong.

She led Lord Alderley to him, introduced the two Bladesmen, and explained her dilemma.

Sir Robert spoke softly. "Bramfield, you say?"

"He has a house between Westminster and London," Lord Alderley said. "Would he go there?"

"And would Philip follow him?" Anne asked. "It seems to be our only choice."

Sir Robert nodded. "I will accompany you, Alderley."

Anne chimed in. "And I will, too."

Lord Alderley frowned at her.

Before he could speak, she said, "Do not say that this is too dangerous for a woman. I have been in constant danger for weeks now."

"And handled yourself well," Sir Robert said with an admiring smile. "You could almost be a Bladesman yourself."

"A Blades*woman*," she corrected. "But I'm no longer interested. Philip is all I can think about. Could we go, please?"

Chapter 25

Philip rode swiftly through the London streets, now barren of traffic except for the occasional drunken fool or eager prostitute. Lanterns guided him, and the crest of the moon peered out from behind a scattering of clouds.

For now, Anne and Lady Rosamond were safe. But how long could that last, with three traitors free of the consequences of their actions?

When he neared the house used by the League, he dismounted at the end of the alley and left the horse tethered to a broken crate. Taking his time, Philip covered the area, looking for anything suspicious. But if Bramfield were still keeping watch, it was not obvious.

And why should he? Philip thought bitterly. The king was not going to act.

When at last he led his horse into the front courtyard, two men materialized out of the shadows on either side of the house. Philip did not hear the sound of swords being drawn, but he remained immobile.

"I need to see Sir David," he said softly. "I have just come from the king."

They pulled him forward, handling him roughly, but he was not surprised. He had taken Lady Rosamond out from under their protection.

Inside, there was light in the front hall, and dark curtains covering the windows. The two men pulled Philip deeper into the house, into a withdrawing room crowded with several men.

Walter, David, and Joseph were among them, as well as two others that Philip didn't recognize.

Walter rose to his feet. "You may leave us," he said to the two guards, who withdrew and shut the door behind them.

"We trusted you, Sir Philip," Walter said coldly.

"And I trusted you," Philip shot back. "But you cared more about the king than the innocent women who had risked their very lives for this mission."

"And you could guard them better than we could?" Walter said with sarcasm.

Philip looked at the two strangers. "I need you gentlemen to leave. I will not say more in front of you."

Walter said, "They will remain."

Philip stared hard at David, who sighed. "Walter, let it just be the four of us for now."

Walter glanced impassively at David, but at last he nodded, and the two men departed.

"I did guard those women better than you could," Philip finally said in a low, heated voice, "because even now they reside within Westminster Palace. Lady Rosamond identified the traitors for the king."

Joseph and David looked at each other in relief, but Walter continued to study Philip. "There is more," Walter said.

Philip nodded, his jaw clenched. "The king will not move against the traitors for fear he will lose control of all of the noblemen so soon after his coronation. He says he will investigate for more proof."

"It sounds like he's being cautious," Joseph said.

Philip felt like he was going to explode. "Cautious? He is leaving Anne and Rosamond vulnerable."

"The League will see them safe."

"The League?" Philip said, looking at David in surprise. "You did not tell them?"

"We were never alone," David said, and then wryly added, "and they felt that I had not done enough to stop your escape."

Walter glanced at David with obvious disappointment. "You had information for us?"

"Someone within the League is working with Bramfield and the traitors," David said. "Lady Rosamond was sent a threatening letter while she was here."

"And the only person who could have known where she was is a Bladesman," Philip added coldly. "Why else would I have taken the women from here?"

Walter's eyes seemed to burn with emotion, but only for a moment. Then he was his impassive self once again. "And yet you came back here to us. Why?"

"Because the three of you are all I have." Philip

tiredly ran a hand through his hair. "There is a rogue Bladesman out there, who knows that at least one traitor is aware of his identity. What do *you* think is going to happen?"

Walter considered Philip. "He will attempt to protect himself by killing the traitors."

"I care nothing for the lives of Bramfield and his cohorts," Philip said. "But if we can capture this Bladesman before he does something worse—"

"You are correct, Sir Philip," Walter interrupted. "I am glad you came to us."

Philip stared at him in surprise.

"I owe you an apology," Walter continued. "I promised to guard Anne, an innocent, at all costs, but I lost sight of this in my quest to aid the king. It was a misjudgment on my part that I deeply regret. The League has never been about politics, but about helping people who could not always help themselves. But I found myself behaving once again as a soldier."

David and Joseph seemed taken aback, but Philip only nodded. "I accept your apology, but I cannot speak for Anne. Yet . . . she understood your motives for leaving her more than I did."

"That was too generous of her," Walter said.

"I agree. Because for me, all I can think about is her safety. If there is corruption in the League, how can she have any kind of normal life?"

"Bramfield has a house on the Strand," Walter said, "rather than apartments at Westminster Palace."

"That will be convenient for the rogue Bladesman,"

Philip said, turning to the door. "And since I already bribed the guard at the city gate to let me in, surely he'll take more money to let me out again. Come."

Anne rode pillion behind Lord Alderley, holding on tightly to his waist as he rode his horse beside Sir Robert beneath a full moon. The Strand led toward the city walls, but they did not have to worry about getting past the closed gates. Bramfield had what was almost a palace on the Thames. They left their horses near the street and crept close to the walls surrounding his property.

At the open gate, near a gatehouse lit from within by lantern light, Sir Robert came up short. "Mistress Anne, you must not look."

"The guard is dead?" she whispered.

Lord Alderley grimaced. "We are too late."

"Philip wouldn't have killed him if he didn't have to," Anne said.

"We don't even know if Philip did it," Lord Alderley reminded her. "Perhaps the king made plans for the traitors that he did not confide in you."

Then Philip had endangered himself for nothing, she worried. "But we don't know that. What if he had to fight his way in? Please, let us keep going."

"I would insist you remain behind, but you are safer with us than on the streets." Sir Robert handed her a dagger. "Have you been taught how to use this?"

"Not formally, but I can get by." And armed, she felt safer.

Sporadic clouds crossed the moon, occasionally letting light shine on the cobbled walkway. The house itself rose three floors, but not a light shone in the windows. It was long after midnight.

They passed another corpse on the approach to the front of the house, and it took her a moment to realize that the yawning blackness was an open door. Sir Robert and Lord Alderley peered within.

"Stay within the entrance hall, Anne," Lord Alderley said. "If you hear fighting, run outside."

She nodded, though she made no promises aloud. She followed them inside, and two high windows in the front wall allowed moonlight to illuminate a two-story hall, lined with ancient statues. She stood against the wall, just within the front door. After looking behind the statues, Sir Robert and Lord Alderley crept down the length of the room, looked into the next, and disappeared into the darkness.

Her nerves were taut, her stomach a hard ball within her. She kept flinching, as if she expected sudden shouts and the ringing of steel on steel, but the house was so silent.

Was Philip—

She could not even think the words. She stared at the statues, as if they populated the hall and watched her with menace.

And then the nearest statue seemed to move.

Before she could even shriek, the man was upon her, hand over her mouth, holding her tightly to him. She hadn't heard a sound, as if he'd just appeared.

"The false Lady Rosamond," he murmured in her ear.

Though she could not see him, his voice was familiar. Was he one of the traitors, come to kill his cohort Bramfield? Or was he the Bladesman who'd assisted Bramfield?

She couldn't speak to him, with his hot hand covering her mouth. His arm pinned hers to her waist. But she still had the dagger clutched in one hand, hidden in the folds of her skirt.

"Your friends are too late," he said almost conversationally. "They're all dead."

Her eyes blurred with tears. He couldn't mean Philip? The ache in her chest expanded until it threatened to stop her breathing.

She moved her mouth against his hand.

"We can't have a discussion like this," he said. "I can't trust you not to scream and alert someone to my presence. But you can come with me, and we'll have a lovely chat later."

He pulled her toward the open doorway, and she started to struggle in earnest. She tried to bite him, and he gripped her jaw harder. Then she let her knees buckle, hoping to pull him to the floor with her. To her surprise, he had to let her go. She rolled onto her back, digging into the floor with her heels to scramble away from him, but her slippers only slid. The shadow man lifted his arm up high, and she saw a dagger glinting in the moonlight.

She lashed out with her own blade, slicing him

across both shins. He howled aloud, and she prayed that someone had heard him. The moonlight suddenly caught his profile, and in shock, she recognized Lord Milforth, the older baron who had told her she didn't kiss well.

"You bitch!" He raised his dagger again.

Just as she began to roll out from under him, she heard the clash of steel over her head. Scrambling up onto her hands and knees, she saw someone standing in the doorway, gripping his sword. Milforth wrung his empty hand, as if the dagger had been knocked from it.

"Anne!"

When Anne realized that Philip was the one to disarm her captor, the relief she felt flooded through her body, leaving her exhausted and near tears. Climbing to her feet, she stumbled back against the wall, out of their way. Milforth lunged for her, but Philip caught him from behind. More men swarmed into the hall, surrounding him, binding him.

It was several minutes before Philip was able to step away from the group. Anne gave him a trembling smile and let him engulf her in his warm embrace.

"Are you well?" he asked.

When she nodded, he pulled back, holding her upper arms.

"How did you get here?"

"With us," said Lord Alderley from behind her.

Candles were slowly being lit through the chamber, and Anne saw Philip's recognition.

"John?" he said in surprise.

"And me as well," said Sir Robert, coming to stand beside Lord Alderley. "Mistress Anne feared for your life, and we were the only Bladesmen to be found."

When Philip frowned at her, she said, "You went alone, Philip! What was I to think?"

"That I might find my own Bladesmen?"

Anne looked past him to see Walter, Joseph, and David surrounding Milforth. "Oh, well that was good thinking."

He shook his head. "Here I was hoping to save the day, and I find you battling a traitor."

"Not a traitor," said Sir Robert, frowning at Milforth. "We found the three noblemen dead within, as if from a robbery. Milforth is a Bladesman."

Both Anne and Philip stared at Milforth, who glared at them all.

"You have no proof of any of this," Milforth said haughtily. "I came here to visit Bramfield and found them dead. I thought your serving girl one of the thieves."

Walter looked at him coldly. "We of the League do not need a layman's proof. We take care of our own, do we not, Lord Milforth? I fear you have made linking you to this crime too easy."

As she watched two of her Bladesmen lead Milforth outside, Anne asked, "But was it really a crime? The three he killed have reaped what they sowed."

"He was their compatriot until he could no longer take the risk that they'd identify him," Philip said, "making him a traitor, too."

With his words, a heavy silence fell.

Walter approached Anne, and to her surprise, he took her hand and brought it to his lips. "My lady," he said, "we erred in our urgency to reach London."

Embarrassed, she said, "Walter, you must not—"

He looked up at her, and there was genuine sorrow in his eyes. "You were fair to us. You are one of the reasons this mission succeeded, and we neglected you."

Anne felt flushed with the praise. "That is kind of you, Walter. I was glad to be of help."

He lifted a candlestand. "I'm going to search the house. We have yet to find Stephen, Bramfield's servant."

"Or Margaret," Anne reminded him. "I pray that she is unharmed."

Lord Alderley glanced between Anne and Philip. "Would you like Sir Robert and me to inform the king of this night's evil deeds? His men will want to examine the bodies."

Anne said, "We can return with you."

"Nay, we cannot," Philip said. "It is over, as far as we are concerned. Anne, after we've looked for Margaret, I need to talk to you."

Though they all searched the house, they did not find Stephen. Frightened servants finally crept into the open, and Margaret was found locked in a bedchamber. Anne held her while she cried, and then released her when Sir Robert offered to escort Margaret back to Lady Rosamond.

Anne felt Philip's hand on her upper arm. "Are we finished here?" he asked.

She looked up at him in surprise, but he was staring down at her with tenderness and urgency, and she found she could not deny him.

Outside, he mounted his horse and pulled her up to ride in his lap. At last she felt safe, not caring what happened next, as long as she was with Philip.

To her surprise, the guard at the city gate let them in without even a question, and as Philip flipped him several coins, he said, "He's becoming wealthy off me tonight."

At first Anne thought he would take her to the League's house, but instead he rode down to the Thames, to the inn where they'd slept in each other's arms. The innkeeper grumbled about being awakened, but at last they were alone in a small chamber. Philip started a fire, and Anne stood before it, wondering if she would ever feel warm again.

He took both of her hands, facing her before the fire, and it danced across his face and glittered in his eyes.

"I never asked where *you* wanted to go this night," Philip said, "because I was worried you would accept someone's offer of escort before you had heard me out."

She smiled, though inside she felt breathless with uncertainty and excitement. "Accept an offer of escort? Do you think I would leave you so easily?"

He sighed and closed his eyes, then brought both

of her hands to his lips. "I was jealous of Walter for touching you like this."

When he turned her hands over and kissed her palms, she shivered in wonder. It seemed such an intimate thing, and she could feel the brush of the whiskers he had not had time to shave.

At last he looked up at her, then pressed her hands over his heart. "Anne, I have never said these words to another, and they have ached to burst forth from my chest. I love you, my sweet."

The tears she told herself she wouldn't cry promptly began to flow down her face, but she was also smiling with quiet joy. "Oh, Philip, I have been in love with you for so long, that I never even realized how this emotion, how these feelings for you, had become such a part of me."

"I always thought I'd know my future when I finally saw it," he said, reaching to wipe her tears, and then cupping her cheek with one hand. "It was you, always you, but I was too blind to see it. I kept thinking that I had to stand alone, to make my own way in the world, to advance myself the way others had wanted me to. But all along I was living in the shadow of these people, basing myself on them, and it was you who showed me true courage."

"Philip, how can you think so little of yourself?" she cried softly. "You transformed yourself from peasant to squire to knight, and you should be as proud as I am. It was you who made me realize that I was letting the inferiority of my position affect me. I was trying to be someone else, living within a masquerade, and then hoping that the League would allow me to disappear within other characters forever. It was almost like running away from myself. But I have to make my own place to belong, and I so desperately want that to be with you." She cupped his hand to her cheek. "Please, Philip, forgive me for using you as Lady Beatrice did."

"What do you mean?"

"Even if you didn't love me, I wanted so much to share my bed with you, to have those memories to cherish. It never dawned on me that Lady Beatrice did the same. I saw how much that hurt you."

"But *you* could never hurt me, Anne," he whispered. "With your every touch you showed me what I meant to you. I never had that with any other woman. Soon enough, I realized that I could not live without you, as even I need the air to breathe. So let there be no more recriminations between us. Will you be my bride, Anne? Will you share my home and my heart?"

She stood on her tiptoes to place a kiss on his lips. "Aye, Philip. I vow with my very soul to be worthy of such a gift."

He laughed and hugged her, then stepped back and tried to look serious. "And I have one more request."

"Anything," she breathed.

"Let our next adventure be the excitement of marriage and the thrill of making babies."

She threw her arms around him and let him lift her from the floor. "Gladly, my love."

Epilogue

Winter was upon them, and Anne stood looking out the window of the manor home Philip had purchased for them, not far from Castle Alderley. Snow softly fell on the hills of Gloucestershire, blanketing the world, but she did not heed its threat. She was snug and warm in her own home, close to her friend Elizabeth, but no longer her servant.

She put a hand to her swelling stomach, knowing with deep satisfaction that she had her own life, her own growing family.

The front door opened and she turned to see Philip and several men enter the hall. She came to them, calling for a servant's aid, as they shook the snow from their cloaks and boots.

When their hoods dropped back, she recognized Walter and David, whom she had not seen since the past summer's adventure in London.

They bowed to her, and she kissed their cold cheeks. "And where is Joseph?" she teased them. "Do you not all travel together?"

"He is with his wife in her time of need," Walter said.

Philip put his arms around her, his hands on her belly. "It seems to be contagious."

They all laughed, and Anne invited them into her home.

As the men were being served food and warm drinks, Philip drew Anne aside to speak privately. "They've asked me to join the League," he said, his smile fading.

She took up his smile for him. "Philip, you had always dreamed of helping people."

"I *am* helping people—our own people. And my dreams of you replaced those simple childhood wishes. I told them I would think about it, but I am in no rush to decide."

He pulled her close, and she snuggled into him, letting him feel her belly and the child within, as he loved to do. She could not be unhappy with his decision.

"I do things on my own terms at last," he murmured against her temple.

"This child might have its own terms," she said, laughing softly.

"Then we'll meet them together."

Every time she thought of giving Philip the chance at fatherhood that he never had before, she felt tears sting her eyes. She was an emotional fountain with the babe growing inside her, but Philip didn't mind. Feeling more at peace than she'd thought possible, she looked back out at the snow-covered world and was glad to be home at last.

Author's Note

The late fifteenth century is rife with political turmoil, with many different kings coming to power. I did extensive research for this book, which is always my favorite thing about being a writer. I hope you'll forgive me for a few liberties I had to take. I could not find the name of the king's Lord Steward, so I created Sir Edward Colet.

Also, nowhere did I find evidence of an underground tunnel into Westminster Palace, but I needed one to cloak my characters' journey in secrecy. I knew in Rome there had been such a tunnel since the second century, so why not London?

Thank you again for understanding, and I hope you enjoyed the adventures of Anne and Philip. Look for Lord Bannaster's story, where he meets the first Bladeswoman, coming to your bookstore soon!

Julia

Avon Romantic Treasures

Unforgettable, enthralling love stories, sparkling with passion and adventure from Romance's bestselling authors

Avon Romances

the best in exceptional authors and unforgettable novels!